SUFFER THE
CHILDREN

SUFFER THE
CHILDREN

JOHN E. ANDES

iUniverse, Inc.
Bloomington

Suffer the Children

iUniverse books may be ordered through booksellers or by contacting:

iUniverse
1663 Liberty Drive
Bloomington, IN 47403
www.iuniverse.com
1-800-Authors (1-800-288-4677)

ISBN: 978-1-4620-6264-5 (sc)
ISBN: 978-1-4620-6265-2 (ebk)

Printed in the United States of America

iUniverse rev. date: 10/29/2011

Contents

To all of God's children.

Be wary of princes, who say they want only what's best for you.

For John David Eshleman and William Raymond Kelly

Prologue

This is a story about today: what is happening, and what could happen. We all need to understand forces, which drive the story. Our children and their children should read this with great care. Although it is set today in this country, the Passion Play can be found in the motifs of the world throughout time. The names and locales change, but the forces and significance of the events are frighteningly similar. Gene Benton is *jeder mensch*. He has the personality quirks and life style entrapments shared by us all. Two divorces, two children, and a good job. His comfortable life is hit by a series of upheavals: some direct and some indirect, some pleasant and some painful. The specter of school violence is everywhere. Remedies are voiced. What forces drive evil? Opposing forces have their own agendas. Who is to be believed puppet or puppeteer? Foreign events impact the domestic environment. Gene's domain crashes around him, as old reason no longer applies. Paranoia prevails. The convolution to resolution defies logic because no one knows the true identity of the players. Why him? Why now? Why not? What's next? When? Read and heed.

Carter, Wyoming

Why is Missus Treadway's class soooo boring? English Literature, not Lit, right before lunch. You know it's boring when the swill they serve at "The Trough" is more appealing than the swill she serves. I mean these guys are dead. Their style is dead. Their stories are dead. I hope no one can hear my stomach over her droning. Is Dorothy looking back at me? She's slowly opening and closing her knees and flashing me a sign. Her khaki rides to her buttocks. She has no panties. Goddammit! I knew there was a reason I liked this class. All the desks are drawn in a circle to allow us to focus on Missus Treadway or, in my case, the girl across from me. Dorothy is licking her lips and I can't do anything about it. She stretches, leans back, and reveals nipples under her denim shirt. The shirt's top three pearl buttons are open and the form of each breast invites more than a passing glance. Cock teaser. I'm starting to chub. Please, don't call on me, 'cause I am not paying attention to the dead head,s only the live one.

The bell arrests Mike's development. Clamor replaces reverie. Motion supplants inertia. Thirty-four juniors of Big Horn High School in Carter, Wyoming gather their wits and books. They shuffle to the door. So many bodies. So little space. The students are loudly reminded of Missus Treadway's English Literature homework assignment . . . neat calligraphy on the blackboard. There will be no excuse for not completing the work. The thirty-four meld into the hallway, school of fish. Each guppy is heading to a specific locker to dump a load of educational hardware, before spewing into the cafeteria, "The Trough."

Dorothy finds Mike and clasps his hand. Part ownership, part affection, and very sexual. They head for their lockers side-by-side in hallway N-2, the senior's hall. The cowgirl and the cowboy are in love. He is dressed in real work jeans with a large silver belt buckle and a red and

1

green checked shirt cut full for the 42-inch shoulders and narrow for the 30-inch waist. The intimacy of their whispering and touching is startled by screaming coming from the main hall. They turn toward the source of the excitement. Now they rush to see what was the matter.

The screaming is in response to the big firecracker pops. Boys and girls are frantically trying to get away from something or to go somewhere. The cafeteria? Then a series of loud yet muffled booms rattles sealed windows. Smoke roils from the side halls and the front door. The lights go out. The freshly waxed tiled floor offers no traction. Leather-soled shoes on ice. The metal lockers are jagged obstacles. When someone falls into a locker, flesh is torn. More screaming, pushing, and pandemonium. The students are trapped, yet being conducted by an unseen force. Can't go forward into the smoke-filled cafeteria. That's where all the shit started. Can't go right or left into the darkened halls. The mass oozes toward the front door. Suddenly three shadows appear. Three Hollywood-Clanton-Wannabes. Encased in smoke. The cowboys are backlit by the sun outside the front doors. Broad-brimmed hats. Long rider coats with the slit up the back from hem to butt. Collars turned up in the back and pointed down on the sides. Skinny-legged denim pants. Boots with spurs. Six jingling spurs sparkling in the smoke filtered rays of the sun. The gun belts become apparent. Huge silver and gold buckles like the ones given as prizes at rodeos. The lines of forty-four caliber cartridges begin at the coat openings and disappear around each side. The three unmasked invaders seem to glide inexorably toward the on-rushing throng. Slow motion. Now three faces. These are kids. Pimples. No facial hair. One with glasses. No smiles as they spin their thirty-thirties to their hips, simultaneously cocking the guns to the ready. The slaughter commences. Slug after slug is discharged from the rifles. Cock the lever. Pull the trigger. Repeat. The action of the rifles seems to set the pace and rhythm for the carnage. Now there is fire and more smoke. Children kill children. Bullets ricochet off the walls, lockers and floors. Those not hit by fusillades stumble over bodies. Some of the fallen have the good sense to stay down and feign death. Now the cowboys discard their rifles and draw the formerly holstered forty-fours. It all appears choreographed. The steps. The pacing. The tossing aside of the big boom sticks. Each and every action planned to the most minute detail and in the proper sequence. Alvin Ailey could not have done better.

The handguns rapidly and independently disgorge projectiles for more death and destruction. Unfettered, the Three Horsemen of the Apocalypse press on. The distance from the front door to the students had been one hundred feet. Now between death and panic is less than ten paces. The crowd spins and heads for the smoky cafeteria, like fish in tropical water. The motion is fluid and total. Backs are turned to the butchers and the retreat is rapid. If the kids can get to the cafeteria and blockade the doors, they may find a haven. Girls are crying out names and pleas for help. The older boys are yelling, cajoling, and shoving the girls and underclassmen down the hall to safety. Stepping over tom and twisted classmates. The tile has been made precarious. Blood and flesh are treacherous surface additions to waxed linoleum. In the dark, slipping and slithering slows progress. Little fishes trying to escape the jaws of death.

There is time to stop and reload. This can be done while striding over the bleeding and dying. Not stopping enhances the menace. The faces of youth, not the faces of innocence. Anger held until the boiling point—and this is it. The doors of the cafeteria are forced open over the protestations of those hiding within. The metal double swinging doors are returned to their closed and upright positions and the top and bottom bolts are inserted into the female receptacles. Tables, folded flat, are stacked three deep against the doors. Braced by chairs, the doors form a shield to match that of the cinder block walls. Now to the rear entrance. Serving carts are wheeled to cover the delivery doors. Stacked on top of each other, the carts create an oddly shaped metal barricade. Above the noise and commotion of things being moved, cries from the outside are audible. Like lambs bleating before slaughter. The cries are silenced by the report of big handguns. Numerous shots are also fired into the front entrance. None get through the table wall. Someone runs to the telephone. The line is clear. Notify the police. From under one tangled, twitching heap of injured, can be seen the hands of two teenage lovers clasped in the grip of love and death. Blood has pooled beneath a denim blouse and khaki skirt with suede trim. The skirt has been pushed to revel that the wearer wore no panties. The male body lies on top. Did he fall last or was he trying to protect his lover. There are two oozing holes in the back of his red and green checked shirt and a large cavity in the back of his head. He was shot execution-style.

A firm voice calls for calm. Local cops? SWAT? The hallway cacophony masks the arrival at the back door. Identification leads to entry. Cries of relief. Sobbing. Stares of silence. Catatonic faces. Panic causes a variety of emotions. The hall is eerily silent. No gun fire, no pleas, no footsteps. The explosion at the front door brings the men in black suits. No gun fire. No one to shoot or who would shoot back. The ten-minute war is over. Now begins the gruesome body count and identification.

Gene Benton's telephone reverberates repeatedly. His tranquility of a mental health day by the pool is interrupted by his sister's scream.

"Dorothy's dead. She's been shot at school. Some crazies came in before lunch and blew the fucking place apart. Killed twelve kids, then the cowards self-destructed. Cops and SWAT all over the place. I need you here now. Please, I'm falling to pieces."

The words are stuttered between the sobs. The volume makes the facts almost unintelligible. Gene gets the gist of what happened and what is needed.

"Mary, calm down. I'll pack now, go to the airport and get to Carter immediately. Once I know my flight schedule and timetable, I'll call you again. Keep your cell phone open and with you. Use the landline for calls to and from your friends and Dorothy's friends. Do you have any tranqs? Take two now. I'll stay on the line."

"No need. It's already done. How else would I have the strength to call you? Hurry, Gene I really, really need you."

"Love you, Mary, I'll be there."

Call the taxi and pack while the checkered van plies its way to my hideaway. At the airport in less than one hour from Mary's call. Check American. Impressed them with the urgency of my need. The fastest way to get to Carter is through Dallas, change and board a plane to Denver, then catch a commuter flight to Boise and rent a car for the two hour drive to Mary's shack in the hills. The entire process will take two time zones and four hours if all the connections are made. The desk attendant promises me that all connections will be held for my arrival. It's the least they can do. I have fifteen minutes to call Mary. She's groggy. I suspect she washed down the pills with at least two single malts. She anxiously awaits my arrival.

The flights and drive are uneventful. The airline was terrific. They can do anything if they want to. They rarely want to. All connections were made on time with a minimum of grumbling from other passengers. All the while I think of Dorothy and her death. There must be time between life and non-life when there is no sensation except dull awareness. No fear. No pain. The moment could seem to last an hour or two if the mind dies after the body, but really might last for only a millisecond when mind brings death to the body. The absence of closure is not an event. The senses don't kick in or out until the nanno second of closure. Physical death versus mental death. The time lag or gap could be substantial. One fast and one slow. Which is which? Sometimes one and sometimes the other. The net of all this is that Dorothy is dead. Her state is irreversible. Now I have to deal with the grieving living, her mother, my sister. I make a note to send a thank you to Miss Janet Cunningham, angel in a blue uniform. My ass is draggin'. My body tells me it's somewhere between later and earlier than my watch tells me.

Mary's directions are terrific. Obviously written with the adult mind in mind. Not like the directions on toys to be assembled on Christmas Eve. From the Interstate to her door is twenty minutes. The lights marking the drive way and a few floods kick on as I arrive. The driveway is extra wide, as is the walk to the front door. Designed and built with the wheelchair in mind. Mary did not escape the scourge of Polio. Jonas Salk's magic bullet missed her. Mary contracted the crippler after Dorothy was born. An infant and the disease were too much for Harry. He drove off to work one morning. Never came home for dinner. Was killed in a drug deal that went very bad, somewhere in Arizona. Three years after she was abandoned, Mary was a widow. The front door is extra wide and the doorbell is extra loud. Mary uses a video and voice system for security and because it's a pain in her ass to get from wherever she is to the front door quickly.

I know to wait for a response. As I press the button, lights are activated around the front door. Bathed in the brilliance of three spots, I am on Candid Camera. In a minute or two she buzzes me in.

"OK, Mary, where are you?" I listen intently as I stand in the foyer. All is dark except for the lights outside.

"I'm here on the porch, Join me for a drink."

I negotiate my way through the living room and den. The furniture pieces are far apart for ease of negotiation. I don't stub my toes, bang my shin, or trip. These are parts of my normal routine in most dark rooms. There is Mary's chariot. Her perpetual companion. Her constant reminder of her half-life. In the shadows I can see the wan smile and sad eyes. The eyes and hair are the visible bond between us. Steel blue eyes and black hair, which has become salt and pepper. Mine is just salt. The L.L.Bean canvas bag settles on the floor. She raises her arms to me. Pulls me to her to absorb her hurt. If I could take one percent of the pain from her by means of a hug, I would hug her for one hundred days until her life became bearable. It's what is expected of friends. Despite the fact that we are siblings, we are dear friends. We have always been straight with each other. Always the truth. Teasing and goading to do better. Sympathy in times of duress. But, no coddling. No bullshit.

"Oh, Gene, it's terrible. My baby is dead. Dorothy and her boy friend, Mike. Slaughtered by some crazies. They killed at least a dozen. In school, for Christ's sake. It's supposed to be safe in school. Teachers, administrators, even the euphemistic Resource Officer. If cops can't protect the kids, who the fuck can?"

"Where did the bastards get the guns and the idea? It was too well planned. The little fucks must have spent days dreaming up all the details. How did they get all the bombs and guns? Where were their parents? Why did no one notice? Did the other kids know anything about the three?"

The questions were rapid-fire. She was beginning to repeat them, because there were no answers. At least I had none. Hysteria commenced. Her voice was louder and shriller with each question. Now the sobs were interfering with communication clarity. I missed many of the words, but got the message. She was pissed, really, really pissed. And she wanted the truth.

"Mary, have you eaten anything today?"

"Fuck food. I want another drink. Then I want to sleep and wake up with this whole thing behind me like the nightmare it is. Fix me a big one, please."

As she turns on the room lights, her tears erupt and cascade down her cheeks following paths well worn by omnipresent pain. She looks like hell. That's a dumb thought. The loss of a loved one is enormous. The sadness of a parent losing a child is incomprehensible. It's just not supposed to be that way. The child is supposed to outlive the parent. But, when the child dies first, hopes for the future, the parent is left empty. The anguish is extreme. The physical torment is visible on the parent, even to strangers.

The bar is incredibly well stocked with two bottles of Balvenie and one each of Talisker, Craggenmore, Dalwhinnie and Glenkinchie. The waters of life in a house with one less life. I find two tall glasses. Pour and add twice the Oban volume in fresh spring water. No ice. Ever. As I turn, I see Mary wiping her face with tissues she keeps in the large undercarriage box. This is her purse. It even locks for safety when she is out of the house. She ain't gonna be purty, jes clean. The flicker of a smile is evident. Release after the eruption. Not the same as sex, but release nonetheless.

She has lighted more table lamps using her remote control system. With the black wand of power, Mary can light her life, open her doors and enter her car. There is also a connection to the police, fire and medical emergency. She is wired for life. The house is wired to her. A truly high tech Clapper and panic button combination we won't see on late night TV for another decade. Mary's was self-designed and installed. She is extraordinarily gifted in the areas of electronics and technology. A hacker par excellence. I am glad someone got Dad's gift. I can barely replace a fuse. And I use my computer for word processing. Mary always said I got the beauty and she got the brains. I think she got both. She has yet to show me how to use this incredible tool as proficiently as she does. But, I have been promised that 'all secrets would be revealed, Grasshopper.'

With the lights on and some faint level of normal returning to her, Mary assumes the role of big sister.

"You can sleep on the couch or in Dorothy's room. It's your choice. Either way you may want fresh linen. Her room will be quieter. The dogs and I sometimes roam at night. For me it's the best time in space. I can talk to all the nutsos and practice my exploring techniques. That's hacking to you. When I roam, I turn on a few lights, go to the kitchen for food and listen to my short wave radio. It can get a bit busy. But, it's your choice."

"Thanks for no choice. I'll throw my bag in the other bedroom. I'd like to shower so that I smell less like the cattle on the hills and more like a twentieth century human. OK?"

"Suit yourself. There are fresh towels and bed linen in the hall closet. All dirty ones can be tossed in the hamper in the closet bottom. I'll be here or in my ComRoom when you're all clean and sparkly."

Odd that she would offer me Mary's room. Maybe having a family body in the space helps her deal with the loss. The closet reveals queen sized sheets and four pillowcases in a set. Somewhat feminine, but, under the circumstances, more than satisfactory. I pull the quilt and comforter to the bottom of the bed, strip the flowery sheets and replace them with pastel striped ones, The pillowcases next. Pull up the covers. Find the hamper, a wicker basket barely visible under a stack of blankets. I'm not used to the thermal protection necessary for sleeping in the cold mountain air. Ready with bed prep, I head for the bath.

This is really strange. While I had hardly taken notice of Dorothy's nest decoration, I am slammed by the fact that this is a woman's bathroom. The female stuff on the counter, the sink, under the sink, on shower windowsill, and in the medicine cabinet. Many colors of eye shadow, six shades of lipstick, skin cleansers and gloss, curlers, three shampoos, crème rinses, lots of cotton balls, astringent, skin lotions, perfumes and parfums, two deodorants, nail files, tweezers, nail polish and polish remover, a cuticle stick, clippers, two toothbrushes, toothpaste, floss, mouth wash, phony eyelashes, eyebrow pencils in four different shades, ribbons, clips, scrunchies, mousse, extra, extra hold gel, body wash and bar soap, disposable shavers in various colors, shaving cream, styptic pencil, feminine pads, tampons, aspirin, decongestant, antihistamine, feminine wipes and an open twelve-pack of condoms. Just by looking, I learned so much about my sixteen-year old niece. Maybe more than I wanted to know. But, I know so little. The little woman-child I hadn't seen for three years. Now I'll never talk to her. Why was this atrocious thing done to her? What did she do to warrant this? Whom did she offend?

The shower water is a real eye opener. In Florida, I turn on the water and step into the shower. Not in Wyoming. Here the cold water is cold. Talk about shrinkage. Adjusting the water temperature to be user friendly takes time, patience, and precision. As I wash I cry. Purging the grime begins to purge the pain. The scent of the shampoo and body wash are not mountain clean. More like field flower fresh. As I towel off, I stare at my surroundings. All of Dorothy's stuff will have to be boxed and tossed. How easily we discard the everyday necessities of the dead. The little things that meant a lot mean nothing now. It was the same with Mom and Dad. Who wants a used or partially depleted supply of a personal item? We shun this, while total strangers might grab it in a heartbeat. To wit, garage sales. Do we shun the item because it is inferior? Do we shun it because it is too personal? Do we shun it because we cannot deal with its memory? Does it matter?

"Well, baby brother looks almost presentable. Clean body and clothes. How is your soul? Pour me another drink, will you?"

I do as I am told. I just make it lighter than before.

"Look at this. These are the amateur and news videos of the police as they gathered then entered. I needed to search the record of the event, so I pulled some strings. Sort of like looking at a car wreck or the ovens at Buchenwald. There are the first uniforms. And there are our local SWAT members. Then the state paramilitary arrives. Who got there first? Who was in command? I copied all the footage and I'm going to edit it to get a time line on the events. Occasionally, I'll break for a Chat room and the short wave. So, pull up a chair and spend the night. Or as long as you can last."

"I've never been able to refuse a beautiful woman, so how can I refuse the secret love of my life?"

"Don't go there smart ass. Come here and give me another hug. Boy, it's good to see you again, even, if you look much older than I do. It must be the hot fetid air of that nether region called Florida versus my pure, fresh mountain air."

Her sarcasm and her smile were back, if only a half smile. Her eyes were no longer dull. The attitude had returned: I can do anything. It's genetic. The DNA of the clans who dwell in the moors and glens. Someone had fucked with her baby and she was going to find out why. Then she would see to it that a very painful, ugly, and slow vengeance was heaped upon the evil-doers. No time to wallow in the self-pity of a loved-one lost. There is work to do. The smoke and blood circus was a start.

"Make yourself really useful and make us dinner. The kitchen has always been your domain. Whatever is there is yours to use. If you truly need anything, Jack's Market is open all night. It's big, but may be common for your elitist taste. I can give you directions if need be. Now scoot. I'm hungry. God, I feel like I'm on a quest. But, I don't know what I'm looking for. If you know, tell me. Otherwise, get thee to the scullery."

I'm hungry, too. Something I hadn't realized until she raised the issue. Certainly the thought of Mary in a kitchen would crush any craving for food. If it comes in a can or can be nuked from the freezer, it's fine for her. If it requires ten minutes prep and an oven, it's gourmet and she can't handle it. Now, I can spoil her by rattling pots and pans, heating the plates and using more spices than salt and pepper. I uncover, and I mean uncover, things that look like pork chops. The preprinted label confirms my assumption and the date of purchase was three days ago. Safe to eat. An entree Dorothy was, most likely, going to prepare. Now, to find applesauce, cabbage and potatoes for mashing. Maybe some beets or green beans, if I am lucky. As luck would have it, no applesauce. But, Red Delicious apples, which can be peeled, sliced, and cooked with cinnamon and honey. Way better that Romes. Big Idaho bakers. Stab the suckers all over with a huge fork for the nuke wave. There is lots of butter and flaky spices that belong on spuds and maybe meat. Canned green beans. A huge onion to be sautéed and folded into the beans. Capped with a few croutons. Well-done herb flavored toast crumbles will have to be the substitute. A feast good enough for the queen and king of silent pain.

"Madam, dinnah is served. May I assist you to the dining room?"

"Be a dear, put the meal on a tray and bring it into my ComRoom. I'm in the middle of some real fascinating stuff. Come see, Look at this. See that big van? The dark one to the right of the trees? Why is it just parked there with no markings? And I can't see a license plate. Now watch. A few uniforms, not locals or state guys, seem to come back to this van as if it were a base. Are they reporting or getting something each time they enter the van? That's one we need to note for further digging. Here. Look. After they come from the van, they give commands to the locals. These van guys seem to have taken control and are directing the show. Who the fuck are they?"

"Enough for now. Take a break. I was in your antediluvian kitchen sweating up a storm to create this monster meal for us. If you don't eat it while it's hot, I'll be insulted and very pissed. So there. Let us have thirty minutes of quiet about the events of today, or was it yesterday."

The meal is hearty with more flavors than Mary is used to. Mary went West to find a life. And then with Dorothy and no husband, she found her economic calling in the world of technology. She fervently dove into the lake of cyber knowledge and taught herself how to swim. In a few years, she became tantamount to an Olympic Gold Medalist. Teaching at Carter Community College, she is recognized as the go-to instructor in the statewide system. If there were a question about computer systems, what is now and what might be, Mary was the source. She lectured around the country. Sat on a few advisory boards. She was offered an important position at the mother ship, but she turned them down. She doesn't deal well with large political organizations and she enjoys a tremendous amount of autonomy here in Carter. In this case the mountain could come to Mohammed, because she was not going to them. Her home reflects her technological, non-familial love. I don't think there was anyone after Harry. We talk about Wyoming and Florida. Our respective business paths.

She wondered how long I would stay. Told her, as long as she wanted. I had taken some vacation time. I had accumulated forty-six days of Earned Time Off. This may be one of the true plusses of Intx that owns my company. The big, Dutch insurance conglomerate believes in earned time off. Not as much pay as their competitors, but more time off. I have seasoned people who can cover for me during a short absence. But, not a long time. Some knights-errant, who have pledged corporate allegiance, would love to put dirks in my side. Sometimes I think Mary was right about structural politics; it isn't the work that will kill you, it's your fellow workers.

"That meal was fit for me, little brother. God, if men only knew their places were the kitchen and the bedroom and that they should be summoned to either at a woman's wishing, what a wonderful world it would be."

"Don't get me started on genders. From birth, the fairer sex makes up the rules as time goes on. Women seek domination. Little girls giggle, big girls wiggle and women rub. The same as in the animal kingdom. Poor helpless schlubs like me are dead meat. First our hearts go, then our loins are purloined, our pockets picked, and souls crushed. We are seduced and abandoned. All we have left is the camaraderie of the jailed."

Her gales of laughter are wonderful. Hyperbolic brother-sister sparring is good for the soul. She knows there is no room for soap boxes in her life and I have long since burned mine. The bond is re-forged. I will clean up the dishes, because that is my function in her world tonight. Besides, she should continue her digging. It is now two AM. Soon I will retire and she should also. With the morning there will be more video to analyze. Maybe some more amateur video from the locals. Clean up is quick, because I clean as I cook. A trick Mom taught me.

When I return to the ComRoom, Mary is sound asleep in the chair. Some videos are on hold, some on continual loop, and some screens are blank. I maneuver the chair to her bedroom and hoist her onto the bed. Even at one hundred-forty-five pounds, she is heavy. I fear the concept of dead weight. A momentary stir, some mumbling, and a small kiss on my cheek. I cover her with a quilt and exit, leaving the door ajar for the dogs.

The dogs, Hither and Yon, are both mixed bags. One of them, and I'm not sure which one, is Shepherd and Rottweiler. He will guard the house and attack intruders. The other dog is a mixture of Puli and Coyote. He will herd the intruders into the garage and butcher them, one at a time, for food. Both are devoted to Mary and were devoted to Dorothy. And after proper introduction, they have come to treat me with the disdain of an acceptable interloper. The introduction required that I lie on the floor and let them smell me from pate to penny loafers, all the time Mary talked to them in soothing tones. After they were done with this primeval form of metal detection, they backed up and went to Mary's side. She praised them. I rose and was permitted to pet them. If Mary likes me, I might be OK.

The ComRoom, Mary's phrase for the room with all the electronic equipment, resembles a decent TV studio of the early nineties. I know it is more sophisticated. She can receive, manipulate and, I guess, send images, data, and sound from this room. When in this room she is perceived as normal, which, for a crippled technowhiz is an important perception. People who have not met her or seen her in her chariot know her words, thoughts, and voice, all of which can appear normal.

I pull up an office chair. I study the console and the various monitors and switches. It's interesting that a foreigner, like me, can ascertain her work patterns by scanning the buttons and switches. Those with the color cleaned off or surrounded by the dirt and oil from innumerable finger hits are the buttons critical to every activity. The gradation or intensity of the color on the button and the amount of finger dirt around it lets the observer know the importance of the button. The frequency of hits. Also, I remember that most consoles are built by and for right-handers.

I stop a loop and restart it. I unfreeze a frame, then refreeze it. I turn on a blank monitor, then shut it down. Go back to the loop and slow it down. Stare at the action. Study it. Stare at the setting. Study it. Stare at the background. Study it. Stare at the interaction. Study it. Study the activity other than that of the focused players. What am I seeing? What am I looking for? I see the cars, people, and school. I see the van near the trees. See the smoke resulting from the explosions. See the police arrive. See men in uniforms leave the van and go to the police. See pointing. Directions given. Orders followed. This is all so painfully expected. My eyes are closing as I stare. To bed, to bed you sleepy head. Yes, Mother.

The sun is bright and the air cold for a Floridian. Daylight happened without me taking off my pants. My shoes, yes. My pants, no. I hear no noise other than nature outside the structure. It takes a few moments to realize I am in my niece's bedroom and why I am here and she is not. Easing from the bed and padding to the door, I listen for the dogs. No dog sounds. Did I really expect noise from protectors and hunters? As I open the door, I smell coffee. Something that Mary can do in the kitchen. Peek in the ComRoom. No Mary. Peek in her bedroom. No Mary. No bathroom water noises. No dogs. My God, I've been deserted. Coffee. The note on one of those yellow half-page pads advises me that she has gone to town to secure any new footage from the stations, and to ask around if anyone else had taken a private record of the events. She hopes to return by noon. I call Mary on her cell phone.

"Hello, sleepy head. I thought you had been drugged by your own cooking. Yes, I have caller ID on my system. I've been to the local station. Not much new.

There may be another personal video at the college. I know the student. I can go to her house, if need be. News conference at eleven AM. Are you OK? You should not eat before your run. Take the West trail. It's easier for out-of-staters. Now, you called." "Good morning, Mary. It's so nice to be talked at by you. What can I do here while you are bouncing around Carter like you're on black beauties? Why don't I tape the network feeds of the conference and any supporting footage they use? OK?'

"Sorry, Gene. But, I cannot be bogged down by remorse. I must learn as much as I can as quickly as I can, so I can put this damnable thing to rest. You know, closure, that latest psycho-term. Can you work the console? After you're up, give me a call and I'll walk through a checklist with you. Now get to your run or you'll be late for class. Oops, sorry."

The run was good. The air a little rarer than I'm used to and much cooler. But I loved it. Shower. Go back to the ComRoom for my assignment. Four monitors. Two on the locals, one on CNN, and one on CBS. Ten forty-five AM. Think I'm ready. Call my master's voice.

"Let's do it by the numbers, Grasshopper. All monitors on?"

"Check."

"Cassettes inserted?"

"Check."

"When I get home, I'll convert all the tapes to CDs so we can play with them tonight. Thanks, you are my friend despite the blood."

The local news conference is led by the sheriff, who relates the events of the past twenty-four hours. His face, expression and words are bland. He talks of safety and security. Isolated incident. Numerous leads. Blah, blah, blah. Nothing concrete. The alleged perps killed themselves. Cameras are not at the same angle. Something strange about some of the faces in the crowd. A few of them are government issue. They avoid camera contact, by moving out of range or turning away. Strange behavior. Normally, they just stand there. Questions are dumber than the answers. Cannot release all the names. Some families are away for the opening of small game season. Will be able to tell more at a news conference set for three this afternoon. The entire event takes five minutes.

A reporter for CNN relays, from an unidentified source, the gist for the notes left by the shooters. They wanted someone to pay attention. Someone to listen to their pain. They were tired of being ignored and hurt. Death rules.

Gulf Beach, Florida

The stress of the six-day trip, the intensity of the stay, and the numerous time changes have taken their toll. I need a vacation to regroup from my time off. Today is Sunday, the day of rest. If I get my mind back into the world of non-family adults and their problems very slowly, Monday will not be too tough. So the New York Times, the local birdcage liner, and the Sunday TV news shows will force feed me. The local paper is a quick read.

"This is Newsmakers, where you learn what will happen."

Somewhere after the item in the newspaper about two twelve-year-old boys, who fell into a sink hole and were rescued by their neighbors, and before the story of a police chase gone awry wherein an innocent driver was run off the road to her death, I hear the deep tones of the senior Senator from Pennsylvania, Baldwin Miller. The voice starts calm and measured, and gradually increases in intensity and volume. The pleasant melody of a professional speaker becomes the fervent tone of a confrontational cheerleader. Staccato surmounts modulation. Senator Miller is decrying the plethora of violence he and his followers have seen in the high schools around the nation. He has all the statistics, dates, and names. They are his litany. His marching orders. The fallen shall be held high. The criminals dealt with. His rambling becomes ranting.

"You are either part of the problem or part of the solution."

This is the rallying cry of the extreme right and the extreme left; each brooks no middle ground. Yes, there are strong black and white areas. There is also a huge, motherfucking gray area known to all as the real world.

Senator Miller is bewailing the issue.

"How could this murderous event of last week have occurred? How could children kill children? Who is the cause of this effect? Who is to blame? Who is accountable?"

15

Then he takes off on the list of much battered culprits.

"The NRA and the loose gun laws make it too easy for anybody to have guns. The champions of unrestricted personal freedom without commensurate individual responsibility foolishly believe we all have the right to carry weapons. The Second Amendment to the Constitution allows people to carry guns if they belong to a well regulated militia. Said militia, by definition, owes allegiance to a government. To what government do the White Brotherhood and the Voodoo Kings owe allegiance. The entertainment industry foists death and destruction on all of us. They target the young and impressionable. Bigger and more powerful guns. Explosives in all shapes and intensities. Car chases, plane crashes, and dismemberment by the dozen. Neutron rays and blades of death. Continual savagery and brutality now come in all shapes and sizes. All for the sake of money or ratings."

"Pornographers, and make no mistake about it, pornography is violence, are the purveyors of hatred. This is a travesty of humanity. And how about the sellers of booze and the dealers in drugs. Wherever the emotionally insecure want to be, other than where they are, the drinks and drugs will send them. These malignancies take money away from children and families. Take resources away from our economy and destroy the work force."

"The schools don't care for the children. They have forgotten: Spare the rod and spoil the child. The school people won't discipline. They adjust. They're afraid of lawsuits from parents. Afraid of gangs. But most of all, they are afraid of failing to be perfect. So they do nothing and promote platitudes that are politically correct. Do you know that the first use of the term, politically correct, was by Chairman Mao? So to be politically correct is to follow a Communist doctrine."

"Professional athletes and their sports associations are the worst. The nearly educated pro athletes, the ones who barely got out of high school and never were graduated from college, want everyone to love them for their athletic antics. But, these same highly visible miscreants claim not to be role models. And the leagues say it's OK to do drugs, just don't take steroids or kill anybody. If you do these two heinous things we will have to suspend you for two games and fine you a dollar."

"And our government leadership is a bad joke. A very sad, bad joke. The present administration and the party that has run the country for the past sixteen years have let the moral fiber of the country degenerate.

Their tactics of power and re-election have been to favor and promote their various personal agendas. Everything today is done in the name of pleasure and for money."

"But we, the people, are the solution to the problem. We must take back our lives, take back our communities, take back our nation, take back our government and take back our rightful place as the moral leader of the free world. And we must do it now."

"We must establish a new life free from the threat of depravity. Our children must be safe. Today, my team is introducing an inclusive, simple, and effective six-point platform for the American people. A platform to help us take back America. Help us ensure a Secure America For Everyone (SAFE),"

"Here are the six points of SAFE:

Number One: Talk and listen to your children and neighbors.

Number Two: Participate in government, in schools, and in your community.

Number Three: Demand security and safety from government.

Number Four: Demand control of weapons and dangerous substances.

Number Five: Demand the highest moral standards from leaders in all aspects of your life. Use background checks.

Number Six: Have faith in your higher power, but guard against the liars.

"Thank you, Bob. Now we'll answer questions."

The guy started off like the voice of reason and ended his spiel with morsels of truth slathered by the hysteria of near facts. God, the Senator's timing is impeccable. As Newsmakers returns, there is Bob Trumet with a nervous smile.

"Welcome back to Newsmakers, I'm Bob Trumet, your host. And today we are talking to Senator Baldwin Miller of Pennsylvania. Senator Miller just introduced a six-point plan, which he calls Secure America For Everyone or SAFE. Our switchboard is completely lit up. But, Senator Miller, before we go to the first caller, let me ask you two questions. First, what do you expect to get from SAFE? Second, how can the people learn more about SAFE?"

I notice the Senator smiling a very genuine, straight-from-the-heart, I-am-here-to-listen-and-serve-see-my-blue-eyes-and-pearly-white-teeth smile. He leans into the camera ever so slightly. Does not stare, but looks intensely as if he really, really cares. His dark blue suit, white shirt, and red and light blue striped tie flag his belief system. Dark hair, solid facial features and subtle gesturing complete the communication of a strong father figure. Then I notice something disconcerting. The eagle at the top of the six-point program, same as the lapel pin worn by the Senator, is depicted in flight, wings spread, and beak and talons open. Is it coming to a safe nest? Is it in a raptor mode?

"Bob, first, SAFE is for the people and by the people. I am just bringing the issues to the attention of all Americans. It's the people who can solve the problems and be safe and secure. They have the power. They have the right. We want to hear from the people. SAFE will be an expression of the will of farmers, factor workers, clerical workers, teachers, retailers, all the hard-working Americans who pay their taxes and who made this country great. America can be great again, because of them, and for their children."

"Second, if the people want to learn more about SAFE, they should search their souls and talk to each other. Then tell us what they want. Do they want security and safety? Do they want to leave their children and their grandchildren a nation that is safe and secure?"

"Thank you, Senator Miller. Now let's hear from our first caller."

"Bob, this is Eli Nachtvogel from Mechanicsburg, Pennsylvania. Me and my wife just want to say thank you and God bless you to Senator Miller. It's about time somebody recognized what the working man and his family want. We want to be safe and our kids to be safe. I just want to say we want to help the Senator in any way we can. Let us know how and we'll do it. We're in the telephone book, Senator. Thanks for looking after us."

"Mister Nachtvogel, thank you for volunteering. It's volunteers that made this country great and can make it safe again."

"Caller two, Senator."

"Good morning, Bob. Senator Miller. You are right, Senator, so right. Where can I get copies of your six-point platform? I want to give them out in my neighborhood, at little Jenny's school, and at the plant where James, that's my husband of twenty-two years, and I work. I'd like to get the church involved, too. Do you have a mailing address? Oh, yes, this is Jenny Creighton from Moline, Illinois."

"Thank you so much Missus Creighton. If you stay on the line, one of the aides will take your name and address to send you some flyers. Now, will you do something for all America? Write and tell us how can we help you feel safe and secure?"

"Next caller, you're on the air with Senator Baldwin Miller."

"Good morning, Senator. This is Bill Lincoln from Biloxi, Mississippi. Let me ask you. How did we get in this state of moral decay to begin with? If we can learn how the problem started, we can learn how to correct it."

"Your question deals with the root of the pervasive moral decay. We believe the root of the problem can be found in not minding. Over time, Americans cared just a little bit less. We didn't take responsibility for our own actions and lives. We let the other guy do it. We let the government take care of us. We let big business take care of us. Our lives had too much of what we thought was comfort stuff—cars, clothes, and self-gratification."

"All of this did not happen overnight. It happened almost imperceptibly over the last fifty years of prosperity. Like sand shifting almost invisibly in the desert wind. After a while the sand has moved completely so that the dune that was on the right is now on the left. No one noticed the change. It just happened. Prosperity blinded us or made us look away. We let it happen to us. And, we had many willing accomplices. For everything we gave up, there was someone who would take it. But, Americans can take back their lives, if they want to. Americans can take back their freedom, rights, and responsibilities."

"Well, that's all the time we have for this spirited discussion. I'm sure we all appreciate Senator Baldwin Miller for sharing his views with us today. And, while we must go off the air, we will keep our lines open for further dialog between our viewers and the Senator. So don't hang up. Until next week, this is Bob Trumet of Newsmakers, where you learn what will happen."

Well, that was disturbing.

Check my computer. I have mail. My first son wants to know about his aunt. How she is holding up Terri is expecting their third. She is convinced it is another boy, because he is so brutally active. They want to know if they can name him after my father. The new one would be William David Benton II. I am pleased and know my dad would be honored. My second son wants to know what is going on. Work bites the big one. The time demands are nearly intolerable. He met a wonderful woman in Edinburgh. They see each other once a month, but this will increase as she travels for the Ministry of Commerce.

My boss wants to know if I'll be in to work tomorrow. He needs to talk about the projects that were started before I left. There is some pressure building to complete them and get them into the field. He wants to talk about some company restructuring that will impact my troops. Martha wants to know when she'll see me. Well, I'm back in the saddle of complacency. Nothing new has happened in my absence.

The light on my phone tells me I have messages. These are new since I swept the system on Friday morning. Some bill collector threatening to ruin my credit. Shit. My credit rating went down the tube years ago when Miss Fit walked out the door with Mister Wonderful after she cleaned out most of our joint assets. She took about one hundred grand in cash and convertibles and I got about half that in debt, excluding the mortgage. I was stupid, or maybe I just wanted the entire mess to come to an end. But the end is never in sight. Now I know how Sisyphus felt.

At five AM, my home away from home is barely visible. My parking spot is still there. That's a good sign. Not having your name painted over over the weekend means you have employment for another week. My office is clean and my desk has three stacks of publications, brochures, and correspondence. The stacks have been labeled by Susan: Must Read Today—Action Required, Must Read This Week—Direction Required, and Must Read Over the Weekend—Knowledge To Be Gained I dive into the same 'ol, same 'ol. The critical mess gets resorted in three sub-stacks: Let's Talk, What Can I Do? and What Is This?

Another of the same boring crap-filled days is in the books. The lead story on the evening news concerns a presidential ad hoc Commission formed to study the problem of citizen safety. The Commission is comprised of the highest profile luminaries the President could find on such short notice. Senator Miller's shot across the bow got the desired reaction from the reigning party. All the President's men scrambled to create this Committee. And now their credentials are displayed for all the world to see.

John Wenger, PhD, professor of Anthropology and Sociology at Brown University, has published six books dealing with twentieth century mores and social actions of international population subsets. He is one of the vocal proponents of the theory, which attempts to establish similarities in domestic and international social ebbs and flows. Not population shifts, but dress, food, living and other manifestations of each culture. The theory is based upon the tenet that historical imperatives are no longer the strong influences as in the nineteenth century due to advancements in communication, transportation, and information. Doctor Wenger is big on the lecture circuit. Sometimes at political rallies. Always promoting a one-world foreign policy. Rumor has it he has been a big contributor to the President's campaigns and may be in line for an ambassadorship.

Leslie Tremaine, a political activist of the downtrodden blacks, received her undergraduate, masters and doctorate degrees in Political Science from Cal Berkeley. She led non-violent (mostly) and successful (always) protests against the university three times during her tenure. Miss Tremaine has fought for better public housing, day care for working mothers, and clinics that care for the substance abusers, who seem to populate her nether world. Miss Tremaine, mother of two, chose not to get married. In fact, she urges single mothers not to feel shame, but to strive and grow. She did it. She showed the way. They can do it. Miss Tremaine is a community leader often where there is no community.

Brett Tucker has been nominated for three Academy Awards. One for her portrayal of a teen prostitute, one for a crusading newspaper reporter, and the most recent nomination for her role as a young widow who fights the system of economic discrimination. No husband. No children. No public love affairs. She has established schools for young men and women who dropped out of high school but who now wish to get a degree. U Graduate Now! schools are run with private donations. A ton of Hollywood money. All given with great fanfare, but no public assistance. Admission, classes, and books are free. Attendance and participation in class are mandatory. The rules are clear and everyone must understand them before they sign on for the courses. Graduates are required to contribute to the schools with time and energy.

Huang Tsai, Ivan The Terrible of Silicon Valley, moved to Fort Worth where he and his followers develop the programs and games known to kids in video arcades and dens throughout the country. Tsai's Troops are not on the cutting edge; they cut the edge. Clothes, language, hairstyles and attitude. The Troops are Chinese, Japanese, Vietnamese, Blacks, Mexicans, and a mix of whites, lower, middle, and upper class brats. All with a penchant for the fantasy world of cyber life. It is their drug. Their booze. And they love to shove their world in the faces of their parents, teachers, and all in authority. Companies that cater to the eleven to fourteen-year old consumers spending the billions acquired by their yuppie parents need Tsai's Troops to be competitive.

Elizabeth Pendelton, Chairwoman of the National Parent Teachers Association, has an alphabet behind her name and a pedigree of experience from years of teaching and school administration, as well as raising four children. The widow has been a face in the media, advocating stricter parental control of the schools. She is the poster child for zero tolerance when it comes to gangs, gang dress, and violence. Under her leadership, the PTA has secured better salaries, more media centers, and many more Resource Officers. Elizabeth has the ear of the President and three years ago did not deny her interest in a Cabinet position.

Roberta Ramierez, President of the League of Woman Voters. Robbi is new inner city power. She is Puerto Rican, Yale-educated, and an attorney. Walked the lines. Sat in after sit-ins were no longer fashionable. Waves the power of a huge block of votes like a beautiful banner when she needs to or wields it like a truncheon if the opposition is recalcitrant. On more than one occasion, she has said that the terrible, high birth rate among Black and Hispanic women is the strongest factor limiting their ascension to economic equality. The fact that men refuse to take responsibility is a huge burr in her blanket. Robbi advocates legally forced responsibility and sharing of the father's revenue. Even goes as far as to promote the concept of work farms with wage garnishment. Although well educated, Robbi continues to speak with a heavy Spanish accent and will lapse into Puerto Rican Spanglish to spice up her speeches. Her husband is always there. Supportive, but in the background.

Chakka Uhuru, inner city National Merit Scholar from Dallas. The wheel chair was the result of a drive-by shooting. Just in the wrong place at 23 the wrong time. Caca pasa. Chakka has risen above poverty, no mother, a second rate school and a near crushing disability. Perfect SAT score and perfect GPA. Valedictorian. Interned with Doctor Wenger. Mother left home to chase the pipe. Father a bus driver. Chakka, or Ka, never frowns. Sometimes comes across as militant. Loved and admired by all. Sympathy is a strong underpinning for admiration.

These are The Magnificent Seven of President Paul Sessler.

Menthen, New Hampshire

A shotgun can be a great hunting gun or a vicious weapon, depending on what one is hunting and the particulars of the gun. First, the length: The normal barrel can be sawed off. This allows the shot or pellets to spread into a wider and unpredictable pattern quicker than is possible with a regular length barrel. Second, the action: Pump action permits the shooter to fire five or six times in rapid succession. Third, the loads: Shotgun loads, or explosive charge, range from dainty to buffalo killer. Fourth, the shot: The shot inside a cartridge can range from BB to aggie. A shooter with a sawed-off pump action twelve-gauge shotgun that shoots heavy loads can make a wasteland out of a living room and the people at the cocktail party. Or a school bus with sixteen children and a driver.

The thirty-one inch monitor in my office is always tuned to the Financial News Network. I rarely notice the details except when I am lunching in my office. Today is just like any other day except I was there.

"We interrupt the regularly scheduled program to bring you this breaking news from Menthen, New Hampshire. Live from Menthen Area High School is Phil Howart. Phil, can you tells us what is happening?"

I raise the volume from five to sixteen. I am afraid to listen, but am drawn to the horrific details.

"Ralph, it is utter chaos. The scene is very gruesome and may not be appropriate for certain viewers. If the sight of carnage and destruction bother anyone, they should turn away and just listen to my report. Here is what we know. Two boys here at Menthen Area High School in Menthen, New Hampshire entered a bus that was waiting to take students home after the day's classes. The two, we believe they were students, closed the doors of the bus and began blasting away with what have been described as pump-action shot guns. They just began shooting without any apparent provocation. The boys were dressed in black long-rider coats, black broad-brimmed cowboy hats and boots with spurs. No names yet. Not for the boys and not for the sixteen children on the bus. We think that's the number. The bus driver was also slaughtered. His name was Elwood Suggins. A driver and custodian with the school district for twenty-seven years. The brutality is staggering. Windows blown out. Chunks of the bus side panels missing. Gaping maws, seemingly cry out in agony. The back door is open because it was ripped from its hinges. Looks like three or four shots. Before I was hustled away by the authorities, I was witness to the results of the massacre."

"Here it gets real dicey. We have some footage limited by good taste and discretion. So what I am about to describe may not be suitable for the young and squeamish. Some viewers may want to turn down the volume. There were body parts everywhere. Arms, legs, and heads had been separated from torsos. I don't think the officials will ever be able to put the children back together. Chunks of flesh and mounds of what looked like hamburger. Entire backs of seats torn away. Gashes in the roof and craters in the floor. The blood was pouring through openings in the bus. Smoke from the burning seats was settling like fog over the dismembered corpses. It looked as if the flesh remnants of the children were rising from the floor of the bus. There were two headless corpses seated upright on the last bench in the bus. Shotguns in two laps. I assume that these were the culprits. The guns and all the children on the bus were silent. No noise. Screaming surrounded the outside of bus. Friends crying out for fallen comrades. Ralph, it looks like a damned war zone. A really bad day in Beirut. The police and SWAT members are here now. They responded in about ten minutes. Nine-and-one-half minutes too late. I am here for the duration, but that's all for now."

I am stunned. Wiped out. Sit in my very expensive chair and stare at the screen. Cut the volume to five. Kids killing kids. This is a bad case of deja vu. The description of the abattoir wear is painfully familiar. From their hats to their boots, these copycats just upped the ante to get in the game from fifteen to nineteen. Slaughter is a game no one can win. What else is familiar? What do I see? What do I not see? Is there a pattern emerging beyond the ages, locations, timing, and garb of the killers? The killers kill themselves. Did they leave notes? Where would they be? Did anybody see this coming? Is my niece connected to this particular event and the entire chain? How? Who is responsible for this and the Carter butchery? Am I unduly paranoid? Are these two isolated events: one real, one a carbon copy?

Home again. By the pool, but no drink. Alone. Serenity. Eyes close ever so briefly. Two hours later I awake and know it's time for dinner. As I am scrounging in the fridge for salad elements and some remnant of meat, out of the comer of my eye I catch the twenty-four hour news channel broadcasting scenes from Menthen, New Hampshire. I stop and stare. And what do my wondering eyes see, but a panoramic view of the school parking lot, school, and athletic fields in the background. This is a lot of repeat footage of the abattoir. The bus looks like it had been parked in the Balkans and was a target for the Allied bombing raids. Can not determine if there are pools of blood or just many small dark shadows caused by the setting sun. What is in the background, near the trees to the left of the school? A dark colored or black van. No visible windows: they, too, are darkened. No activity around it. Suddenly, a government issued body and face enters the side door. What's inside? Now another GI android. Another. Five in total. The van moves. Exit the group. Now the news conference. I turn up the volume.

"Ladies and gentlemen. Thank you."

The news conference is led by the sheriff, who relates the events of the past eight hours. His face, expression and words are bland. He talks of safety and security. Isolated incident. Numerous leads. Blah, blah, blah. Nothing concrete. The alleged perps killed themselves. Questions are dumber than the answers. Can not release all the names until we notify all the families. Will be able to tell more at a news conference set for tomorrow at eleven AM. A stringer from Boston asks if it's true the boys left suicide notes. Did the boys want to be better, kill more than the three kids in Wyoming? Or, did they just want someone to pay attention. Someone to listen to their pain. No answer. The entire event takes five minutes. The crowd of reporters and authorities disperses. The similarity to the Carter news briefing is quite unnerving.

Now the questions are coming faster than my brain can log them. They spin into absurdities, double back on themselves, and are reinvented as something totally unintelligible. School kids, the brutality, the van, the faces, the evasive answers, suicide notes, news conferences. It's too much for me now. I need release from the tribulation of intellectual recrimination.

I have to stop thinking or I'll cross the razor's line between sanity and insanity. Light into darkness. Episodic depression is frightful in two ways.

First, it can disable the sufferer. Second, it resembles the long-term variety. I endured the test market version once and its return is always a possibility. I've been in both camps and I prefer the summer variety to the gulag of winter. Have to be on my guard to avoid the long-term version. I remember the days of single rooms, sunrooms, and soothing music. Casual clothes and no belts. Nights of lights-out-at ten and bed checks at eleven. We were chaperoned as if we were hormone-driven teens rather than disoriented adults. I think there was some bed hopping during my one-month stay at the funny farm. I got nothing, but the young kid in room three-forty-five seemed to be very friendly with his next door neighbor, the topless dancer with the crack habit and pimp for a boy friend. Mediocre food and great meds. Rest and relaxation. Counseling. Individual and groups. Exercise was permitted after one week. Twice daily for me.

After three weeks, it was time to reenter the fun world, the world of the multiple agendas, the con men, and governmental deceit. The people in the funny farm are crazy but mostly honest. The people on the outside are dishonest and crazy about it. I was stacked, packed, and jacked. My mind was clear and I was buff. That was fifteen years ago. Now I'm soft in places, which were once firm. But, my mind is clearer than ever. And my emotions are well grounded. Sometimes, when I'm under pressure my cognitive capacity expands exponentially, but in a very haphazard way. The light saber pierces the darkness only to become engulfed by it. My fear is that having pierced the darkness, the darkness is let loose and will flood my mind forever. No more light. Ever. Insanity is a large package of C-4 I carry with me. I am making no sense now. I quit.

The telephone saves me from emotionally going away. The caller ID tells me it's Mary on her cell phone

"Hello, Mary. How are you?"

"Hello, Gene. Listen, there are two things you need to know. First, Dorothy was into some weird websites and chat rooms. She was known as Girlfromoz. Yes, she went to the usual info rooms and some very adult rooms. She also went to a few rooms that are beyond the edge. These are places where the lunatic fringe rambles and rants. Places that are monitored by authorities. The feds are there to listen, just listen. I heard through the cyber grapevine that one time the feds knew about a major bombing before it never happened. And that is why it never happened. So, Dorothy was into a chat room of an underground militia, one for a radical third-world group, and a few that featured discussions about the rights of all Americans. This is strange and frightening. If she goes in, she must learn something. And when does curiosity become belief? Also, when she goes in she leaves a trail, which can be followed by anyone who knows how to use the system and the processs. The could be curious or they could be hunters. What does this have to do with the Big Horn slaughter, I don't know? But, I think there has to be some connection. Whatta you think?"

"I think you need to slow down and take a breath. As a matter of good health, take five deep breaths then tell me about the second item."

"I sold my place and quit my job. I have to get out of this place so I can think clearly. I got a great deal on the house and the land from some developer who is looking to build mountain condos for the bored rich. I've been in negotiations for about a year. He just met my price. The university paid me through the end of next year. I am now on sabbatical. Then I retire and become a consultant. So, I have a big wad of cash little brother, enough for about fifteen years of living very large. And, here is the best part. I'm now crossing the Tennessee border on my way to you. I know you have room and will enjoy my company. Oh, yes the dogs are with me. As is all my equipment. So we can set up a ComRoom and continue our investigation. Well, what do you think? I mean I spent a small fortune on my home on wheels. The RV dealership made it road-ready for the trip. God, I had no idea tires were so expensive. And mechanics get forty-five dollars an hour in nowhereville Wyoming. The dealership could have closed for a week after I paid my bill. But, they made my van safe for me to drive the distance from where I was to where I want to be."

"Mary, it will be wonderful to see you again. Will you be able to find my cave? It's intentionally obscure from the eyes and ears of the world. 1, like my much older sister, love my privacy. You know, back roads and a hidden driveway. Even the mailbox carries only the road number. I'll clean up the room I reserve for guests. The dogs? A ComRoom? Jesus, Mary, thanks for the advanced notice. I'm sorry, that was really snotty. It's just that this all comes as a huge surprise. Of course you're welcome to stay as long as you wish. I look forward to seeing you. What is your ETA?"

"About noon tomorrow good buddy, back atcha. How did I find you? God, do you mistake me for a dullard and dolt? Almost like my brother. I fed my complete address and your complete address into the MapsUSA and I get a very detailed map of roads, turns, miles and time. Plus, I have GPS. You are not invisible, you know. The dogs can stay anywhere you want. By the way, I assume that I'll have no difficulty parking near the house? My toy is thirty feet long."

"I'll meet you at the door. Drink in hand. We'll worry about the house on wheels later when you are relaxed."

I am reminded of the schoolboy in England who was asked to use the word, marvelous twice in the same sentence. He replied: 'My sixteen-year-old sister got pregnant and my father said that was marvelous, bloodyfucking marvelous.' Well, she is not pregnant, but Mary was coming to stay and that was 'marvelous, bloody fucking marvelous.' My mind is bouncing with consternation. Real schizoid consternation. The push-me-pull-you from Dr. Dolittle. I have to work hard to avoid the pit of the passive aggressive. How would she fit into my life and I into hers? What about the hounds from hell? What about her stuff? She gets her own room and my office, albeit meager, would have to be the ComRoom. I can't help her set up the equipment. Do we need another telephone line? Yes. Do we need more juice? How about surge protectors in the lightning capital of the Western world? Don't want the toys to fry.

I feel put upon, but don't want to put her out. She has been through the ultimate rejection. Death of a loved one. I want to protect my life, yet open my heart. My world with all its patterns, sameness and security is about to be turned topsy-turvy. I am not sure I can handle the change easily, but I look forward to the challenge. Hell, if Mary can handle the loss of her daughter, I can handle Mary. Maybe, I am meant to help Mary in her struggle.

She is exceptionally prompt: 12:05 PM. She drives a boat. *Strasseshiff, auf Deutsche* for huge vehicle. One story tall, longer than I had thought, and wider than I had feared. The door opens, the driver's seat turns and a lift plate appears. The seat is the wheel chair, which she glides onto the plate. The plate is lowered via the hand controls. A ramp flips over and permits exit to the ground. I rush to greet her. She is all smiles and hugs.

We enter the house. The double front doors ease the awkwardness. I take her to her room with the bath attached. The doors here are a squeeze. This has to be remedied as soon as possible. Retrieve four bags. That's it. All her personal needs. Four bags. Dad used to say that a true Scot could pack and disappear from the English in ten minutes. It may have taken Mary thirty, but she is a lot faster than either of my wives.

Hither and Yon seem content to stay in the mobile hotel. They have their beds and water. And they smell Mary. We will run them three times a day until I can think of a space for them. My back yard seems big enough for the two. Just not as big as they are used to. Maybe they can stay with Mary, in the house, when I am gone. God, I'm resizing my doors, building dog runs, and making a new nest. I guess the intrusion is not an intrusion, but rather a massive revision. Onward, ever onward.

"Well, that meal was terrific, little brother. Do you cook all the time, or just for visiting dignitaries? Seriously, I know this is awkward, to say the least. And I truly appreciate your welcoming me with "Outstretched Arms." I needed to get away from the scene of my angst and devote myself to uncovering the issues, both criminal and familial of this situation. I have a plethora of discs. I need to sort through all of them. Align them in chronology. Analyze the visuals and the words. It will take me only a day to unload all my stuff. It may take two or three days to hook up and get everything in running order. Next, I'll have the boat emptied except for my babies no later than Saturday. I hope you don't mind. But I desperately need this time and space. I won't interfere with your comings and goings. Where you go and what you do are your business."

"Mary, understand this. It will take me a while to get used to all of us. I love the idea that you thought of here and me. I am just a little traumatized. That and any crampedness will melt away, my soul will become warm again, and we will learn to coexist. God, that sounded so sappy, didn't it? I, too, want to get some answers. Dorothy may be the key or simply an innocent bystander. We won't know until we dig deeply. Now here is a brave step. Let's get the dogs into the house for a brief visit. Smell the space and me. I've never had pets. So, this will be more difficult for me than for them."

We exit and retrieve her children and protectors. They remember me. Thank God. I get to keep my hands, feet, and throat. Now I learn that Hither is the mix of Shepherd and Rottweiler. Yon is the Puli and Coyote blend. Hither weighs about ninety-five or one hundred pounds, I guess, depending on the size of the mailman's leg he just ate. Yon weighs a skimpy seventy pounds. Hither plods at a gait. Yon walks then sprints. He can cover forty yards in three-point-two seconds. If he only had hands and could run the curl pattern, Mary and I could retire on his contract with the Dallas Cowboys. Yon can leap over or crawl under any fence. Yon has been known to walk along roofs and the top rung of a split rail fence. This is the Puli. Hither would run through the fence rather than jump it.

A good special teams player. Fears nothing, because everyone, except Yon, fears him.

The two never sleep at the same time. They are devoted to the protection of Mary. They eat once a day. In the morning. They expect water all day, particularly in this new heated environment. They like to gnaw bones. Some of their favorites look like femurs. For all their physical prowess, what I respect most is their uncanny way of always keeping Mary within distance. This is why they must come into the house as soon as possible. When she is away from them they pace. No barking. Just pacing like the Bengal tiger caged in the zoo. You can feel the tension. A spring about to be sprung. Humans don't own dogs like these. The dogs let a few select humans into their world and nurture them to animalhood. I am glad they are with Mary. I think I'll be glad they are with me.

Big Pass, Kansas

"We are honored to be with you people in Big Pass. We want to hear what you have to say about the safety and security of your families. What do you want? How can we help?"

Senator Miller begins his grass roots campaign. At this first town hall forum, the original six points are on display. The poster is huge, about 30 feet by 40 feet, and the dark colored eagle is a powerful, almost threatening symbol. Miller is cheerleading input from a new constituency in a small town. Every small town represents a part of constituency much broader than his own in Pennsylvania. He is apparently running for some office higher in the food chain than that of Senator.

"Before we start the discussion, I'd like Pastor Carl Waters of the Main Street Methodist Church to lead us in prayer. Pastor Waters."

"Heavenly and gracious Father, protector of your faithful children, keep us safe from harm, and grant us the courage and clarity to open our hearts and minds to hear your word and to do such things that please you. We ask that your guidance be with us tonight as we strive to return to the basic tenets of human decency and Godly love."

"Thank you, Pastor Waters. Now, the combined choirs of East High School, Big Pass High School, Central Vocational School, and York County High School will lead us in the National Anthem. Boys and girls."

As the anthem dies down, the applause and whistling swell to a deafening level. National pride runs deep in the heartland. As the audience shuffles and sits, there is a great deal of waving, handshaking, and general greeting. The noise and commotion are exhilarating. A real pep rally. Just no football game. There is a commonality to the look of the townsfolk. For the men, flannel, denim, or khaki work shirts are the norm. There are a few T-shirts underneath, each with a logo or a message. The hats are blue, green, or red depending on the farm equipment of choice. The hats are not removed. Black lace-up Stride Rites are to this set what Gucci or Bally loafers are to their distant cousins in Chicago. The women have on their size sixteen-eighteen checked or striped dresses and sensible shoes. They carry handbags, not purses. The hairstyles reflect the owners' desire for simplicity and neatness. Cut short, but not butch-dyke.

The faces of both the men and women are right out of a Rockwell or a Homer. Ruddy complexions. Enough lines to make them interesting. Blue eyes abound. Light hair. The women have bigger hips than the men reflecting that they are breeding stock. The men look like terriers: wiry, piercing eyes, and quick darting actions. Very few fat men. When you work on a farm fourteen hours a day six days a week, you burn up all the food calories. There are numerous teens in the assembled throng but no small children. Many young folk. This is their future.

"Welcome, ladies and gentlemen. May I say how gratified I am to see such a huge turn out? Maybe we should have up-linked this event to all the high schools in the state. I hope that by now all of you know the original six points of the platform. We have taken the liberty to provide leaflets with the six points, our mission, and our telephone numbers. Also, so that I don't forget our purpose, my team has given us this reminder poster behind me."

"Before we take our first question or comment, let's remember to relax, have fun, and treat your neighbor with the respect and dignity you would like from him or her. There are no network TV cameras here. Obviously, the big city power mongers, or is that mongrels . . ."

This draws the desired hoots and whistles.

"Maybe those fine folks don't think much of what you want. The microphones are so that we can hear each other. OK, who's first?"

"Senator Miller, my name is Jack Williamson. My wife, Luanne, and I have three children and we are scared stiff. We see stuff on the television news. We call them the three Gees: guns, gangs, and godlessness. My family wants to be safe and secure. But, how do we get there without more violence?"

"Mr. Williamson, thanks for being the lead-off batter. Going first takes courage. I don't think this great nation of yours needs another revolution. I say, get involved in local governments. This is the entry port to the sea of political change. If you can influence local governments and the state government representatives who live in your town, they will influence the national government. The problem, as we see it, is that in the past fifty years politics and political power have shifted away from the local, law abiding citizenry to those who live in an ivory tower called Washington. New rules have been handed down to you good citizens. To wrest power from those in power is not easy, because those in power will not go quietly into the night. But you good people know everything worth having is worth the effort. Plants don't grow without fighting the soil, elements, and vermin. It takes a lot of effort. It's the same with reclaiming your country. It's worth reclaiming, so it's worth the effort."

"Senator Miller, Marva Locker. I would first like to thank you for coming to Big Pass. You're the first national politician we've seen in three years. Our own Senator, old what's his name, never seems to have the time to stop by for coffee and pie. Even during the County Fair."

The applause and cheering are thunderous.

"Anyway, what I'd like to ask is, once we've begun the process, how do we know that the people in Washington won't just shut us out like they've done in the past? And second, do we need new laws?"

"Thank you, Miss Locker. I'd be honored to be invited back to Big Pass anytime. Just one question—What kind of pie will I get? I'm partial to apple or peach."

The laughter reverberates throughout the auditorium. Even a few cheers. He has won their hearts. Their minds and votes will follow.

"Seriously, it will take a lot of work. Quitting is not an option for you. You will probably have to elect new leaders. Men and women, who believe as you do."

"Now to your second point. No new laws are needed. What is needed is firm enforcement of the laws already on the books. There are state and federal laws, which regulate and control dangerous things like guns and drugs. There are state and federal laws, which establish prosecutorial guidelines and punishments for abusers of the gun and drug laws. Let me ask you to think a minute about guns, because that's the thornier of the two subjects. The Second Amendment to the Constitution clearly states that gun ownership is based upon the need for a militia."

"Let me quote: 'A well-regulated Militia, being necessary to the security of a free State, the right of the people to keep and bear arms, shall not be infringed.' The militia would, in turn, act at the orders of and owe their allegiance to the government. In the period of international revolution, this was the government's way of maintaining individual freedom and controlling any wide spread abuse of weapons at the same time."

"Today, there is not a right thinking American among you who would call for the removal of hunting guns. Rifles and shotguns are for sport and self-protection. Do we need automatic weapons? Do we really think it's a good idea to make automatic weapons available to children and the emotionally unstable? What's wrong with licensing these weapons like we do cars and doing background checks on the people who want to own them? These two steps would go a long way to ensure the safety and security of the decent, honest citizens. We do not need the Posse Comitatus and myriad of paramilitary, neo-Nazi, white supremacists, that feel they and they alone, can protect us. Who will protect us from them?"

"Surely we don't need the rampaging drugs that are threatening the future of our youth. We have strict laws outlawing cocaine, crack, crank, meth, smack, and every other imported or hometown destroyer. But, our police have their hands tied by the judicial system that coddles the criminal. The police can't do this and the police can't do that. The rights and freedoms of the criminal are held above the safety and security of society. Use the laws that are on the books. Encourage the courts to act without fear. If they will not, get new, responsible judges who will.

"Remember: the judges are elected or appointed by elected officials. They all owe their bench to someone and that someone ultimately is you. The future is in your hands. This is what we believe. What do you believe?"

The admirers were on their feet. The applause lasts well over two minutes.

"Thank you, my friends. I hope I'm not being too presumptuous to call you my friends. I am excited. I feel the energy of goodness. I feel the strength of conviction. I feel the concern. I know there is a better way and you are the answer."

"Senator Miller, God bless you. You and your wake-up call. How do we protect ourselves against the liars, deceivers, and charlatans? Oh, sorry, my name is Ida Hess. This is Thomas, my husband of twenty-nine years. These are my children, Tom Junior, Grace, Richard, Sarah, and Mark. And I have six grandchildren. We didn't bring them along tonight, 'cause they're all full of spit and vinegar. And this is a serious grown-up night."

"Ida, thank you, and God bless you and your clan. Well, protection against liars. This country is blessed with the highest degree of technological expertise in the world. And, because of a free market system, the cost of this technology is reasonable and even inexpensive when the benefits are weighed against both the actual costs and savings generated by use of the technology. There is a wealth of information about places, companies, and people in files throughout the world. Let us use the information for safety and security. You can do it. The sooner, the better."

"It is possible to establish a national clearinghouse of information—of personal files—to be checked by the proper duly-elected authorities? We have a system already in place. This single source would have more useable, important information than the Internal Revenue Service or the credit companies, and it would be substantially more accessible. If we can establish this data bank, we can control our destiny."

"OK. That pretty much covers the basics. Can we take a half-hour break for restroom and refreshment? Then we'll reconvene for further discussion. Those of you who must tend to little ones at home. We understand if you leave now. The children must come first. This evening is for the children. We thank you for coming. If you would be so kind to leave your names and addresses in the books by the doors. We'd like to send you literature about what we are learning and doing. Also, please take a few of the pamphlets in the baskets. Give them to your friends. Let them read the material at their convenience. If something strikes a favorable chord, tell them to let us know. Write to us or call us on the eight-hundred number. Those of you who can stay, please be back in the auditorium in thirty minutes. It's now eight-forty-five. We'll restart our discussion at nine-fifteen."

With that, Senator Miller takes a big drink of water, smiles, and waves to his enthusiastic supporters. Then he turns to the dozen men and women behind him. They form a small discussion circle. All of this while the rafters are shaking from the applause, shouting, and stomping. The place is going wild. He is on his way.

The morning's work has exhausted me. I think I'll avail myself of the executive health spa. Pump a little. Steam a little. Nap a little. Eat late and light at my desk.

My nap lasted a little longer than I had planned. Finished eating by three. Mary e-mailed and asked that I pick up a few things at Electronic Land. She is putting her equipment together and needs items listed by description, number, and manufacturer name. What is on the electronic news and in the national financial newspaper? Nothing and nothing. The usual plethora of dearth. Stare at the work. Double and triple check the overall impression. Look for flaws. The spinach between the teeth of the naked woman. Looking for any inconsistencies is mesmerizing. When I gaze intently, I drift into a trance-like state. Time and place mean nothing. Two seconds become an hour. An hour is a millisecond. I am in my office. I am on the beach. The telephone comes to my aid. Like the light that pierces the darkness. This time the darkness is shattered.

"Gene, have you seen the local paper today?"

"Mary, I don't get a second copy at the office. What is so important?"

"Senator Miller had his inaugural town hall meeting last night. Somewhere in Kansas. There was a picture and small UPI article on page six of the National section. The text is banal. But, it's the picture. There is the good Senator waving to the crowd. Behind him I think I see a face or two that are familiar. They may have been in Carter. I can't wait for you to see the shot. We'll need to get a blow-up of it and dig into the details. I can do some cross matching with lifts from the videos of the other tragedies. Hurry home."

Gulf Beach, Florida—ComRoom

My used-to-be office looks as if it has been redesigned by Rube Goldberg. Boxes stacked and seemingly held together by bailing wire and duct tape. Cables run all over the place. Under, over, in front of and behind the boxes, the desk, the worktable, and the control panel. The small room is noticeably much smaller. The walls have been moved in eighteen inches to two feet by the equipment. Like a Poe short story, this shrinking of space is disconcerting. Screens on, off, and flickering. Broadcast and cable stations visible in the comer. Floor lights on low so as not to interfere with viewing the screens. In front of a large monitor displaying the Internet is Mary's keyboard. The wheelchair can't be driven easily throughout the small space because of the intertwined clumps of cord on the floor. Mary has devised paths. The cables are tagged so that she knows the workings of the intricate system. This, I assume, will facilitate repair. The floor looks like an old English garden maze. There is a visible entrance and exit, but they are one in the same. My office has become Mary's electronic womb. The dogs have somehow wormed into the small space and lie protectively near their queen. She is in hog heaven.

"I was trying to fire up this puppy. But, couldn't. So, I'm fixin' to stand by to get ready. The stuff you bought at the store will complete my project. Please put the bag on the table somewhere. But, don't move anything."

"How will anything new fit into this space?"

"It's not so much that this is additional, rather faster and stronger replacements. I'll be able to eliminate about half the cables. The ones you bought can carry more. Do more and take up less space. You'll see. By the by, take a gander at page four of the National section of today's newspaper. Upper right hand corner."

There he is in miniature. But, looming in my soul larger than life. Senator Baldwin Miller. Waving. His face is a study in fatherly authority. His family is behind him. I'm not sure that anyone looks familiar. Faces too small and out of focus.

"OK, so what. Now what?"

"How do we get the original or the negative of that picture? If we can get it, I can play with the images and we can learn who is standing in support of the good Senator. It's a wire photo. Can you contact them? I have no pull with the news media. You do, don't you?"

"I can call a guy in New York and find out how to get the shot."

"Could you do that now?"

I learn that I can call a Jim Larson at United Press International. Jim will find out who took the shot and how to get the neg. He will then get back to me. I can talk to Jim in two days, because he is out of town. Mary is disappointed.

"I'm going for a swim. I need to cleanse."

"Yes, baby brother, you may swim now. Be careful and don't drown. Maybe I'll send the dogs to watch over you. You know, protect you from yourself."

I commence my laps. Nothing purges like a long swim. Swimming is a solitary activity. I like that. I had the pool built for exactly that purpose. The birdcage extends from the house down the far side of the backyard. Still have enough space for my flower garden. Over one hundred blooming plants and flowers. The colors, textures and aromas are calming and seductive. When I'm not swimming laps, the pool will accommodate only two floating chaise lounges. Headrests, arm rests, cup holders, and the fixture for an umbrella. My aquatic LayZee-Dads. The wide side of the river stone pool deck is closer to the garden. God, the single life encourages self-indulgence.

The pool has no diving board. No deep end. Just a constant four feet deep, sixteen feet wide, and sixty feet long. Forty yards to a lap and twenty-two laps to a half mile. This is good, enervating relaxation. A great way for me to maintain some semblance of a shape other than pear. Somewhere between lap eight and eleven, I break the wall. Get my second wind. There is a reasonable cadence to my strokes, breathing and kicking. It may not be the fastest combination, but it's comfortable.

My lungs no longer feel as if they are about to implode. The desired warmth seeps into my muscles. This means it's all working. I hear the hounds and catch a glimpse of their antics at the next turn.

Are they dancing? They are running back and forth with my laps. They're bounding poolside, barking uproariously. Sprinting, ducking, and lunging as if they were herding animals or small children. Are they stupidly happy or concerned that I am in some sort of trouble? Does this mean that they care or that they are worried that if I drown they won't be fed?

Through all the barking and scrambling, they never take their eyes off me. Finally, I stop and call to them. They see that I am not in danger of drowning and that they will be fed. The ruckus stops. They both cautiously approach the water by the narrow side steps. First, Hither puts a paw in the green-blue medium. Then another. Part in and part out. Yon backs up and springs in. The resultant waves cascade over the canine partner. Hither lunges ahead. They both swim toward me, the target of their anxiety. They do not attack, although the clawing and clamoring pushes me under. God, to be killed by the saviors. How sadly ironic. Now they begin to push me toward the stairs, which lead to dry land and safety. Their noses are prods. Strong with soft tips. And they really do doggie paddle.

Their wet bodies are much smaller than they appear in the house. Their fur or hair, depending on the animal, is matted by the water. This causes them to gain weight. This new weight would pull them under if they weren't so powerful. Their paws are like canoe paddles. Their faces and eyes are not menacing, but rather show concern for my state. They're convinced I was in trouble. Once on land they shake dry. I towel dry and we go our separate ways. They run the yard. Out to the hedges and back. I plop in my chair. They win. They seemed to have fun asserting their authority over the homeowner stranger.

"Well, did all my boys have fun in the pool?"

"Mary, these dogs are amazing. I think they actually care for me. Either that or they see me as a great toy not to be lost, broken, or drowned. What would you like for dinner? Given the fact that I am wiped. Let's make it simple to prep and clean. You know, your kind of meal."

"How about a big bowl of everything in the fridge?"

"You got it. And we'll dine poolside."

After dinner I stretch out on the couch to read some trade journals. The tedium of their text has a narcotic effect, which is particularly powerful after exercise, at the end of the day, and on a full stomach. I drift off with the last magazine resting on my chest.

Hiking is a phenomenal way to go outside to get inside. The Appalachian Trail is one of the great gifts Americans share. I've walked the Georgia section several times. Each time, I experience something new about nature. The topography, the trees, rocks, path, and the sky are different every time. Then there are the people. Similar goals from dissimilar lives. All the time I walk I can think. Wherever my mind leads me. I have settled family disputes. Understood the inner workings of the primitive computers. Contemplated love in its many and diverse forms. Argued with myself. Prayed a lot. Stared at the stars and comprehended my insignificance. All these things are possible when I am alone on the trail. As I reach a crest, I survey where I've been and where I must go before I make camp. The clouds are darkening. Wind picking up from breeze to puffs. The roiling clouds sporadically obliterate the sun heading earthward. Everything happens quickly out here. Or, at least, it seems so because I am distracted by inner thoughts and outer beauty. No time to rest. Down the other side of my conquest. Down is just as difficult as up. Different muscles. Slope is slippery. Switchbacks are severe, because the down side is steeper than the up side. Switchbacks can double and triple the distance traveled. I must pick up my pace. One of the great things about hiking alone is the aloneness, which is also the not-so-great aspect of hiking. I miss the camaraderie of another's presence, but I don't miss the required interaction. I've been out here alone, in a small group, and with seven others. Alone is best. The weight of the pack is no different. But, my schedule is my own. Four miles a day. Eight the next. Three nights out. One week alone.

It's almost dark. The combination of no sun, the heavy clouds, and the overhanging trees has created a forest primeval for my trip down the other side of the mountain. The branches bow. The trees bend. Bark and twigs from the forest floor are kicked up against my legs and into my eyes. Vision beyond twenty feet is impaired. The rustling of the leaves, the cracking of thunder, and creaking of the trunks and branches are a threatening cacophony. Footing is precarious. The rain has increased the moisture on every surface. Damn! Falling to one knee causes the pack weight to shift nearly over my head. Pushes me precipitously downward. I am now rolling. Well, more like flopping. Arms and legs are going every which way. I try to grab anything to slow the inevitable process. The pack weight, my weight, and momentum rule out any possibility of stopping. Just tuck and roll. Prevent breaking an arm or leg. Cover my head to limit damage. Stumps and fallen branches dig into my torso. Really hurt. Suddenly there is nothing between the earth and me. I have fallen over some edge or into a hole.

Crash. It was a hole. I landed feet first but am jammed into the crevasse. Stuffed like a hand in a glove. Wind knocked out of me. Gasp for breath. Rain is beginning to cascade over me. Can't unhook pack. Arms pinned against my body. Have to wriggle and squeeze my arms over my head. Great fucking effort for very little result. Struggle to right my body and to pull it up using the vines. Pack jammed to the walls will not move easily. It's about eight feet from the top of my head to the cleft to the outside. Test the vines. Slippery, but they appear to hold me even with the jammed pack. I better be quick about it. Exit before the water loosens the vines' grips on the cave walls.

The pack is lodged in the wall and creates an extreme impediment to upward movement. Slowly I begin my ascent. One inch at a time. At this rate, I'll be out of the tomb in an hour and a half. Or drowned. Dig toes of boots into earth walls. Pull on base of vines. Very gradually I rise like Lazarus. As vines break or pull away, I pause and rest on my toes. I can't lean back or I'll drive the pack deeper into the muddy wall. I must press my body forward. Face flat against the muck. If I rush and pull too hard, the vines will come from the sides. If I wait, the rainwater will weaken the vines' hold in the walls. Damned if I do and damned if I don't. Purposefully, I hoist my body. Pausing only to seek a stronger vine or a deeper toehold. The rain is gushing over the opening's rim. The thunderclaps are deafening. So close that I can't even think the word, one, between the flash and the crash. The storm must be right on top of me. Maybe inside my personal hell. If I look up, muddy water with leaves and sticks blinds me. If I look down, I can't see my next step. Or next vine. The rain. The noise. The position. I'm scared and about to be fucked by Mother Nature. The vines are barely holding. The toeholds are crumbling. I freeze. The rainwater is building in the bottom of my cavern. If I wait much longer to escape, the water will overtake me. I'll drown. Can't go forward. Won't go back. Muscles are beginning to bum and ache. I hear voices through the storm's rage. They're almost laughing. Males seem to be calling. I call back. Help. Help me. I'm down here. Stuck. Can't get up or out. Help. Two shapes appear at the mouth of my earthen coffin. My boys. Dad. We're here. Reach out your hand we'll help you out. Dad. Dad. Gene. Gene. Can you get up? Get up. Gene, get up. My eyes slit open. It's Mary holding my hand gently.

"Gene, wake up. You've been involved in a frantic dream. You're OK. Here, wipe your face. You're sweating up a storm. What was it all about? You were reaching out and up as if for someone or something. Like the moment before death. Reaching out to God. Calling out to be saved. From what or whom?"

"Mary, it's a dream I've had many times before. Except this ending was different and much more rewarding. I think I understand it now. I know my boys love me. And, I think I love me. Many thanks for being here. At this time. Right now. Now, I think I'd like to get out of the sweatbox. Change the linens. Have a weak drink and go back to sleep."

"Not before you see what I've found. I hate to one-up your psychic revelation, but I think I just tapped the vein to the mother lode. Get showered and changed. Then come to the ComRoom. Yes, it's important."

I do as I am told. The dutiful bro. The entire changing and cleansing takes fifteen minutes.

"Now what is so important?"

"Chat room heaven. Here are a few of the places Dorothy went late at night. She was Girlfromoz. A few of the wrinkles in her soul. I'll skip the stud pages and fuck rooms. But check this out. Here is the first: Houseafire. Scrutinize the message board and you'll get an idea about the purpose of the room and the personalities of the Chatty Kathies and Kens."

I sit and stare at the screen. Scroll and click. Houseafire seems to promote anarchy. Do away with all governmental restriction and repression. Protests and violence are directly below the surface. RichBitch wants to know if guns will be made available to all or just the leaders. What will happen to the good parents and the benevolent leaders? WarEagle tells her to either play on this team or the enemy's. He will make war when he is ready and at the site of his own designation. Destruction will rule. FarmerJohn praises WarEagle for his courage, but warns him against the foolhardiness of the ego. From the many planted seeds, only a specific crop will spring. If we work with natural forces, we will be stronger because we share the strength of our ancestors and allies. We will overthrow the powers that regulate our lives into slavery. To rush ahead unaware of our fate, friends, and foes will ultimately bring about the crushing of our cause. Look to the East. The land of our elders. Look to the farmers. Farmers nurture. We will rise up and recapture our heritage of freedom.

"Shit, that's nothing but sophomoric drivel. Noisy tin drums. They barely talk the talk much less walk the walk. Just weirdos who love the sound of their own printed word. And, incidentally, don't any of them use a spellchecker? They are not telling anybody anything."

"Open your eyes and ears. These people are trying to tell anyone who will listen. They are filled with angst. They may have information they want to share but do not want to be caught sharing. Take this room as a place that could contain one piece of a very big and strange puzzle. Here is another: BoldWorld."

The future of man is in his hands. He must take control of his techno-faculties. The space around men and women is theirs to rule. Those who deny this are the enemy of the future and the enemy of the people. SeeingEye pines for the time when governments and big business serve the people. The time when we are connected with the other planets and other life forms, which have been kept from us and we from them. Our PCs will be the connecting points. This will require a liberation and international distribution of the resource. Governments will have to work together or they will be abolished by the People's Committee. The planets are aligned for an event, which will bring recognition to our struggle. FaithBlinded wants to provide food for the millions who are starving because of governments' lack of interest. No money, just foodstuffs and basic ingredients which are now rotting in the granaries and warehouses all over the word. Storm the silos. Feed the people. Before we venture into space, we must feed the children. Weapons of power have been stashed throughout the world. Look and listen. Read the signs and follow the map.

"Just more claptrap. Little voices in the night sounding bolder than they are. Verbal testosterone. Silhouettes on the shade. Smaller than life. This is so much bullshit. Mary, your information gathering nee conspiracy theory is like the old adage that if you put ten thousand monkeys at ten thousand typewriters, they would produce Shakespeare's entire body of work. This may be true given two or three millennia. But, within the time constraints of life and reality, the monkeys would produce gibberish. It's the same with the interpretation of these volk-sprachers. If they say enough over a long enough period of time, some morsel of whatever they say will very likely occur. We used to have street crazies, who would pace all around and mutter nonsense. The crazies are now accessible via the

Internet. Look, Mary, I'm exhausted from my dream. I need my rest. See you in a few hours if you are awake when I arise. It's not that I don't care. I just can't see the handwriting on the walls. As of now it's just graffiti. Take this kiss."

The workday was eleven hours long, before noon. The afternoon was longer. By the time I got home, all I wanted to do was go to bed. I am not required to exchange niceties with my sister, as she is not so with me. We cohabitate. The Early Network News was mumbling softly about tonight's American Forum from the studios in New York City. The President's Commission on Citizen Safety has been convened to hear the outcries of America. The Magnificent Seven will take telephone calls from anywhere in the country. For ninety minutes, including limited commercial interruptions, the politically-correct-celebrating-diversity group of over-promised intellectuals will tell the factory workers, laborers, and members of other service sectors how to behave and what to think. All within the confines of a safe and sterile television studio. Jesus H. Christ, what's wrong with that picture. Limited reality, maximum governmental control, and no humanity. Other than these shortcomings, the program is truly beneficial for the American public. I will watch nonetheless. I also watch train wrecks.

"Good evening, ladies and gentlemen. Tonight you will be a participant in a breakthrough public forum. A revolutionary format of national proportions. Tonight, the federal government's Commission on Citizen Safety wants to hear from you, the citizens of this great nation. You see around the table seven of the most distinguished people of our time. People from all venues. Men and women selected by your government as those best able to give the administration advice in the area of citizen safety. Advice from you through them to the President. Let me introduce them. From my left: Doctor John Wenger, noted teacher and lecturer in the field of Sociology and Anthropology. Leslie Tremaine, social activist and leader. Brett Tucker, founder of U Graduate Now! High School. Huang Tsai, software and program pioneer. Doctor Elizabeth Pendelton, Chairwoman of the National Parent Teacher Association. Roberta Ramirez, President of the League of Woman Voters. Chakka Uhuru, National Merit Scholarship winner."

"This panel needs no further introduction. Just call the eight hundred number presently on your screen. Operators are waiting. The panel members will answer the questions by providing their own interpretation of each subject. Each panel member will be allotted ninety seconds to answer each viewer's question. We urge you to gather your entire family into the television room for this, the first of four open forums. So, without further ado, let's take our first question."

"Hello, my name is Raymond Smalley. From Littletown, New York. My question is this: Because humans are, by their very nature, violent animals, is it reasonable to anticipate that a free society can mitigate or eliminate violence?"

"Thank you Mister Smalley, first up will be Miss Leslie Tremaine."

"Sir, I disagree entirely with your basic premise. Humans are not violent by nature. Rather they have within them the capacity for violence when they feel threatened or when they are hurt. Fear begets or triggers violence. All animals have this defensive reaction to harm. Humans have, throughout history, subverted the defensive capacity into an offensive action, such as a preemptive strike or an attack long after they perceived they have been injured or wronged. So, to avoid violence, humankind's imperative must be to ensure that no segments or sub segments are hurt or wronged. No more fear equals no more violence."

"Thank you, Miss Tremaine. Now on to Huang Tsai. Mister Tsai."

"We must cleanly separate violence from action. Violence is rooted in evil, because it causes injury, harm or destruction. Action has no moral value. It can be good or evil depending on its roots and consequences. Situational ethics apply to action. Man acts. But, man is not violent. Most people, particularly the older, unenlightened ones, will not take the time or exert the energy to be active, but not violent."

"Elizabeth Pendelton?"

"Yes, humans are and can be violent. We, who are leaders, must set the example of restraint and control. This example in our daily lives clearly communicates to our peers and our children how one should live. To sustain control and thereby provide a safe and secure environment for our children, we must elicit the involvement of governing bodies. The governing bodies must institute a system of protective measures, which will not adversely impact the law abiding, but will protect us all from the violent. Violence has been and will always be a part of the psyche in certain segments of humankind. But we can control it with appropriate measures and constraints."

"Miss Tucker."

"Education is the key. Pure and simple. Humankind, uneducated, is savage. The broader the education base, the better. A thoroughly educated society can take human kind beyond the jungle to understand that violence serves no short-term or long-term good or benefit for society. Opening of education to all people is critical. This will require greater private and governmental involvement in the education process—from pre-school to college. By investing in education, we can be sure to ultimately eliminate violence engendered by ignorance."

"Mister Uhuru."

"Well, education is fine up to a point. But, sooner or later, and most often sooner, all the education in the world falls flat if the educated are not held responsible for their actions. Therein lies the core of violence. I can be loving, neutral, or violent. But in all cases I must be responsible. If responsibility is truly enriched in each and every one of us, there will be no violence."

"Miss Ramierez."

"It's amazing. Some of us are skirting the issue of the root of violence. We cannot just usher in a police state and slap control on everyone until they listen like good boys and girls. I, like my learned younger colleague, firmly believe in the concept of responsibility. And I look to the male of the species to lead the way as he has over the centuries. And all of it starts with accountability. Men have sustained a pattern of domination without accountability. Today its manifested in illegitimate births and the abandonment of the children. These are violent actions because they harm the psyche of children and women. But, if men are required to be responsible, their actions would lead to the elimination of violence."

"Doctor Wenger, you're next and our last contributor to this question."

"Mister Smalley, it is reasonable to hope that we can eliminate violence from our society. I believe that if we look at the trends in this country and throughout the world we can see this day coming. What brought about these favorable indicators? Education. Solid and very thorough education for all. Constant state-supervised curricula which has led to a fuller realization of one's place vis a vis others and society in general. It's that simple. It is easier to be angry or violent with a stranger than with ourselves. Education will eliminate violence."

"Lets take this moment for a commercial break. We'll take a second call after the break."

I could see each panel member bristling at the others. All the while keeping an ingenuously concerned face to the camera. A mask. There were more moral high grounds in that studio than during a papal election. And tons of ego agitation. The shuffling of papers. The tapping of pens. Arms folded and unfolded. Seat shifting. Knuckle cracking. All the signs of unrest. Unrest caused by panel members having to listen to the canned responses of their associates. God, these intellectual sphincters are out of kilter with each other. Each is so sure he or she is the right voice that each is dismissed by the others as totally wrong. Dialog among the crazies. Gibberish and gobbledi-gook.

I quit. To bed before nausea sets in.

Lutztown, Pennsylvania

Recess. Playtime. Fresh air time. No teacher staring down from the blackboard time. At one o'clock in early May it's pleasantly warm in Lutztown, Pennsylvania. The sun is bright because it is spring. A bright sun is integral to the planting season. It's been this way for centuries. First the Indians, then the political refugees flocking to Penn's Woods, then the Amish and Mennonites, the religious refugees. They are married to the land. The old ways don't really die; they are just modified ever so slightly every century. They never quite fit with the mode du jour, but the old ways don't clash that much either. The Amish and Mennonites try to keep to themselves as much as possible to avoid confrontation. Farming is one way to isolate. Their own school is another. However, with each generation a few more of the young ones go out among the English, taste the fruits, both bitter and sweet, of the foreign world, and never come back. Hope springs eternal. Some people hope for change and some people hope for no change. The children just hope to be first to the slide or the swing. A game of kick ball can be started on a Monday and completed during Friday afternoon's last recess of the week. This day is no different. So they think.

The first shot kicks up the soil near the big slide. The second rips an arm off Leslie Taylor. For a brief moment the schoolyard is deathly silent. No voices, no yelling, not even Leslie. She is stunned to stone. There is no motion. The kids are frozen in time and space. Paralyzed. Not panicky, yet. The crack of the foreshadowed event is so great that even the teachers sitting on the benches sipping coffee are stunned still. Then the outburst. The rain of death from one hundred yards. In the time it takes Missus Fellenbaum to put her mug of decaf on the bench, there is a shower of bullets, all concentrated on the four swings and two teeter totters. Six little bodies are simply heaped onto the ground. Blood pours from the torsos like grain from punctured burlap sacks. No movement. No sound. As she stands to rush to the fallen, Missus Fellenbaum, mother of one, teacher for twelve years, loses her right leg from the knee down. Then her face is removed from the front of her head by the impact of a huge slug. She falls before she can scream in personal pain or distress for her children. Another lump of former human is on the ground.

The cloud of doom rains on the kick ball game about fifty yards to the left of the swings. Because the players are dispersed on the unused baseball diamond, the carnage is not intensive. Still, Jimmy Leonard playing second base, Henry Brubaker at one shortstop and Gwen Wenrich at the other short stop bounce as they fall. Gwen tries to crawl or slide to second. It's impossible to crawl with only one arm and one shoulder as the functional parts of a body that is traumatized by pain and impact. Her white barrettes flung from her hair by the impact of the slug float in small pools of blood where she fell. Face down and still, Henry appears to have the kickball resting on his back. But, the big red blob is nothing more than the contents of his internal cavity dragged through the hole made by the bullet entering below his sternum and exiting above the base of his spine. His once yellow shirt is now the same crimson as his jeans. Jimmy is seated with eyes open. No motion from the battered life-sized doll on the base. Just a dime sized hole replacing the polo player monogram on his shirt. A through and through as the New York City cops would say. Death was instantaneous. Missus Mikler screams in panic and dives under the concrete and oak bench spilling her coffee en route.

The cloud of black rain continues its rush to the building. The teachers and children can't see or hear the familiar pelting of big raindrops from the nourishing early spring rains. They can hear the windows and their frames being shattered. Splinters and shards fly twenty feet into the bright sky. The brick walls of the forty-year-old structure lose chunks and chips to the hot metal shower. There is no one inside except the administration staff and the janitor, Les Rutt. At the instant of the downpour, Les was entering Missus Mikler's class room to empty the waste basket, check the paper towel dispenser and touch her chair. This latter was his reason and the first two were required by his job. He adored Ruth. But, she was married and he was just a school janitor. His entrance was his exit. His body unceremoniously accepted three slugs and was thrown against the blackboard. The impact of the unplanned meeting of body and slate cracked the slate at the letter, G, written in cursive Italics, capital and lower case. Ruth had written the letter three times on one panel. Three children at a time were required to come to the board and copy her work. Then they would return to their seats and repeat the process from afar. This method would be repeated until everyone could properly, without coaching or example, write the alphabet. This week was G-H-I. The lesson stopped today. Les's body and blood erased a great deal of hard work by Bobby Slotkin, Jack Messersmith, and Georgianna Kunzler.

The children outside are in a true panic modality by now. Most of them are running aimlessly, screaming at the top of their lungs. A few of them are standing stalk-still and staring. Nowhere in particular. Billy Stow trips over Mary Ruth Martin's body and scrapes his knees and hands. He whines in pain. Mary Ruth's body did not move. She said nothing because she had no jaw. Assistant Principal Gerald Dance leaps into action. A rare activity for a life-long bureaucrat. He runs on the outer rim of the gaggle of panic. Herds the children by waving his arms in a constant upward and outward motion directing the little ducks to the side of the school away from the frenzy. He calls their names, imploring, demanding and pleading for them to run to the safe place. This activity is both good and bad. Most of the children respond as required and flock to the comer. Some simply stand immobilized by panic and the pandemonium. The standers present obstacles to the others seeking safety around the comer. Small jumbles of small bodies crop up, then dissipate as the on rushers rush on. As the herd clumps, each clump becomes a target for renewed onslaught. The herd is culled on the basis that they are there. Not genetics. Not race, creed, or color. Just presence in the yard.

Mister Dance presents a substantial target. And although he is active, his motion is not rapid enough to reduce his vulnerability. One slugs twists him completely around. He staggers backward, but going forward ever herding. He moves around the tightening circle of innocent humanity. The second slug drives him face down to the earth. He pushes himself up to his knees. Screams to the children to run and hide. Turns to see if the other teachers are following his lead and takes the third and final round about one-half an inch above the bridge of his nose. His dandruff encrusted scalp is lifted from front to back, the mental machinery spews into the air, and Mister Dance flops on his back. Gerald Dance, too young for one war and too old for the next, dies on the playground. The last of the students and three teachers scurry around the building to safety. All is well except for the eleven third graders, two teachers, a janitor, and an

Assistant Principal. In less time than it takes to write the three letters of the week, fifteen universes are obliterated. There is no life on or in them.

"How come reloading takes so damned much time? You'd think the companies that make these guns would have figured a way to shorten the time it takes to remove the spent clip, insert a fresh one, and get a load into the breach. Shit, somebody could get hurt or killed just getting ready to re-fire."

George Greiner always complained about something. Nothing was ever good enough for him. His ego and his father told him he deserved perfection in people and things around him. God knows his father deserved perfection. His dad beat this in to George Junior. George Senior was always getting the short end or the filthy end of the stick. People and businesses tried to cheat him or take advantage of his good and giving nature. He was Number One on the union grievance list in both quantity and complexity of complaints against Lutztown Machinery. Somehow the union covered for George. Took his grievances to the company and covered his frequent post payday absences with alibis. George Junior learned from the master. Now the gun didn't work to his ideal.

"Shut up, you pussy. You're always bitching about something. Now you have a chance to make everything right. For people to take you seriously. Make your mark. And what do you do but piss and moan? Ya' know a little less bitchin' and a little more finger twitchin' would do you a world of good."

Freddie Douts was a bully. George needed this. But, Freddie was extreme. He had a tattoo on his back that read, 'Take no prisoners and rip the watches off the dead.' Freddie loved to hunt. The more gentle the game, the better he liked to kill it. Rabbits were perfect. There were over twenty guns in his household on Duke Road. His formal education stopped with the tenth grade. The state minimum. He went to work with his dad and two older brothers fixin' stuff around other people's houses, mowin' lawns, plowin' driveways in the winter. General handyman activities. The quality of their work was satisfactory. Never exemplary. Their living was modest, but the family needs were more. Or, so they were convinced. And, while there was never enough for better basics, there was always money for personal indulgences such as many rifles and hand guns, regular visits to the local saloons, and several partially repaired tractors and trucks. Viewed from a normal plateau, the Douts clan lived just above the poverty line in a junkyard.

Freddie was the baby and spoiled rotten by his dim-witted mother, who was also his father's cousin. Therein lies the root of the problem. He got what he demanded. Stomped his feet. Screamed. Pushed. Even hit. Mom took it. Dad looked the other way because Freddie was just following a fine family tradition. Freddie even beat up his older brothers. All he was good at was bullying. And he was damned good. He was a regular on the county sheriff s sign-in sheet. Four times he had been charged with breaking and entering and vandalism. Four times he had been excused and four times his family covered the cost of the damages by doing odd jobs around the property. Freddie always promised to be good. He lied.

"Yah, George, you're nothin' but a big pussy. Cryin' because you've been fucked by everybody. Well, now it's your turn to do the fuckin' and you're still bawling. Maybe we shoulda' brought along your titty bottle to make you feel good. You don't hear me bein' a baby."

"Shit, Al, all you ever say is what Freddie says. Can't that pea brain of yours come up with its own thoughts. You're nothin' but Freddie's echo shadow."

Alvin Slaughter was dumber than a box of rocks. On top of that he was fat and ugly. A great three-way combination that endeared him to his chronological peers. If someone can be the butt of jokes, Al was the prime, fat-bunned tightly puckered aperture. His folks even picked on Al. They thought it was just cute teasing. He was hurt by it all. His sister rarely acknowledged their relationship and never wanted to be seen with Al in public. He was good at and for nothing. Barely read. Loved cartoons with the big pictures and those on TV. Could write his name and little else. No hygiene habits. Same clothes everyday. A fucking mess who didn't care. But, Al was a great follower who harbored as much hatred for the outside world as trust in Freddie. He made Mortimer Snerd look like an independent thinker. He was a parrot to all the venom Freddie could spew. All the cruel words that made Freddie feel bigger and better made Al feel alive. Someone cared. His idol cared.

The three warriors against life had embarked upon a path of social and personal destruction driven by anger and their desire to do better than the punks in Carter and Menthen. If those assholes could kill, George, Freddie and Al, could destroy. Quality was more important than quantity. Sure, anybody could shoot fifteen little weenies in a hall or school bus, where they couldn't run. These three had sworn to shoot in an open area. More motion. The targets could duck and cover. More difficult for the hunters. More credit for the shooters. Plus, they wanted to take out some pigs. Those rotten motherfuckers who had chased and harassed the three over the recent years. Shooting the kids was bait in the trap. It was payback time. They were secure in their keep.

The bunker from which they shot had a rock wall eight feet high at the rear. On the other side of the wall was a straight drop of thirty feet. So attack from the rear was out of the question. The earthen front had three slits carved into it. The slits were nine inches high and two feet across. Between the bunker's front wall and the rock wall was trench ten feet long, three feet wide, and seven feet deep. There were little steps at each slit so the boys could fire then step down into the safety of the trench and reload or get a new gun. The trench was a good replica of those in World War One.

They each had two automatic rifles and a handgun. The rifles' clips held twenty-five rounds. The handguns were matched; blue-black forty-four caliber Ravens. Fourteen in the clip and one in the pipe. Boxes of ammunition appropriate to each boy's weaponry sat in three small wooden boxes at the right side of the appropriate slit. There were cooler chests of food and water. The food was of surprisingly high nutritional value. No junk. Fruit. Bread. Meats. Eight gallons of water. A large pee hole at the south end of the trench and plastic bags for the collection of shit. The bags would then be lobbed over the rock wall. Like defenders of a castle. This operation had been planned and prepped scrupulously for weeks.

Freddie and George had never been to the library before the planning. But, this time was special and the old ladies even showed them how to use the computers. Got on the Internet for books and pamphlets that they could take home and study helped them with the details. They stole the material with the diagrams from the local Army and Navy store on Prince Street. They had thought of everything and were very proud of their efforts. They knew people would talk about them for years to come. They would be immortal, while all the smart-ass turd balls, who had made their lives miserable would die and be forgotten.

"Put down your weapons and show yourself." The police bullhorn screeched from the side of the school.

"How stupid do the cops think we are? Show yourselves. Show this. Yah, show yourself and be shot. Hey, assholes, why don't you come up here and make us show ourselves? Pull down our pants and show you the big ones we got."

The bullhorn stolen from The Big Store had proven its worth in one use. Now the three teenage gladiators could taunt the authorities. The thugs were truly above the rest.

"Al. George. Now it's time to show them how serious were are. Take your weapon with the scope sight and cause some real damage to the badge bandits."

The three carefully slid their versions of sniper rifles through the openings and targeted three different policemen. In rapid succession, twelve shots exploded from the face of the hill. Two cops went down and the third dove under the squad car.

"Hey, dummies, why don't you put down your weapons and show yourselves? How big are your balls?"

The taunting bully was feeling powerful.

Al was so excited he had peed himself and George's face was twitching as if he had some form of palsy. Freddie was in complete control and the hormones rushing through him were giving him an erection. Power was an aphrodisiac and killing was the ultimate power. He wanted to masturbate, to capture the moment, but he knew these two fools would not understand his action. So he gave each one a big hug and small kiss on the cheek. They were his army. They knew, but didn't know, they were going to die. It's what he wanted and what he had planned. Die in a blaze of glory. Defending the keep against the evil authorities. The oppressors. Three righteous avengers. Dying for their honor.

The first shot from outside tore into the center slit and made it a little wider. The second and third shots hit around the opening. No damage. Then there was silence. The boys remounted the steps and returned fire. Spray and pray. They extracted their weapons and sat on the floor of the trench. Four more thumps around each cleft. Once more a return of fire. Withdraw. Ten minutes went by and there was a tremendous fusillade around the firing portals and the top of the trench. As the two boys were about to mount the steps to return fire, Freddie waved them off.

"The fucks are just sighting us. If we fire back now, they will rain holy hell at the slits. So we wait, because we can wait. We have ammunition and supplies. We can wait until they offer us the respect we deserve. Remember, we're better than all of them. We're on top."

Freddie had the situation under control.

"What if they just wait forever?"

"George, you're bellyachin' again. Shut the fuck up."

"Al, pass out water and an apple for each of us."

Dutifully, Al did as he was ordered.

Twenty minutes passed. Freddie crept up the center step and peered out the slit.

"Holy fuckin' shit. You guys gotta see this. There must be ten squad cars, four fire trucks, half a dozen ambulances and three SWAT vans. They know we're for real. I guess the first priority for them is to remove our kill. Then settle in for the siege. Now don't both of you jump up here at once. You gotta see this."

First Al, then George was impressed by the reactions to their actions. Hell, they even knew some of the firemen and two ambulance drivers. Certainly they were on speaking terms with the local cops. Not the state troopers or the SWAT members. They counted the vehicles the way a hunter counts the points on a buck's antlers. They were smug with their accomplishments but failed to notice the black van parked beneath the elms about two hundred yards away from the cars and trucks. They didn't see the man to the side of the black van giving orders and the men taking them. Blissfully unaware, euphoria set in. Big grins and laughter. No one really knows when the end is coming.

"Well, men, let's let them know we are still here. Fire at will. Empty your clip. Drop back and rest. At the count of three. One. Two. Three."

Three boys, three slits, three scoped rifles. Three shots. Al dies instantly. George loses his right ear and is screaming in pain. Freddie can't see because the bullet from the police rifle kicked dirt into every opening in his face.

"Fuck, man I'm hit. Help me."

Then the explosions. Grenades that stun and tear gas that blinds. The trench is filled with confusion. Freddie and George are twisting and scrambling, in a daze, seeking fresh air and comfort from the pain in their heads.

"George, shoot at the top of the trench. Above the slits. That's where they're coming. Shoot anywhere and you'll get a few. Like this."

Freddie knew the end was near. Somehow the police had gotten up the hill. Maybe because the boys couldn't see down the slope, only outward from the slits. Freddie emptied his clip and started to pull his Raven. Four slugs slam him to the bottom of the trench. Four slugs from behind. George never got off a shot as one well directed magnum stilled his complaining forever. The impenetrable had been penetrated and justice was meted out. Two men dressed in camouflage had come over the back wall and ended the skirmish. The two shadow shooters disappeared faster than the smoke cleared. Back over the wall. Down the drop. Into the waiting van. Exit stage left. The play is over. Draw the curtain. No audience applause.

The school will never be the same. The town will be forever changed. The Amish and Mennonites will plow, plant, grow, harvest, and consume. This permanent cycle would not be altered by a little bump in the road.

The shock-quasi-news media mavens were all over this horrific episode like paint on a house. Not real time on-the-scene coverage, because it all happened so fast. From start to finish in less than forty minutes. Enough time for the police to set up roadblocks designed to both keep out and keep in. Before the TV trucks and their crews could figure a way around the circled wagons, the slaughter was over. The bad dudes dead. The black van on the road again. There were no in-progress pictures, motion or still. And the police had removed the dead and wounded. All was very clean, except for the pools of blood, glass and brick shards, and body fragments. Hysterical children and adults were receiving treatment in ambulances and then escorted to their homes. So it was up to the aggrandizing imaginations of the targets, three passersby, and the reporters to create a complete story. The who, why, when, where, what and how differed slightly by network. Some facts were constant, but the overall thrusts and underlying factors were so unknown that speculation served as truth.

The county sheriff and a major in the state police fielded all questions. Some of them as badly as Marv Thronberry of the original Mets. One reporter dared to ask how this could all happen so rapidly. How could the police arrive so quickly after the start of the shooting? How could a command center be established? How could it be drawn to a conclusion without the usual standoff and siege? How did the police know to scale the escarpment behind the salient? Who was in charge? All the unanswered questions were referred to a later news conference in the Lutztown High School Auditorium. Tomorrow at eight AM. Thank you. Exit stage right.

Television shows were interrupted all night to bring the audience blood suckers all the latest non-news. A loop repetition of the day's events. Profiles of the killers, the school, and the families of the slain. Fluff with just a smidgen of reality to justify the intrusion into the safety and security of dens and living rooms. Mary is in the ComRoom. I am reading some incredibly bad magazines and drifting off to sleep.

Gulf Beach, Florida

Jim Larson of United Press International returned my call and was very pleasant once I introduced my connection to a mutual friend and my request. He gave me the name of Mike Duncan, a freelance photographer, who was responsible for the shot of the Big Pass Rally. Mike was home-based in San Diego but was emailed, modemed, and wired to the world. Jim felt sure Mike would be willing to part with a dupe neg or a blow up of the original. UPI could not put any pressure on the shooter. The shooter just leased the shot to the wire service. There was never a purchase agreement. I thanked Jim and called Mike.

"Mister Duncan, this is Gene Benton. I was referred to you by Jim Larson at UPI. He thought you could be of help to me . . ."

"Hi, Mister Benton. How do you know Jim Larson?"

"Jim is a friend of a friend. He thought you might be able to help me. Actually my sister and me. You see we understand you took a photo of Senator Baldwin Miller's SAFE rally in Big Pass, Kansas the other week. The photo made our local fish wrap along with the obligatory caption, which said nothing. We're interested in getting either a copy of the negative or a blow-up of the original shot. Is that possible?"

"Really? Well, I have a number of great shots from the rally. I took about fifty. How do you plan to use my work?"

"We don't want to use it, just review it. Explore it."

"Why?"

"That's personal. But I will send you a notarized affidavit that the photos or any parts thereof will not be used in any way. And, of course, we'll pay you for your time, material, and pain and suffering for letting loose your babies."

"Payment is a given. What I must know before I agree to anything is why."

"The why should be of no consequence to you, Mister Duncan."

"Please, call me Mike. And, the why is of paramount importance to me."

"OK, Mike, the why is personal and somewhat convoluted. Here goes. My niece was one of the children killed in Carter, Wyoming. My sister is a computer whiz. She captured all the footage of the incident and analyzed the pee out of it. To her, there are a few faces that are unexplained. People, who were there for some unknown reason. People in the background and the shadows. I realize this sounds paranoid. You know the grand conspiracy theory. Who really killed JFK? She now claims that she recognizes some of the same faces at the Big Pass rally. So she is making a quantum leap in her thinking process. She just needs to confirm her suspicions. I understand this all sounds crazy, but I owe it to her to help find answers. Put to rest much of the anger that rages in her soul at the loss of her daughter. Does this make sense?"

"Somewhat. Or, it may be the best damned smoke screen I've ever heard. It seems harmless enough, if you'll fax me the signed document you mentioned and agree to pay one hundred dollars for each negative and shot I send you. All at my discretion."

"That's steep, considering we just want to look at them. And how do we know we will be getting negs of everything you shot at the rally and not just the ones you want to send us or the supposed good ones."

"I'll gladly send you dupes of all the shots. As I said, there are fifty. So you can see every dark corner, shadowy profile, and out-of-focus countenance. But, first I'll need the letter and the money. No checks."

"What assurance do we get that what we're getting is everything we ask for."

"MY word."

"And your understanding that if you are less than truthful, you'll have a tough time selling another photo to the wires services. Notice I used the plural."

"I don't take kindly to threats, Mister Benton."

"That was not threat. It was a promise. A threat involves violence. OK, I'll discuss this with my sister and, if she agrees, draft the letter for both our signatures. Hopefully I can fax the letter to you by tomorrow for your notarized signature. Then I'll overnight the money to you. And you can overnight the negatives back to us. Is that fair?"

"Sounds fair. I'd like to get this deal wrapped up very quickly."

"Do I sense a cash bind, Mike?"

"That's none of your business."

"I need your fax number and a physical address. FedEx will not deliver to a post office box and FedEx is all I use."

Not really, but there's no reason he should have it easy.

"Only one number. Just press the pound key during the message. It automatically kicks over and I receive. And the address is 1221 Hunsicker Avenue, San Diego, California, 80045. By tomorrow then, OK?'

"OK. One way or the other, you'll hear from me."

Mary says yes before I tell her all the details. The amount is chump change relative to her anxiety. Besides, she is convinced the photos will unlock the riddle or, at least, shine a light on the path of knowledge. I draft the letter, e-mail it to her at home. She makes a few revisions. E-mails it back to me with her signature already on it. Attached is a copy of her driver's license confirming her name and signature to be notarized. Not quite kosher, but close enough for my bosom buddy (bad choice of words) in payroll. The letter is notarized and faxed a day early. Hell, within two hours of my conversation with Mike Duncan. It comes back signed, but not notarized in thirty minutes. I re-send another original and demand notarization. The second response has been dutifully executed by someone named Rahjid at The Mail Bin. Mary has wired the necessary funds to my account. A series of clicks and I am instantly, but temporarily, richer. My bank is still open. So I leave work for an hour, get the five thousand dollars in hundreds, and take it to FedEx. I don't want to use the office system. No need for anyone else to know. God, I'm getting paranoid. Send the complete package including the appropriate return envelope to my new best friend. Then I wait. Will he return the negs? All the negs? Just how trustworthy is this unknown but recommended individual? What leverage do I have if he fucks us? Very little. So I wait anxiously. My time limit for him before I take corrective action is seventy-two hours. My first step will be to call. Second step will be to get Jim Larson to call. My third, and final assertive action will be to fax a second letter outlining the points in my law suit. We are a litigious society.

Before lunch of the second day, the mail boy delivers a FedEx package addressed in my hand. The sucker is thick. Yes, I can't wait. I'm like a kid who gets a toy or hamburger and fries. Dad says don't open the package until we get home. Fat chance. The photos and negs are strewn over my table. I can put the negs in sequence by roll, but I don't know which roll was shot first. There apparently were three. Then there is the hand scrawl.

"This is everything. More than I had thought. Sixty-five in total. I won't ask for more money, 'cause a deal is a deal. I would like to know what you've found. I plan to cover Senator Miller's campaign for my pictorial of grass roots politics. If I know what you want, I will be sure to get it for us."

Somehow the math doesn't compute. Three rolls of twenty-four would be seventy-two. Two rolls of thirty-six would be seventy-two. No matter what combination I try, I can't get sixty-five. Is he holding something back? Is he just a bad shooter and seven shots were wasted? Should I call Jim Larson and dig deeper into Mike's talents? All at my discretion. The prick held some back. As many as seven. Are these critical? For now, this will be our secret. Back in the envelope. Home to Mary.

"The mother lode. You done real good, boy. Now I need to scan all of these in sequence. Which roll was shot first?"

"Tried to figure that out but failed, Mary. Does that really matter?"

"When you're performing an autopsy, you must eliminate all extraneous factors. It will take me hours to scan and format the photos and even longer to get the material ready for enlargement and fact extraction. What's for dinner? By the way, I invited a dear friend to stop by this evening. I promise she won't hit you."

"Her name is Karen Leach. I met her through the Internet a bunch of years ago. Then, numerous times at conventions for the teaching nerds, like me. She was a vendor then. I had forgotten that she lived up the road in Lake Wetton. I think you'll like her. She is smart as hell and takes no shit from kids or men. Very quiet divorce about three years ago. You may have even read about what caused the divorce, but at the time you did not know the players or the result of the activity. Karen discovered, just in time, that hubby dearest was using their finances to amass a snow mass big enough for skiers. His plan was to move the nose candy to the Northeast and unload it. Feds and state narcs short-circuited his plans by about two days. She was in hot water for a while. He tried to implicate her to lighten his hit. Fortunately, the mental giants saw through his lie. Used him to get the sellers in New York, Baltimore, and Boston. The entire operation netted about forty missing links in the coke chain. Mark, that's the husband, is in the witness protection plan somewhere. Karen lives an almost protected life. The feds just keep a casual eye on her to make sure that she is safe. That's probably more than you needed or wanted to know. But, she can be hostile. So be kind and somewhat invisible."

"Thrown out of my own house. The last time that happened was that Labor Day party at home when the folks were up in New England. You remember the party that started on Thursday before Labor Day and ran straight until noon on

Tuesday after the Holiday. Thirteen fifty-five gallon drums of empty bottles and beer cans. Food to feed Ethiopia for a week. Hundreds of people at the house. Many of whom I never knew. Well, two guys who were there as guests of Artie Mann, the Yalie, thought I was too drunk and obnoxious and threw me out of the house. My return and introduction caused the little snot bags to turn red. Now, eons later, some dolly I've never met is forcing me into the back bedroom with the door closed just because she had a bad marriage. She is probably a dyke anyway. And, yes I'm pissed."

"Her car lights. Be a pleasant dear and get the door. And be nice or I'll deal with you later."

These were the words and tones of my mother. The small knot from years ago appeared in my stomach, just below and behind the actual gut. I must do right. If I just do as I am told, no more and no less, I'll be safe. Try not to speak too much. Because of the tension, I'll stutter for sure. Fuck, I hate old emotional recordings.

It takes three twists of the lock and corresponding turns of the handle to open a door I've opened quickly and easily about ten thousand times before. My hands are clammy. I'm sure I am sweating and look pale. As the door swings inward, I turn on the porch light. There she is. The object of my neurosis. The raison d'etre for all my nervousness. A vision. A nightmare. I stand and stare for roughly six hundred hours. Her smile could light RayJay. Her light olive countenance is warm. Almost inviting. Her delft blue eyes pierced my emotional body-armor and resuscitated my long-dormant soul. She is my sister's friend. Initially, perceived as an intrusion, she is transformed into desirable in about four tremendous heart thumps. Seems like ten years. I flash back to the high school sophomores who were geekettes when I was a senior, but who were incredibly desirable by the time I finished Brown. Did they really get better looking or did I just become more discerning? Karen reminds me of the neighbor who gets better and better looking with each Fourth of July picnic and Christmas party. She is dressed nicely, yet comfortable looking. Not lazy or sloppy. Low maintenance. Self-reliant. Beautiful in a long-term way. The enormity of her presence quickens my pulse to well above 80.

"Hello, my name is Karen Leach. I've come to see Mary Benton. Is she at home?"

She extends her right hand. My corresponding appendage obediently rises from my side. My limp fish is now in the firm grasp of a warm, non-threatening soft hand. I barely move my arm. She has to do the greeting shake. Our hands are directly over the doorframe—doorframe that protects me from outside-driven emotions. I am safely inside the house and this attractive, but threatening psychic force is on the outside, but abuot to enter.

"May I come in?"

I am snapped back to real time and space.

"I'm t-t-terribly sorry. Forgive m-my rudeness. Of course Mary is here. Please, come in, won't you."

I think I have achieved perfection, as in perfect asshole. I have become a teenager. The only two things missing are acne and my voice cracking. The stutter, the perspiration marks at my underarms, and hand clamminess signal that this quivering mess of a male before Karen is totally out of control. This hasn't happened in years. Since I met the daughter of the Chairman of Intx. And all she wanted to do was coke and fuck—with or without my wife. If I speak loudly and quickly, she won't notice how awkward I am behaving. Yah, right.

"Mary, Karen is here. Let me show you to her ComRoom. An ever decreasing space she shares with two very large dogs and more electronic stuff than my mind can deal with. Would you like a drink? Beer? Hard liquor? Coffee? Tea? Soda? Water? Can I get you anything to eat?"

I lead her down the hall. I continue to yammer, never giving her a chance to answer. I am soooo nervous. Finally, we have completed the odyssey to the open door.

"Watch out for the cables and wires. These are the dogs, Hither and Yon. And, Mary."

"Karen. So nice to see you. Come on in to my lair. I'm just scanning some photos and negatives. A mindless process. What have you been up to? How's the job? We have so much to catch up. Where to start? Where to start?"

That is my cue to exit.

"Excuse me, will you. I have some work to review. We're looking to add to our staff. I'll be in the den if you need anything. It's nice to have you in my house, Karen. Please make yourself at home."

I turn on the TV after I pour a tall, strong one. The teenaged trembling will stop in a few minutes.

This is the evening of the second installment of the President's Commission on Citizen Safety bestowing rhetoric on the unwashed. Broadcast once again in a safe hideout away from the contamination of truth and humanity. Tonight is also the second of Baldwin Miller's town meetings. He's really taking it to the streets. This time Bricklersville, Tennessee. It seems that the stations from Nashville and Atlanta will send crews. Nothing live. Just filmed reports with highlights and post-game interviews. Is he becoming The Mouse That Roared?

"Mary, Senator Miller is conducting a tent revival in Tennessee. Should we get the footage?"

"What the hell do you think?"

"I'll call Tony Seton at Channel Ten and see if he can scrounge the footage, used and unused from his counterparts in Nashville and Chattanooga."

The phone call takes thirty seconds. He'll be glad to oblige. He even knows two of the guys. The tapes will be down here in a few days. Can't reveal urgency. Just idle curiosity. Now I owe Tony six hours of handling the incoming calls during the County Wide Charity Telethon in September. Quid pro quo.

Click! This is no more fact-finding or pulse-taking than a college professor's lecture. People ask and are told what to think. With Sessler's stooges there are various versions of reality or truth. Each caller is posing a question. I wonder if there is some sort of immediate electronic poll conducted with each query. Who in the television audience believes which of the panel the most? Which one of the responses touched the greatest number of hot buttons? This being the assumption, the extension is that this data will be reviewed and analyzed by others. The final report, most likely, would become a white paper for the President, who could then urge Congress to pass laws. These laws, being the voice of the people, would be designed to provide new or strengthened safe-guards for the age. The assumption seems reasonable and the extension logical. But, then again, I've been married twice and bet on the Saint Louis Cardinals to win the National League Pennant each year.

I surf to CNN to see if any of Senator Miller's barnstorming is being aired or analyzed. Financial news greets me. I leave the security of my den and venture into the witch's lair.

"I'm fixing some cheese and fruit. Would you two like some, or a drink of any kind?"

"Gene, that would be very nice. A plate of whatever you're having and some iced tea for me. Karen?"

"That sounds perfect. No sugar. Just lemon in the tea."

Now that I've promised, I'd better deliver. Gouda, Brie and Caraway Swiss. Water crackers. Green grapes, orange slice,s and strawberries. Two large glasses of cold tea with lemon in one and lemon and sugar in the other. A small carafe for refills. God, it looks like a feast for Caesar. Delivered.

"If you need anything else, let me know."

Well, I didn't stutter. But I must have acted like a little boy with a terrible crush on one of his older sister's friend. So? Back to the den just in time to see them go live to Bricklersville, Tennessee.

"This is Mary Fulton, live in Bricklersville, Tennessee, the scene of the second in Senator Baldwin Miller's stops on his nationwide tour. The purpose of the tour is to promote SAFE, Secure America For Everyone. Senator Miller plans to travel to small towns throughout the country, asking people what can be done to, and these are his words, keep them safe from the rampant violence that is threatening the very essence of the country. We've talked to a few of the people who attended the rally and here are their comments:

"The man makes sense to me. He asked us for our views. You can tell he listens. He's got people on the stage taking notes and he promises to incorporate our wishes in his program."

"It's about time the Washington bigwigs came to us and asked what we wanted. Maybe we ought to get the ideas on the ballot and tell Congress and the President what to do. I mean, that's what they're in Washington to do anyway."

"I think SAFE is a good idea. I just don't believe our elected officials can agree on anything but higher taxes. Not all the people are going to agree on everything. But, this is really important. It's worth a try, because we have nothing else. This country is going to hell in a hand basket and we are the only ones who can stop the destruction."

"These are just a few of the comments. It does seem that the Senator from Pennsylvania is stirring up a lot of interest in his program. It also seems the Senator is running for a higher political office. This is Mary Fulton, CNN, Bicklersville, Tennessee."

"Ladies, may I clear?"

"Yes, Jeeves, I mean, Gene."

"Sister you're so kind. Then I am to bed. See you tomorrow, Mary. It was nice to meet you, Karen. I hope to see you again soon."

"OK, how about tomorrow evening? I'll bring the dinner and the three of us can get to know each other better. No separate rooms. Fair enough?"

Her smile was genuine and inviting. I had to refocus so as to not stutter or make an ass out of myself, again.

"That sounds terrific. About six?"

"I look forward to the evening very much. See you then. Good night."

I was enticed, promised, and dismissed in thirteen words. My emotions were aflame. My mind spun like a hurricane. I went to bed.

The Net

There is an edge in Mary's voice I've never heard. She seems to be talking in circles. She is using the home phone, not her cell phone.

"Gene, this is no longer weird. This is frightening. A few of my suppositions and suspicions are closer to the truth than I had hoped. The faces, the people, the process. It's more than we want to know and way much more than I can deal with."

"Hey, you're talking in crypticese. Slow down and give me details."

"I can't over the phone. When can you come home? It's really important we talk and you see what I've found."

"This afternoon is slow. Whatever I have, I can push to tomorrow. Let me clean up some stuff and I'll be home in about an hour. OK?"

"See you then. And thanks for indulging me. You won't be disappointed. Fearful, yes. Disappointed, no."

A few odds and ends to clear up. The drive home is mindless except for the stop at Food-A-Rama. About to pick-up something for dinner when I realize that's Karen's duty. I get two bottles of a '92 California Merlot.

"OK now, big sis, what is so damned important to pry me away from the fun factory?"

"Sit and just listen. After you went to bed last night, I stayed up and went back into the nether world of chat rooms. I was Girlfromoz again. I went to three new ones, BloodNourishment, JonnyGetYourGun, and HandsHeldHigh. They were similar to the two we entered the other evening. Somewhat more violent, as you would expect from their names, but all seem substantially similar. Well, I went from room to room, and chatted with the occupants. One sweep. Then I went back to HouseAfire and BoldWorld. And, I uncovered something strange. Immediately after my, Dorothy's, posting in HouseAfire came a posting from TruthSeeker and immediately after the posting in BoldWorld there was a posting from BrokenArrow."

"Yes, and what does that have to do with anything?"

"Please listen, then we'll talk. I found TruthSeeker and BrokenArrow had posted immediately after I had in all three rooms. This is too much for coincidence. I posted a second time. Then I went back to HouseAfire and BoldWorld for Dorothy's third visit and found my new best friends had come in after my second posting. I have not posted anything inflammatory or confrontational, yet these two have spotted me, or Dorothy, and they are now tracing my every step. If they can trace me, I have to believe they can backtrack my entry and locate my system and physical situation. Said another way, I'm willing to bet they, whoever they are, know where 1, we, live. If they know where we live, they can monitor our lives. Our computer activity. Our telephone conversations. Fuck, even our garbage if they are so inclined. I'm not sure what that does for them, but it scares the hell out of me."

"Whoa, big girl. Take it easy. You have taken an ever slippery trip down the anxiety trail. What you have discovered may or may not have any basis in reality. From this, you make a set of assumptions which are just that, assumptions without irrefutable confirmation. From these assumptions, you have made a number of SWAG, Scientific Wild-Ass Guesses. So, at the end of the process, we are in a Twilight Zone. Now, we are to act and react as if the ubiquitous and ever evil are right outside our windows about to unleash a death ray. I love you, but you stayed up all night and are suffering from sleep deprivation, which fuels your natural grief caused by the loss of your daughter. So, before we go off sealing the house in an electronic cocoon, you need to get some sleep and we need to review all the information in the cool light of a well rested morning."

"I realize this must sound bonkers. Like I was finding evil behind each and every door. But, I'm not through revealing my discoveries. This has way more substance than the Kennedy Conspiracy Theories. So, just be quiet and listen to this."

There was a definite edge to her voice and demeanor. She was tired, afraid, angry, and frustrated. So, I listened.

"Remember all the photos from that guy in San Diego, Duncan? Well, we hit the mother lode of too much coincidence. I scanned them, got them in some fashion of sequence, and examined them. Look what I found."

She wheels to the keyboard and starts to work her magic.

"I'll pull up shots of Senator Miller's rally at Big Pass. Shots of his entourage on stage. Two shots of the audience. What do you see? You see three male faces that are in both places. On stage and in the audience. Obviously not at the same time. Blonde. Ruggedly handsome. Very powerful looking. They look more like bodyguards than political advisors. Now I'll move the pictures of the three to screen left and pull up some stills we got from my friends in Carter. See those guys near the black van. They are the same three. Faces, body shapes and sizes, clothes. It's a match."

"Mary, slow down. You are running so fast in circles all you can see is your own backside. In the blow-ups, I see the fuzzy outlines of what may or may not be men's faces. Fuzzy faces in Mike Duncan's photos and really fuzzy faces in the stills taken from videos in Carter. These imagess are so many generations removed from the original they don't even know their great-great-great-grandparents' names. You're asking for a connective leap of faith I cannot make. And, here is the big question: If we assume that the faces are somehow the same, what the hell does that have to do with the chat room retracing? Jesus, Mary, you've gone over the line. This is like an episode of some drug-induced parlor game, except it's no game to you or me.

"Christ, Gene, stop being so dense. The retracing is real. It's the why that's unknown. The men in the pictures are the same. They are storm troopers for someone. We just don't know for whom. I'm on to something. And, if you don't believe me or won't help me, I'll get help elsewhere. I'll call Karen."

Her voice is now at shrill intensity. Her eyes are welling up with tears. Tears of frustration and fatigue. Her hands are trembling when they are not vise gripped on the arms of her chair.

"Look, let's agree to put all this aside for a few hours. You get some sleep and we'll review all the material this evening. OK?"

"You're stalling me. You'll soon see the folly of your ways tonight. I'll show the material to Karen. She'll see my wisdom. Plus, she is objective. And you won't be able to refute the truth of an objective third party."

Yes, I am stalling. Why does Mary have to set up a me-versus-you battle zone? That shit goes back forty years. I didn't like it then and I really don't like it now. Particularly in my house and including an uninvited houseguest. Maybe I should go around to each of the comers in every room and mark my territory with pee. Whoa. This is not good. We're fighting about something unknown, which is like the argument dealing with thirteen or twenty angels on the head of the Friar's sewing needle. What does all this mean? Can somebody really trace back the entry to a Chat room? Could somebody learn where we are? And, therefore, who we are? Or is it the other way around? Once they find us, what's next? Do they just keep us under surveillance? Beat us up? Kill us? Do they tap our phones? How do we find out? I saw an ad for a device that can show if a telephone is bugged. One of those anti-theft systems for international travelers or guys who just think everybody wants to know what they are thinking and talking about. There's profit in paranoia. How come we're so important that somebody would want to spend time and money keeping us under watch?

And those black and white. What a crock. The distance of the subject from the lens makes details impossible. Just hauntingly vague similarities. No face shots. Only profiles and three-quarter looks. Second, we all know there is an unlimited number of big, blond guys in all of this country. But, do they travel in sets of three or four? And just happen to be in the land of the outdoor blondes, Wyoming and Kansas?

There is no logical connection between the images. One set was at a shooting. The other at a political rally. One set was functioning in the capacity of crime scene control. The other as the entourage of a politician. However, I accept the fact that if they had been at the shooting and the rally, they should be the subject of my sister's inquiry. But, were they? There's the rub.

And, there is absolutely no connection whatsoever between the blurry pictures and the Internet Chat Rooms. That is as clear as day. And should be so to Mary. She is grasping at straws in a desperate drive to understand what happened to her daughter and why. I help her to her bedroom. She slides out of the chariot, I cover her with a blanket, and she is asleep in two minutes.

The damned doorbell. Good God Almighty, it's Karen and it's six.

"Welcome, Karen. It's nice to know the Avon Lady has been replaced by the Dinner Lady. Let me show you what's where in the kitchen. I'll awaken Mary in about an hour. She threw an all-nighter last night. I forced her to take a nap. OK. Here are the pots, pans, and lids. The mixing bowls. Utensils. Spices. What else do you need for now?"

"This all looks fine. Let me get started. Then join me."

Mary is groggy. Wants to bathe and change from her stealth rags to company dinner clothes.

"My sister will be along before eight. Hope that helps your planning."

Karen is smooth in the kitchen. Black beans, yellow rice, and pork. These are her grandmother's recipes. She is very proud of her Cuban heritage. Her maiden name was Rocha. Was married. No children. Not sure she wants kids.

Works as an associate in the trust department of a very upscale local bank. Karen lives north of Gulf Beach on a lake. A forty-five minute commute. When she is away from the pressure she is far away. She is about five feet four inches high. Maybe weighs one hundred and five pounds. Khaki shorts and a blue man's shirt tied at the waist and sleeves rolled up. Sandals. She must have changed at the office. Raven hair, slight olive complexion, and delft eyes. Skin so smooth it is almost luminescent. Legs are flawless. Her hands are thin and fingers long. The puffiness of the shirt conceals her breast size, but she has a small waist and an apricot butt. She glides from counter to stove to sink to trash. Next to Karen, Salome must have been a stumbling, pigeon-toed knock-kneed, clodhopper. I am mired in a school boy crush. If Karen asked me to help, I would probably do myself bodily harm.

"Karen, let me ask you to help Mary. She seems to have gone off the deep end. She is talking about her entry to chat rooms being back tracked by some sinister force, but does not know why. And she is convinced she has found some connection between some faces in Carter and Big Pass. Remember the images I brought home last night? Well, she scanned them and claims to have found the faces of men who were at the Carter, Wyoming slaughter and at Senator Baldwin Miller's rally in Big Pass, Kansas. Now, here is the triple crazy part. She firmly believes these two factoids, the retracing and the faces, are related. Joined at the hip from birth. She could use the help of a friend, not a brother, to help her come to her senses. Maybe she should see a grief therapist for a while until she no longer considers these connections real. Would you listen to her? Then tell me what you think. I'd appreciate it. I know she would."

"I'd be glad to spend some time with her after dinner and try to find out what is troubling her. I know she must be going through hell. First Dorothy, her best friend and daughter, dies. Then she sells her home of fifteen years. She quits her job of twelve years. She moves to a place that is geographically different and where she has few friends. All of this in less than two months. She hasn't had time to grieve or to get her life in order. Her soul must be bouncing around inside her like a single pea in an empty gallon mayonnaise jar. Mary was an acquaintance a few years ago and our friendship grew long distance, occasional trade shows, but in a somewhat removed mode. I'm not so sure I am the right one to analyze her discomfort. Why don't you do it? You're her brother."

"We've already fought over these issues and she needs an objective set of ears. Someone who is not blood or a mate."

"Looking around, I guess I am the only one who fills that description. How convenient."

"If you would prefer not to get embroiled in this mess, I understand. If the positions were reversed, Mary would also understand. I am only asking. Your response can be either yes or no. How and when you do the listening is up to you."

"After dinner then. Where will you be while I am giving Mary the third degree?"

"Come on, it's not supposed to be like that. And, I'll be in the den. Out of your sight and out of my mind."

"Why, Gene, how cute. You're blushing. That's even cuter."

"OK, you two, what kind of shenanigans are going on in here?"

"God, caught by my big sister. Don't tell mom and dad we were flirting. Nothing happened. Really nothing at all."

"Karen, so good to see you. Hell, it's good to see anyone other than this tapioca brain. Come here bro and give me a big hug. You, too, Karen. A big hug. I'm famished and the aromas emanating from this strange room are causing me to salivate. What is this room called? Ah, yes . . . kitchen. What's for dinner?"

"The scullery and only the house servants are allowed to be here, ma'am. Black beans cooked with bay, cinnamon, clove, and garlic. Yellow rice cooked with peas and peppers, then sprinkled with fresh onions. Pork cooked in an orange and plum mélange and splashed with Cointreau. Plus, fresh Cuban bread. Washed down with Rolling Rock beer. This latter is not Cuban, but my own choice. Gene, would you set the table out by the pool?"

It's amazing how much of one's personality comes out at the dinner table. Not the breakfast table or the lunch counter. I guess when you see someone eat and they see you, there is not much to hide, except bathroom habits. I mean how you cut, in-take and chew your food is basic to existence. And the manners of the table and meal consumption range from, as the Germans would say, fressen to essen. The former is food consumption like an animal. The latter like a human. But, even within the human species there is a significant disparity between how those of the classes handle cutlery and chew their food. How many plates, forks and glasses are at each place at one time? So, if everyone's place setting is the same, the only notable differences will be the conduct. In a casual setting such as poolside with family and friends, the guard of propriety drops. Nonetheless, I can tell a great deal about the people at the table or the woman across from me. And I like what I see. The conversation is day-based and job-related until Mary interjects her findings of the morning. I volunteer to clean up, as they want to retire to the ComRoom so Mary can reveal her treasures of truth. Clean up is very quick. Karen even brought her own refrigerator storage containers. The machine will wash the dishes and glasses. The pots and pans are scrubbed and stacked to dry overnight. They're not going anywhere. I pour an adult beverage and head back to the pool.

"Gene, we have to talk. Mary showed me what she found and I believe there is some measure of substance in her theories. I'm not entirely sure what is happening or why, but I firmly believe that you two and this place have been tagged. You know, like a bear. Captured by the Game Commission, tagged with an electronic beeper and then let loose back into the wild. The authorities track the migration, feeding, and mating patterns this way. Well, in your case they are just keeping tabs on Mary and you or just Mary. I think the latter. You're just here. Come with me back to her ComRoom and maybe she and I can do a better job of convincing you of what may be going on."

"As I was telling Karen, I believe that whoever retraced the entries made by Girlfromoz just recently learned that the person behind the mask has moved from Wyoming to Florida. I cannot begin to know if they know that Girlfromoz is now a second person. So I believe they hooked on to Dorothy and are just following the person they think is her. That's the only solution I can come up with for is what they do. Let me explain. I think they retrace every entry to every chat room that may be a potential threat to society. Hell, they probably set up the chat rooms to attract the crazies. They started by simply monitoring activity. This is similar to the authorities that monitor the sex chat rooms. This monitoring can be a useful intervention tool to protect children and the unsuspecting."

"Unlike thought police, these back trackers don't want to control how the chatters think. But, they do want to know who is thinking what. Who may be hinting at the next violence? Some chatters may already know this. So they are bold and brazen braggadocios. Baby bull-shitters who couldn't walk the walk in my chair. There are some that speak the truth and are looking for converts and followers. Then there is the vast majority, I believe Dorothy was one, who are just naively fascinated by all the talk. So, unable to ascertain just who is who, the re-tracers trace everyone. At least until the real persona is revealed. I also believe the authorities are some level and form of government agency that willingly ignores free speech. Sort of like the infiltrators of the Communist Party in this country in the thirties, forties, and fifties. It's more like a cat and mouse game. You know, the cat lets the mouse play until the cat is ready to pounce. All the time the mouse is under primitive surveillance. The kind that never blinks."

"Now, what are they doing to monitor me, us, here, in Florida? I'm willing to bet your next paycheck they have us under some form of surveillance already. Electronic. Probative. I don't know. I do know that they have Karen under protection, which is another word for surveillance. Maybe they have not labeled us as threats to society. It gets foggy here, so I can't go on without sounding like an ass."

"We must take some action to protect ourselves from further electronic invasion. I know how to wrap the computer systems and avenues so as to confuse the authorities. They can break the wrap, sure. But, that takes more time and a lot more money. And, we may not be worth both. So, it's very likely they'll just give up and chase more desirable game. I could take care of that. Karen convinced me we are not under telephonic watch. That was my paranoia. But, the house may be bugged. I hope not. We really need to secure the primary entry port, the computer. I will still be able to visit chat rooms, just not be followed home from new ones."

"And look what Karen was able to do with the pictures. See this left three-quarter shot from Carter? See the left three-quarter shot from Big Pass? Check out the hairline, the nose angle, the ear lobe and the strange cut of the eyebrow. This guy was at both places. We're sure of it. And, I am willing to bet your paycheck after the next one that this second guy was in both places, too. See his jacket lapel. Notice the button loop at the top. Also note the strong similarity of the side cowlicks in the guy's scalp. So, what do we make of this? We're not sure but it does not sit well. Why would a gun toter be a political advisor? Unless he, or they, are not advisors. Maybe they're bodyguards. That's pretty heavy protection for a Senator on the pre-campaign trail. Maybe they are thugs hired by his staff. Then why the hell were they at Carter?"

"So far we know of electronic eyes and ears, and multiple personalities on TV. But, we have no connection, if there is one. Well, what do you think little brother?"

"You have made compelling arguments for the conspiracy side of the argument. I will suspend skepticism and acid logic for the moment and agree that you may, just may, be on to something. If you are on to something, I'm just not sure what it is. I am not smart enough to understand the how's of the computer Internet world. And, I am not sure that your plan to combat it is viable. If you are correct, and I stress the word if, we would be well advised to maintain contact with the original chat rooms, so that the authorities don't realize that we know about them. This will mean not masking the trail and thereby letting them follow us. Do not give them any reason to think that we know they are there. They should not know that we know. I am not convinced the house is bugged. My guess is that we are safe from that for now. Most importantly, I believe much more digging is in order. This you can do. I cannot. Maybe you can team who is walking the walk. See if you can discern any threats. This sounds crazy. Maybe you can find out what's next. Christ, I'm beginning to sound like a true believer."

Mary lets out a scream of delight. She has a convert. Someone who will work with her. Karen smiles.

"About the faces in the crowd. This is weirder than I thought possible. I have to admit there are some real similarities in the faces. It's just that their situations are so contradictory as to defy connection. We are due to get some video from Tony Seton soon. Perhaps we can find some corroborating visual evidence.

"If we can get a cleaner image, I can ask Mike Duncan to do some deeper digging. Mike must have access to shots of other political rallies. Maybe he knows someone, who knows someone, who knows someone, who can put names and job specs with the faces. He has expressed an interest in helping and getting rich in the process. This would be a good way to find out if he is serious about the former. Hopefully, I'll get the video tomorrow. You can commence scanning for faces. And, then compare them with those already in your electronic file. I am not convinced this will lead anywhere except the proverbial blind alley. But, you have the time and equipment and certainly the motivation."

"I still see no connection between the chat rooms and the similar faces. I believe they are simply isolated facts occurring at random in a similar time frame. Sort of like a rainstorm and burning cookies on a Saturday afternoon. There is no cause and no effect. There is no link. The events just happened at the same time. But, sis, I am on your side. Each new piece of evidence will lead us. We can not lead the evidence, OK?"

"You must be exhausted. I am tired and you did all the legwork. I am going to swim a few laps. Clear my head so I can concentrate on the 'morrow. Ladies, it's been a great evening. Let's do this again sometime soon."

"We will, 'er are. Karen is coming back tomorrow evening when we get the tape from your friend, Tony."

"I said I hoped to get the tape tomorrow. If it's available, he will have it delivered to my office and I'll call you at home. You can call Karen. God, this sounds like a junior high school club meeting. Now, I need my swim. Do you think the dogs would like to join me?"

"Doubtful. You swim. I'm going get ready for bed. You were right, I'm whipped."

"Does that invitation extend to me? I even brought my suit. Where can I change?"

That was sudden and smacked of planning. Except many Floridians keep a spare swimming suit in the car. So if she wants to swim, she's welcome.

Midway into my second lap, there is a splash at the other end of the pool. My partner in the kitchen and now in the world of Aquaman. We pass about midpool. I don't turn on the lights at night if it's just me. There is enough house light and moon glow for me to follow the lane markers. Make the turn. See her stroking aggressively. Trying to catch me? Why? This is not a race. It's a form of nonalcoholic relaxation to tire me into a deep and long sleep. She is approaching in my lane. I move to avoid collision. We maintain the distance and I avoid the contact for the remainder of my ten laps. Then I'm out of the pool, wrapped in a bath sheet breathing deeply to stop the panting and to get my pulse rate down to the low sixties. Bath sheets are the only things I own from Needless-Markup. They are big enough to cover my entire body and thirsty enough to create the Amazon Dessert.

As Karen pulls herself from the pool I can't help but notice the incredible body, which had been hiding in the bloused shirt and khaki shorts. The bikini top and bottom are adjusted for modesty. She swims without a cap. The entirety of her countenance is exquisite. I hand her a bath sheet. She envelops herself in it.

"You swim well."

"Thank you, but what you mean to say is that I swim well for an older man."

"That is not what I said. Do us both a favor and don't ever put words in my mouth. I would never presume to do that to you. Don't you ever, ever presume to know what I am going to say. Fair enough?"

"I apologize. Fair enough?"

We just had a territorial fight and no one lost. I was a little bloodied, but not bowed.

"I came out here for three reasons. First, I wanted to swim. Second, I wanted to talk to you about Mary. I don't think she is well. I think she is ill or becoming less well. I really have no recent standard to which I can compare her present state. The last time we were together was two years ago. Today she is much less vibrant. Everything is measured. There is much less physical spontaneity. Her mind is sharp, but she looks tired and pale. Her arms are flabby, which is not what I would expect from someone in a wheel chair. She doesn't have much strength. She dropped several things while we were together. Pens just fell out of her hands. Twice her hands shook as if she had some form of palsy. And her breathing is labored as if she has asthma. No hard coughing, just wheezing when she tries to take a deep full breath. And there is another thing. The dogs. They seem to be hovering too close to her. Close enough to give her comfort. Impart their strength to her. Have you noticed any of this?"

"I was unaware of her condition. Life, in general, has been quite hectic since she and the two dogs moved in unannounced. But, since you mentioned it, I'll take a closer look at her before I go to bed. She seemed to be strong and feisty when I was with her in Wyoming. Maybe she is just very tired. Needs a good rest."

"Oh, come on. Have you been so self-absorbed as to not notice your own sister? That's incredibly arrogant. I asked her if she was OK and she dismissed the question. I even asked after the shaking and she told me she was fine, just tired. She is just as arrogant as her brother when it comes to people caring about her health. I believe it's a cover up for something real

76

and threatening. What could be wrong? Has she seen a doctor recently? Who was her doctor in Wyoming?"

"I don't know the answers. I am sure the stress of the past months has caught up to her. As she and I both told you she is most likely just tired. And she needs a vacation from stress. I can call the university tomorrow. Maybe they can help with a doctor's name or some other releasable information. When I can learn anything, I'll find a doctor for her."

"I am embarrassed that I failed to notice what was obvious to you. I appreciate the fact you brought this to my attention. And, I'll let you know what will be the next actions. Now is the appropriate time for each of us to separately tuck ourselves in. I'm not throwing you out. I'm tired and took this afternoon off so tomorrow will be a day and a half, literally and figuratively. I'll retrieve your food containers and meet you at the front door."

She heads for the guest bathroom. I straighten up the lanai, make sure the gates are locked and leave one sliding door open for Hither and Yon to roam. But, given Karen's observation, I doubt they will leave Mary's side. It's great to have guard dogs that really guard. Three small containers from the frig. Head for the front door. She is there. Hair wet and her shirt and shorts pulled on. I open the door and walk her to her car in the moonlight. Bright enough to see the suit in the small canvas tote next to the bra and panties. My imagination revs. Be still my teenage heart. She has her keys in her right hand.

"You never told me the third reason you came to the pool."

"This."

She drops the tote, turns around, and slithers her hands around my neck. Our lips, ever so slightly apart, caress softly. She turns back and enters her car. I am agog. She drives off with my heart.

Front of the house secure. Outside lights turned on. Front and side alarm systems activated. Back one off for the hounds. Inside lights off except for small table lamps in den and dining room. The routine is necessary when you live in the home invasion and burglary capital of Florida. Though I suspect the dogs would be alarm enough. Pass by Mary's room. See light from the bedside table. Knock gently. No answer. Knock again. Same non-response. Enter delicately. The dogs raise their heads an inch off the bed. One at her feet. One at her side. The door side. Seeing me, they return to the rest position. The lamp illuminates Mary's face, shoulders and arms. A dull yellow-gray-white flesh color. This is not the hue of health. She seems thinner somehow. Thinner than she was in Wyoming. Then I hear her snore. Except it is not a nasal or throat sound. A chest wheeze. Very delicate, but very disconcerting. Is this real? Am I just experiencing what Karen implanted? Confused and concerned, I exit to my room.

I call Wyoming State University main campus at eight o'clock their time and am directed to the faculty administration office. There I am told to contact the local campus in Carter. There I am put on hold for five minutes while some student tries to determine if the information is available and if she can release it to me. She asks me to call back in one hour and ask for Dean Tomas. Dean Tomas will be able to help me. Sixty-two minutes later Dean Tomas is very pleasant, yet vague about what information he has and what he can give out without the permission of Professor Benton. Finally he allows that it would be all right to give me the name of her doctor in Carter.

Doctor Byers is busy at the time of my call. His nurse will find Mary's file and have the Doctor call me. Too much fucking delay. I implore her to pull the file and tell the doctor that I will call back in thirty minutes. Doctor Byers is very aware of the physician-patient right to privacy. The last time she saw Mary was a year ago, when Mary was in for her annual check-up. She was experiencing infrequent chest pains. The usual tests were conducted. Doctor Byers wanted Mary to see a pulmonary specialist at the university hospital on the main campus. Never received the results of her visit. Never saw Mary again either. Would be willing to forward her records to her new physician in Florida. I call Karen and relate my trip thought the maze. She will find a doctor for Mary.

About two PM, a messenger delivers a package from Tony Seton. I call Mary and tell her to call Karen for a continuation of the investigation. I'll cook so the ladies can work their computer magic. I try to sound as serious as Mary and I try not to sound excited that I'll be seeing Karen tonight. It's almost like a date—with my sister as chaperone.

The afternoon has its quota of bull shit.

"Karen is bringing the makings for a huge multi-flavored salad. You should be prepared to sweat and slave over running water and a cutting board. She is also bringing fresh bread, which she demands must not be toasted, just warmed. The funniest thing, Gene. She asked if it was all right if she went swimming again after dinner. I got the strangest feeling I was a parent approving a date. Tres bizarre. Be careful little brother. Cupid may be stalking you."

"Very funny but not likely, older sister."

God, I hope she is right. The thing I fear most is growing old alone. The thing I would miss most is the companionship of a very close and dear friend, preferably of the opposite sex. Some hippie once said that love is good friends who fuck. I miss love. Easy big fella. Stay in reality. Don't go off star struck like some weak kneed teen, only to have your dreams dashed. Just relax and take it one day at a time. Make no plans or promises. Karen's car is in the driveway. She had the good sense to not take my spot. Also, she is in the best possible escape position. In the door and down the drive in less than fifteen seconds.

"Hello, honeys, I'm home."

"We're poolside. I decided to take today off and play with the dogs. I also cleaned out the last remnants of Wyoming from the wheeled house. I think it's time to sell it and get a vehicle which is more conducive to street travel and which does not label me as a carpetbagger. Let's make that our weekend project, Gene. Getting the heap to a dealer and disposing of it. It has served its usefulness anyway. I've already checked on the Net and learned its supposed value. Also, we should consider getting pontoons for the chair and some hand paddles for me. Then, I could go in with my babies and have some mobility. I am suddenly excited about life! Now, down to the serious side of why you have intruded in our world. You do have the tape, don't you? Thank you. Will you excuse us while we go to work? You are banished to the sink, cutting board, and spice rack in that place you call, what is that word, kitchen? Call us when dinner is ready, if you would please."

She is smiling and giggling. Acting almost childish. The day of rest and play with the hounds has worked its wonders. I knew it would. The prospects for a pleasant evening are grrrrrreat.

Poolside

For the native and knowledgeable, there are old fashioned fresh grocery stores and roadside stands, which purvey produce delivered by farmers with old flat bed trucks. It takes time, energy, and a little more money to find and shop at these places. The result is worth the effort. Karen obviously considered salad and its creation to be some form of artistic expression of her persona. So, she knew where to shop to impress the eyes, ears, nose, and palate. She had brought two large brown shopping bags of numerous and various ingredients for our fresh feast. Now the pressure was on me to produce the proper produce product. If my finished creation were less than her benchmark, I will have injured her soul. But, if I can energize the senses beyond her expectations, I will have won her heart.

I empty each goody bag. Cornucopia is an inadequate description. Cherry and plum tomatoes. Bib, Romaine, and Boston lettuces. Yellow and green peppers. Watercress. Parsley. Celery with hearts, baby carrots, and radishes. Pecans. Bean sprouts. Kale and verdiccio. Pea pods. Coconut to be shredded. Grapefruit and mandarin oranges. Red cabbage. And, two loaves of fresh bread. One nine-grain. The other a rich sourdough. I've been to Calistaro's bakery before and I know how fantastic their bread is. At least I know one place where Karen shops.

Place a tea towel in the front of my waist. Roll up my sleeves. Pour a drink. Turn on the old time rock 'n roll to a blare level. The Stones, The Eagles, The Temps, and the Topps have come to my house for dinner. I call the ladies in waiting and warn them that, for the full flavor, dinner must commence by the time Mickey's big hand reaches twelve and his little hand reaches seven. Else all will spoil and turn to In-Sink-Erator fodder. A tremendous, aces up, one in the hole, multi-flavored salad, Rolling Rocks, and warm bread on the lanai by the pool. What could be bad?

"Let me tell you what we have extracted from Tony Seton's tape. Clear and identifiable faces. Three faces. Two blondes and a coal head. Three places. Carter, Big Pass, and now Lutztown. Beyond the question of who, is why. If we can learn who, most likely, we'll learn why. So that's where we should begin. Can we call Mister Duncan tonight? There is a three-hour time difference. Let's see if he truly wants to get rich. I can e-mail him whatever he needs to start his investigation. What do you say, bro?"

"Mary, before we go off inviting others to swim in our paranoid pool, I'd like to see the iron-clad evidence and listen to Karen's counsel. What do you think, Karen? Are we on to something other than a slippery slope?"

"I think Mary is right. And I stress "think." There do seem to be a number of similarities in the pictures. The real problem is with the lack of fidelity in the Carter shots. There are also the various angles of the headshots. If I had to swear in court to a definite match, I couldn't. But, I would be willing to bet two quarters. And that's five times my highest ever bet. I would like some other form of confirmation. Not just another video from another rally. It's expected that the same guys show up at the same rallies. What is unexpected is if the same guys that were at Carter would be at another shooting. It's the "if" that bothers me. And I'll throw another log on the fire. What if these guys were at Menthen and Lutztown? We'll never know for sure, but it's cause for speculation."

"Jesus, Karen, I think you're on to something. How do we get tapes and photos of those events? Gene, maybe Mike Duncan can help us."

"First, let me look at your findings. Then we'll decide if action involving Mike is right. If Mary's point about the cat and mouse game is accurate, if someone can watch us while we search for them, we had better be damned careful and discreet. If this is true, and I'm beginning to think it is, whatever we want to say to Mike Duncan, I should say and send from my office."

The pictures of the guys at both rallies were a match. No doubt. No big deal. The pictures from Carter could complete the triangulation. But, I'd like another expert's view. I take the disc of the pictures and head for my office. Mary and Karen are safe with the two dogs. Out the lane. Left to the second light and right on to Ellerton drive. Six miles on Ellerton to Interstate I-775. Twelve miles to exit nine. Down the ramp and left to the third light. Into the parking lot and my space. I've traveled this route a kajillion times during the morning. Rarely, if ever, at night. Although it is dark in the early hours and tonight, the dark now seems threatening.

One nice thing about driving in the dark is the ability to see cars. There are fewer of them and they are well lit. Can't see the driver too clearly unless there is light entering the front of the car, but each car was obvious. A small, dark colored pick-up truck was behind me up to I-775. Then I spotted a sports car in my rear-view mirror up to the parking lot. Is all this imagination? Am I being followed? By whom? Is this such a big deal that someone can put someone on my ass? Maybe we are on to something. Maybe I am just being a paranoid parrot. I love Mary and maybe she is just getting to me.

Duncan is not home, but his voice mail gives me his e-mail address. I send the data and explain what we are looking for. Tell him to call me at the office number tomorrow as early as possible in the morning. Deal done. Lights off. Guard waved at. Car entered. Head for home. Retracing my route, like the back trackers who Mary is convinced have followed her to us.

The lights in a second car behind me are those of a small pick-up truck. Black. The grill is vaguely familiar. The truck pulls to the left and passes me only to turn into the mall beyond the Interstate. It's closed. That's strange. On to I-775. Now its urgent that I get home. My safety. The safety of Mary and Karen. Speedometer registers eighty. To my left and about six car lengths behind me I note the front end of a coupe. Or is it a sports car? I quickly slow down to forty-five. The small gray car slows down. But, not in lock step with me so it gets very close to me in the left lane. It is a sports car and I spot the young blond male driver before he has a chance to slow down and drop behind my field of vision. He has been made. He knows that I know he is there. I know that he knows that I know. The game of cat and mouse has taken on a new twist. Just who is the cat and who is the mouse. When do they change roles? Who is watching the game? Who has the rulebook? I am sweating.

"Gene, you're pale. Are you frightened? What's wrong?"

"Nothing's wrong, Mary. I'm just tired, that's all. I need to swim and rest. In fact, a long night's sleep would, no doubt, do you a world of good, too. Why don't we all go to our respective beds and sleep. A fresh outlook on this issue would help us all."

"Jesus, you don't have to be so rude. I'm tired any way. I was headed for bed. Karen is out by the pool. She was hoping to swim. Remember I told you."

"Fuck, I forgot. OK. Sure. Sorry."

"Good night, cranky bag."

"Yeah, good night."

I change into my baggy blue and red striped suit. The boys bought it for me last Christmas. It's a hoot. I look and feel like the Piltown Surfer. Grab two bath sheets. Exit the master bedroom doors to the pool. Karen is wrapped in her own big towel dangling her feet poolside.

"Sorry, Karen, I forgot about our swim. Before we thrash about in the aqueous solution, let me ask you about Mary. How do you think she is doing? Were you able to find a doctor? What are the next steps?"

"I made an appointment for Mary with Doctor Hanan. Nine AM the day after tomorrow. He is the best internist in the area. Or at least that's what his peers say. His office has faxed or will fax her doctor in Wyoming for her files. I stressed urgency. All will be accomplished. Consider me your native guide to the local medical profession. I am owed some favors in the community and she is worth all of them."

"Yes, I think she is ill. Very ill. Although she put up a front of good spirits, it was a front. She had on too much make up. Back in the ComRoom and at dinner her hands trembled. And she was sweating at the table when both of us were cool. Her mind is incredibly sharp and her heart is strong. I just think other parts of her body are worn out. It's this quest that gives her the drive to be aggressive. Take away the investigation and we would take away her will to live. She is more than tired. Sadly, she is dead-tired."

"I really appreciate your help. You have gone beyond the call of friendship or duty. I'll take the day off and drive her to the doctor."

"She insisted that she would get herself to Doctor Hanan's. Her spirit is indomitable and she is incredibly stubborn. I suspect that this is a genetic trait. I've already made a date with her for lunch after her appointment. Then she wants to cruise the RV lots and beat up some salesmen. I admire her, so we had better back off. What about your . . . ?"

I hold my hand over her mouth and hand her a napkin upon which I have written, 'From here on we will need to whisper.'

"I e-mailed him the material, told him what we wanted and asked him to call me tomorrow at the office. But, there is something else. I have this very strong feeling I was followed to and from the office. It's almost as if someone knew when I was leaving. It was not a hard-on-my-ass tail. Rather it was a soft one. One car a few cars back. It's like they knew where I was going. But, they got sloppy. I saw one in ta second. I think it was a young blond man. Clean cut. That's all. I am becoming very convinced they have us under surveillance. I think Mary is right. I think they have bugged the house. They are listening. We can talk about things. But we must whisper about this. This is just a precaution."

"Let's dive in and fake drowning."

"That's the idea. I'm tired so maybe I won't fake it."

Dive in and begin the toughest part of the evening. The first two laps are the most difficult. The initial exuberance after the dive must be tempered by the desire to achieve appropriate rhythm. The rhythm is absofuckinglutely critical. The number of arm strokes. The depth of the dig. The power of the pull. The beat of the kick. The push of the legs. The bend of the knees. All dictate breathing and energy loss. All of these are the major, apparent factors, which impact the ease at which I swim. The faster I can get all of these elements to work together in synch, the slower fatigue will set in. As I get increasingly fatigued, my body wiggles. I don't turn my head properly to intake air. My shoulders shift. My hips sink. The lack of rhythm accelerates the onset of fatigue. My mind wants to quit long before my body. So, I am constantly fighting mental fatigue. All of this thinking and chess playing occurs in the first two laps of my swim. I will not race. I will swim against the biological, emotional, and mental clocks that are within me.

Karen has a good pace. Her strokes are measured and her breathing is every stroke. By the end of lap three we each found our respective rhythms. I have ratcheted down, but not much, so that I can swim with her. Catch a glimpse of her with each breath on the return leg and peek under water. Swimming side by side, even if unintended, breeds competition. If I speed up, she speeds up. If she picks up the pace, I follow so as not to follow. Seven laps together and we make the final turn. The arm pulls and kicks are just a tad quicker, deeper and more powerful. Head for home. Should I win? Should this be a race? Yes, absolutely. Swimming is always about winning.

No conversation for the first minute. Gasping for breath. Grasping every cubic centimeter of air to force into the lungs. Holding on to the side of the pool with head lowered does not facilitate air intake. I learned this years ago. So, I stand upright, face pointed to the sky and force my lungs to work hard sucking in salvation.

"That was great. You're quite good. Did you ever swim competitively?"

The initial sentences are short and choppy. The voices are low. Almost at a whisper. Not hiding anything. Just not capable of normal volume or yelling. Particularly at my age. Questions very often so that the other person must speak and give you a chance to breathe.

"Always been around water. Prefer pools for this type. The gulf is for fun. How about you?"

"In a previous lifetime. Love the water. If I could come back as anything, I would choose to be a dolphin or porpoise. Grace, speed, strength, and intelligence. Not a bad combination. Plus, they live in my medium of choice."

She stares and motions me to move close to her. She whispers.

"Do you think they can hear us in the pool? I mean, can we talk about what's going on without being heard?"

"I believe only the house is bugged. Besides, even if the lanai were bugged we could stand real close in the pool and whisper in each other's ears. Then no one could eavesdrop."

I am standing directly in front of Karen. No touching. I move to her right ear and begin.

"I appreciate all that you've done for Mary. I'm happy she has such a good friend. I'm afraid I have not been able to give her the attention she deserves. She is sick and I can't fix it. Hell, I can't even find a doctor to help. But you did. Thank you."

My lips are about a millimeter from her ear. I can smell the combination of pool water and her perfume. She wears some new fragrance. Tabbac covered with some mid-level spices and a hint of citrus. Perhaps she chose it after great deliberation. I have luxuriated in the full-strength aroma since I met her. It's in her hair and her clothes. It is her aura, enduring and endearing. I do not touch her ear lobe or the delicate folds that lead to her inner self. My inhaling and exhaling do. The temperature of my breath enhances the sensation of the zephyr wafting over her skin. She senses heat and motion. I can see the fragile, baby hairs in, on and around her ear and on the nape of her neck stand up. They are reacting to external stimulation and internal chemistry. We do not touch. The dynamic tension of physical and sexual interest restrained is a fearsome force. She moves closer. Our bodies are held together and separated by the meniscus of the water between us. I don't have to move for her to converse.

"Thanks are not necessary. I do what I please for those who matter to me. Mary is a special person. I'm lucky to have her for a friend. On top of all that, she's brilliant. I can learn much from her. So, we share. That's the basis of friendship. Sharing. Do you think that those who are listening are also looking?"

She is not whispering in my ear, but rather talking to my neck. Her breath is hot. This method of communication, at and not to, increases the tension and therefore the sensuality of the action. Her lips ever so slightly touch my throat. She skips her partially opened mouth from side to front and around to the other side. Then her dry tongue retraces her path back to my right. Her mouth moves up my throat. Across cheekbone and cheek to about an inch below my eye. Lips seem to be driven by an internal engine. Still no hands. No holding. No grasping. Her breathing and my heartbeat are quickening. Hastening toward some conclusion. Is this a race?

The languorous medium of the swimming pool is perfect for the physical anxiety created by our strong and obvious feelings. Her lips glide down to mine and brush across the dry opening of my mouth. I am quivering and panting. Still no hands. No holding. Her lips return and stay. I return the tender pressure. The contact lasts an eternity. I feel her hands glide from nowhere to my neck and up to my cheeks. Her fingertips are feathers. The palms never touch my electrified skin. My hands and arms respond to her advance. They seek to recapture control. They gently grasp her upper arms and draw her onto me. I feel her wet bikini bra squash against my chest as my fingernails trace small circles on her shoulder blades. The tongues are now dancing. Moisture, hers and mine, covers the inside of my mouth. Breathing is deeper and faster. A flash back to the initial stage of our swim. She withdraws her hands from my face and drops them to her suit bottom. She lowers her body into the water as she tugs and wiggles out. At the same time she unties my suit, separates the Velcro fly, and removes my last vestige of modesty. Arising, she resumes her oral attack. Battle is enjoined. I am ready. I have been ready for minutes. Hell, like all male babies, I was born ready.

What had been gentle exploration becomes pressurized groping. Suddenly she pulls hard on my shoulders and springs up above my face. She wraps her legs around my hips and lowers her body onto me. The pressure of entry is painful. She grimaces. Partial access. Withdrawal. Greater access. Slight withdrawal. Complete insertion and thrashing begins. The agitation churns the water. The bra is unsnapped. Her nipples are sand-papered to hardness by rubbing against my chest hair. Kisses have reached the frantic stage. She is pumping. I am pushing back. She leans back and I take a breast with my teeth. I nip. She jolts. I nip. She jolts. I nip. She pulls back and gives me the other breast. I nip again. Her whimper is barely audible. The pumping is slowed down, but the thrusts are deeper and longer. She devours my mouth. Eyes open a slit. Her skin glistens in the pool lights. Rhythm picks up from a waltz to fox trot to jitterbug. Then she is frozen in time as she clings to me. Pulsing. Throbbing. Her thrusts are powerful. Almost painful, except this pain is pleasure. Three. Four. Five. Six. She collapses onto me. All the energy of a wet blanket.

Not fatigue. She is spent. The race is over. I had finished the race about thirty seconds before she did. The greatest joy for me in the race is not the finishing. It is watching my partner finish. I love women. They are beautiful. Their bodies. Faces. Eyes. Hair. Smiles. Laughs. Their process to arrive. As they finish the race of sexual fulfillment, they are magnificent. A combination of Madonna, vixen, sister, and friend. All the pent up emotions of centuries, some repressed, some exploited, spew uncontrollably. Unashamedly. Good for them. Good for me to be there and help them get to where they want to be. Years ago I learned that woman love sex as much or more than men. They have been denied that love for at least two millennia. I no longer worry about completing the run up the hill before my partner. My goal is to help my partner get to her goal. Her kisses covering my face and head are tender. We have conquered the race and each other. The next step is to learn who we are. Something for tomorrow. For now, to bed. To sleep, but not to snuggle.

Breakfast isn't awkward, because Mary is never awake when I arise for my daily grind. Karen leaves at the same time. She must go home and dress for success in the financial world. I will call later today.

One message on my line. Call number one. Three forty five AM from an unknown number.

"Hey, Mister Benton, Gene, I received your e-mail, opened it, and examined the pictures. Who are these guys? I mean, why are they important to you? Whatever. I can dig into the job, but it will cost you. I mean money and a piece of the action if this leads anywhere. I mean, I can use a big break and the attendant celebrity status. Not to mention all the jobs that this could bring in. So, why don't you call me when you get this message? No, make that call me after eight your time. We can expand this dialogue as you guys in the suit world like to say. As I understand it, you want me to learn who the three mugs are and what they do for a living. Is this accurate?"

Yes, he understands just enough. That's what we need to know. He continues.

"I suspect I can. They're not familiar as of now. But, who knows what I can find if properly motivated. By the way this one set of images is really washed and grainy. Are these the same guys as in my photos?"

We think so, but that's where he comes in. Can he extract clearer images from what we sent or does he need the original tape?

"I can start with this, but only get so far. I'll need the tape to confirm reality. Why do you need this confirmation? I mean, are we looking at a major national conspiracy or what? My fee is seven hundred and fifty a day plus expenses. And I need three days up front. I bill partial days at five hundred. Fair enough?"

I'll send a money order and the tape by FedEx tomorrow. One more thing he must know. We talk and correspond only at this office. That must be perfectly clear. There can be no deviation.

I call Karen. Her voice mail tells me she is away from her desk. Leave message. When I was twenty, simply panting over the phone was sufficient to communicate feelings. At my present age and the experience of two marriages and several affairs, expression of carnal desires is not wise. Don't dare send flowers.

Ask her to dinner away from my home. Get a gander at her crib. All done with a dash of teenage eagerness. I am unfuckingbelievably nervous. Once it was the pre-first-kiss jitters. Now it's post-coital anxiety. Did she have as good a time as I did? How we have changed. Is this change for the better? Morning rushes by me as if I were running backward. Lunch consists of red meat, pasta, tea with lemon, and a nap. Am I an athlete in training? Thank God for the spa. Back in my tower of almost power. Karen has called. Message says no dinner tonight. She has some huge project to complete and get in front of some important clients by eight AM. But tomorrow night would be great. Meet her at Stone Crab Charlie's on the beach at seven. Dress casual. Food can be sloppy. I even get a kiss and a hug. I am excited. It just doesn't show, because I am seated.

Afternoon is as expected. Review some projects in the works. Talk to the supervisors about performance, plans for expansion into a department, my review of possible prospects for their groups, and some long-range wool gathering. Home by six.

Hither and Yon are bouncing around like little kids who have to pee. They do. I let them out. I check the ComRoom for Mary. She has been in bed all day. Exhausted from the week's activities, she says. She is pale and seems very weak. Help her out of bed to the shower. She will join me in a bit. The dogs are barking furiously. Investigate. No squirrels. No rats, rodent or human. The back gate is open. Damned pool guy.

Dinner is simple. Mary wants soup and toast. Her stomach is bothering her. She claims she is well rested.

"Did you two swim well last night?"

The probe is inserted.

"Yeah, I love to swim before sleep and it's fun to have a partner."

"Did you sleep well after your swim?"

"Like a stone. Dropped off in less than ten minutes."

"You two were quiet this morning."

Busted!

"We tried not to disturb you."

"I was up most of the night. Couldn't sleep so I worked on the Net. Went back to the chat rooms."

She now begins to whisper. She was not told of the possible bug, so she must have deduced something on her own. Maybe it's just the exhaustion.

"I think I discovered something very, very disturbing. I think I can predict where the next school shooting will occur. It frightens me so much I can't get excited. That's why I'm so calm. Let me show you what I've found."

She is too calm. The sky before a hurricane is dead calm because it knows what's about to happen. All hell will break loose. Ferocity. Destruction. Pandemonium. She is sky calm.

"Here, look at this scroll from Bloodnourishment: Look to the FirefromGod."

"Now look at JonnyGetYourGun: He will free us."

"Last, HandsHeldHigh: Shoulders carry the load."

"What's so important about those three quotes is that they are all entered as the last line from TruthSeeker. Always. I believe this guy is one of the monitors of the five chat rooms. And here's the kicker. I have the sick feeling this guy is doing more than listening. He is broadcasting. And through broadcasting, he leads or, at least, guides the others."

"Mary, a week ago I would have thought that was crazy. Today I could not say that. But, I will say that this is very unlikely. Sort of like the theory of black particles. How can we prove it? Can it be proven?"

"There is no litmus test. A way to see if I'm right is to sit back and let something happen. If it happens as we silently predict, we will know we were right. If it does not happen, we were wrong. If we were right and do nothing, many kids will be slaughtered. If we're wrong and do nothing, no one gets hurt. This is a conundrum. What to do? What to do?"

"Here is another thought. If we alert the authorities, I doubt they will listen to us. Then they will do nothing. If nothing happens, we are branded as loonies and no one will ever listen to us. If the kids are killed after we warned the school officials, we become the prime suspects. They'll ask how we knew? Who did we tell? Who are we really? No one else would step forward and admit that they ordered the killings. Not even the killers, who are oh so proud of their actions. If we know there will be violence, how do we know where the violence will occur?"

"That part may be easier than we think. The fire from God could be Lucifer or Saint Ignatius. He will free us could be Lincoln. Abraham Lincoln set free the slaves. And where is the land of Lincoln? Illinois. Shoulders that carry the load is Chicago, the broad shoulders of the nation. So, we have St. Ignatius High School in Chicago, Illinois. We just don't know the when"

"Wait a minute, sis. Taking all those factoids could also give you a high school in Lincoln, Nebraska near the Broad River or Shoulder Bend. What about Lucifer? You might even have Prometheus. Or Moses as the freer of people. We would have to check all the high schools in every state, in every town, and in every district to determine if any fit all the clues. And, in which order. If these are clues, that is. Or simply incredible intellectual leaps based on the emotions of two people, who don't know where they're jumping. Besides all this, remember that the three shooting incidents have occurred in small towns, Carter, Menthen, and Lutztown. Chicago and even Lincoln don't fit that part of the puzzle. The cities are too big. So where are we?"

"We have to do something to stop the slaughter I know will occur! We owe Dorothy and every other school child that much. We can't just sit back and let it happen. That would make us as guilty as the shooters and the entire evil force. Passivity is no excuse."

"Fair enough. Let's go to the Net and do some deep digging. We'll start with a list of metro areas with less than a quarter of a million people. Census information will be the key. Note any relationship to fire, free, and shoulders. Then we'll check the states containing appropriate metro areas looking for names that have any relationship to our key words. Then we'll cross reference the resultant lists with schools with the same commonality. The last step will be the toughest. State school systems are available, just hidden. This will take a few hours using the right websites. But, it is the only way to do this that I can think of. Are you up for it?"

"We can both go on line, if you go to the office. I'll be fine here with my boys. I'll take states east of the Mississippi. You got the ones west. See you in a few hours. Are you up for it?"

After four hours, I have four possible targets and head for home. Mary has five on her list. We have a baseball team. Now what? It frightens me that we are pursuing a course of action based upon some very questionable assumptions. What if TruthSeeker is anything other than our bleak assumption? What if the messages are a deeper code? What if there is no significance to what was on the scroll? What if they are baiting a trap? What if? What if? What if? Between anxiety and fear lies the great void of indecision. We must do something. But what? Narrow the list? How? Call all nine targets? How we do warn them of our unsubstantiated fear based upon shaky hypotheses?

"By telephone. I'll call the school principal and speak to him or her very calmly. I can do this after I get back from the doctor's. A woman's voice will be a better vehicle than a man's. Plus, this is really my mission. Your work for now is done. Now clean up and go to work. I have an eight o'clock appointment with Doctor Hanan. So, scoot."

Gulf Beach, Florida

The external call came at nine. The police officer just said to come to the hospital. Mary Thomas Benton had been in an accident. The police had gotten my name and address and both telephone numbers from her wallet. Strange how using her full name objectified everything. Mary was no longer my sister. She was Mary Thomas Benton in the emergency room of County Hospital. On a good day, this trip would take forty-five minutes. Today, twenty-five. Lights flashing. Horns blasting. Screaming for the snails to get the fuck out of my way. Changing lanes every three hundred yards. Darting in and out of traffic. Eased through two red lights. The no-cop God watched over my trip. Screeched to a halt in a spot normally reserved for some member of administration. I yelled at the guard where I was going.

This must have been a slow morning for the ER. Or maybe they are just really efficient. That concept is disturbing. How did they get to be so good at moving bodies in and out? Practice is the appropriate answer, but not the one I wanted to hear. No gurneys in the hall. No one in the admitting area. No one waiting for an injured loved one. Just the expected paging and telephone ringing. Officer Davis met me halfway down the hall. Young. About six feet tall. Solidly constructed. Kevlar vest. Dour look on his face.

"Mister Eugene Benton?"

"Yes, I am he."

"Mister Benton, your wife has been in an accident. We brought her to County via Medivac from downtown. She was admitted about eight forty-five. We called you right away. Let me get Doctor Kenney for you he has all the details."

"Officer, Mary is my sister. She has no family except for me. Moved here from Wyoming. Lives with me until she can find a place of her own."

"Sorry."

"Mister Benton this is Doctor Kenney."

Christ, she looks like she is no older than twenty-five. I wonder if she is good or just eager and strong enough to put up with the hours and bullshit. Maybe a combination of all three. I hope. She is homelier than a stick, barely four feet eight inches tall and skinnier than a beanpole.

"Mister Benton, your wife has been in a serious auto accident. She has multiple breaks in her legs and right arm, skull fracture, and her left lung is crushed. We're not sure of the amount of internal damage. But, given what we know, I have to believe that she suffered very extensive injuries that will be problematic. We'll have a better fix on this issue in a few moments. Doctor Miller, our resident internist, is examining her now. Why don't we see what he has learned?"

"Doctor Kenney, just for clarification, Mary is my sister. I am the only family she has. Both her husband and daughter are dead."

"Sorry for the error."

"No problem."

"Doctor Lopez, this is Mister Benton, Miss Benton's brother."

"Sir, we are doing all we can to sustain your sister. The internal injuries have been very extensive. Spleen, both lungs and liver . . . all damaged. She had been weakened by the polio. So, her ability to fight this massive trauma is not strong. Miss Benton is holding on. Barely. Frankly, I'm not sure we can do more for her than just help her hold on. So, we're in a bind. We can keep her alive. But for how long before her body just quits? We don't know. No one knows. We do know that she is not suffering. And won't."

"Doctor, are you asking me to consent to pulling the plug? Because, if you are, I'm not empowered to do so. I am her brother and only living relative, but she never provided me with the authority to assist her demise. However, if there are forms to complete by which I could legally assume that power, I will sign them. Just in case. This assumes that her life is in a true downward spiral. And you would be responsible for that determination. In court if need be. Or should we just wait and let nature take its final course?"

"I believe we should wait for at least four hours. By then we'll have a better assessment of her condition and our ability to stabilize her. If you would like to see her, you may. She can't recognize you at this time. But, if you would like, she is in room six."

Just like you never hear the bullet that kills you, I don't remember what Doctor Lopez looked or sounded like. I remember the room. No matter what is done, a hospital room is just a functional, sterile booth in which humans are placed when they enter this world, recover from trauma, or repose before departure. There was this bandaged mass of near life with tubes and such into and out of her body. She was formerly known as Mary Thomas Benton. Smart-ass older sister who tormented her adoring baby brother every day. Bull-headed young woman who left the East Coast sanctuary of her family to start a new life with a low-life. Mother of a now dead daughter. Re-builder of her own life. Teacher of adult youths. Seeker of truth. Lover of dogs. This life was in the pre-departure repose. And all the king's horses and all the king's men couldn't put Mary Thomas Benton together again. Maybe the doctors were not frustrated and angry because they had faced similar situations many times before. They had to act detached and professional. Not me. I was pissed. I wanted answers. How? Why? I can do nothing but wait for the inevitable. I'll be in the hospital. Talk to Officer Davis.

"Do you know what happened?"

"We know that the RV she was driving failed to negotiate the ramp at Exit Fourteen from the Interstate. This is one of the exits that leads to the west side of downtown. Do you know why she was on the road at that time?"

"She had a doctor's appointment. She had been weakening lately and thought it was a good idea to have a check-up."

"Well, the vehicle seemed to run straight on a curved exit ramp and stove-piped on the concrete barrier about six feet from the road. Seems she was moving right along and just failed to negotiate the turn. Investigators are on the scene. I'll have a full report by tomorrow. We've impounded the RV. You can retrieve it in a few days. That's all I know now."

I call my office and leave voice mail for appropriate people. Then I sit in Mary's room and wait. And wait. I think Godot is next door. No sound other than the whooshing of air being breathed for her and the mid-pitched ping of the monitor. The magazines are three months old, which is fine because I never read them anyway. I can feel the sap oozing from my body as I slump forward in the uncomfortable easy chair by her bed. My head rests beside her arm. Put the magazine down and hold her hand. No response. Just my hope. The flurry around me startles me awake. I sit up. Spittle had run down the right side of my chin. A nurse was checking dials, print-outs, and the screen with all the lines. The ping had become a constant ring. Trouble was evidenced by change.

"Sir, excuse me. But, you'll have to step aside."

Through the building-wide intercom she barks, "This is Winters in room six. We have a Code Blue. Check monitors at station. Call Doctor Lopez. Stat."

No matter what she tried, there was no change in the change. All bells and whistles indicated that Mary was in permanent stillness. I had failed on my watch. Doctor Lopez confirmed what I knew. I completed the requisite forms and went back home. Stunned. Numb. Soulless.

The dogs could sense something terrible had happened. They paced, whined, and moaned. Feral sadness is deeper, more powerful than human sorrow. Not as noisy and far fewer recriminations. I can see their sorrow. It's thick like fog. Dark like a thundercloud. The pacing. Constant motion. Then the dogs plop. Stare woefully at the ceiling for twenty or thirty seconds then arise to pace. This cycle continues for hours. There is nothing I can say or do to change their natural process of grieving. Should I start to clean up? Pack-up her belongings like I did for Dorothy? Not today. Tomorrow. Now answer the telephone.

"Gene, I just heard. What happened? Are you OK? I'm on my way over, if that's all right with you?"

"Sure. I'm not sure I'll be good company with snappy patter. But I could use your presence."

The hug at the door was designed to begin the restoration of my soul. Thus the rebuilding commences. With friends or family. Her tears were a strange comfort. I got to hug her back. Helping her was helping me. No food. Iced tea by the pool with the dogs. Karen was good for them, too. They liked her. We talked about Mary's life as we knew it. I shared bunches of I remember when's. Childhood. Our teens. When she left to get married. Et cetera. Et cetera. With each memory, I realized how little I knew of her adult life. With each story, the pain diminished and the new void was filled with fondness. The idea to continue Mary's work came from somewhere. I just spoke it. Karen thought it was a great idea. I gave all the details. As best as the apostle can relate the teachings of the master. Finally, the list of nine possible targets and the very complex philosophical issue of what to do with it. We were both lesser zealots than Mary. We had not lost a daughter. We were almost objective. It was agreed to do nothing.

Wait and see. There were too many ifs and what ifs inherent in Mary's work. I needed sleep. I needed to sleep alone. No touching. Just alone with my sadness and guilt. Karen slept in Mary's room. The dogs paced and plopped and paced and plopped.

I have taken a few days from work. Frankly, that's no big deal. Nothing going on that my troops can't handle or that I can't change when I return. The call to the police stirs some embers. They ask that I come down to the station. Breakfast with Karen. She will be by my side for the next few days. Then I have to decide where we go from there. For now two reeds in the wind are strength for each other. Off on the journey. Police station. The morgue. The mortuary.

"Mister Benton, it seems that the steering and brakes on the RV simply wore out at the same time. And she was not strong enough to control the vehicle when this happened. The failure coincidence happens occasionally on older vehicles. Your sister's RV had one hundred and sixty thousand miles on it and was twelve years old. So, frankly, failures to the brakes and steering are not an unexpected event. The tubes and wiring were old and they failed. We are sorry about your loss."

What's wrong with this picture? Mary had the bus truck completely serviced and checked out before her trek to Florida. She even bitched about the amount of money she spent. The service center would have checked brakes and steering. I want to understand this inconsistency. We check the papers from the glove box. Big Bob's RV Center had replaced the brake fluid lines to the front wheels and did a six-point check on the power steering and found that no repair or replacement was necessary. Karen agrees that something is amiss and calls the service center on her cell phone. Harold, the service manager, tells her that he remembers Mary Benton. She had the RV serviced every three thousand miles. Kept real good care of her second home and was very fussy with mechanics. She had told them to give the vehicle a thorough going over. As if their kids were going to drive it to Florida. She wanted no problems. When she pulled off the lot, Harold felt that the RV was ready and safe enough for his mother or his kids. There was nothing wrong with the steering. The brake lines to the front wheels were replaced because they were a tad worn. Nothing real serious. Just a precaution because of the long trip.

Now I am scared. There is contradictory knowledge that only Karen and I can share. Can't tell the local cops that they are wrong. Don't want to stir up some a major brouhaha with investigations and media digging.

Don't want the perps to know that we know. Best to remain silent for the time being. Get many more of the puzzle pieces on the board before we ask for serious help. The Scots have a saying: 'Sometimes you have to lie in the bushes and wait before you scream like a banshee.' We will lie.

The morgue agrees to release the body to Mossers Funeral Home. Mossers will turn Mary into ashes. I will buy the urn. The RV remains in impound. No reason to reclaim it. It can be sold by the insurance company to the junk yard. They will send Mary a check. Who will cash it?

Back home we start to pack. Boxes upon boxes of personal stuff. The ComRoom is to remain as is. I have no idea what to do. It's more than I need or want, but I can't dismantle it. Not that smart. Karen suggests that she go shopping for dinner. She'll cook. I sit with the boxes, memories, and dogs. They come to me and rest on my lap. Sadness of loss has replaced pitiful woe. The next stage for them is acceptance and moving on. What am I to do with them? Will I adopt them or vice versa? They can stay because they are the last vestiges of a family which was part of me. They are good company and this place might just need vicious security.

Dinner goes quickly, silently. Clean up is by rote. Sitting by the pool, I whisper my real fears. Fears, which I had not taken seriously before, are like daggers in my heart. Was Mary killed? Is the house bugged? Who are the guys in the pictures? Is there a connection between Senator Miller's campaign and the shootings at the schools? What is on the websites? Who are all those characters? Can we predict the future? Should we? What principal would close a school for a week on the insane supposition that mayhem might happen? What the fuck have we gotten ourselves into? I have no answers. Just lots of questions, which produce even more questions, which produce even more.

Karen takes me by the hand and pulls me close. I can feel her heart in syncopation with mine. The warmth of her breath and embrace calm my trembling. We turn off the lights, close the doors, keeping one open to let the dogs have run of the house and back yard. The bed is comfortable and lovemaking tender. Grasping at mortality, I am so self-involved that I forget who Karen is or why she is there. This she must never know.

Four AM coffee is an old pattern that can return me to a pre-trauma state. Feed the dogs. Throw tennis balls for them to retrieve for me to throw for them to retrieve. Check the back gate. Fetch a lock for the latch. Remember to call the pool service and my garden genius and leave a key hidden for their use. No duplication allowed. The dogs are the guards.

They have already been introduced to the regular workers. It's the strangers they will pursue. Their attitude now that Mary is dead will make them unpleasant with interlopers. A huge battle will commence upon intrusion and the bad guys will die. Oh, well. Oh, well.

Check my voice mail at the office and access my e-mail from the ComRoom. Mary and Karen showed me how to do this off-site magic. Maybe I'll never go back to the office. The voice mail is soporific except for the call from Mike Duncan. I am afraid to listen to his message over this line. I'll have to go to the office right now, before the throng arrives. I can be there in thirty minutes or so and won't be noticed by anyone but security. Scribble note for Karen, who sleeps sensually in my space.

"Gene, this is Mike Duncan. I've learned something about your buddies. They work for the Federal Government. National Security Agency. Very strange operatives working outside their anticipated area of expertise. Their names are Brent Forbes, Roger Thompson and Alan Campbell. All Ivy League educated. Are assigned at the whim and fancy of the director who reports only to the President. Their histories are fuzzy. But, it's safe to assume they have been all over the world. Hot spots only. Places where the national interest needs special, very prejudicial attention. I know that Brent and Alan were in the Middle East for about two years. You know, the usual stuff. Organizing small groups of dissidents to work together for a common good. Overthrow some bad guy or protect some one who loves Uncle Sam. Men with no pasts bother me, because you never know where they are going. Now, Roger is a piece of work. The only place he has been is the Nonunion of Soviet Socialist Republics. He visited most of the small but very angry states. The ones that have all the nuclear war heads and oil, but no food and clothing. The ticking time bombs. Somehow these three were put together to protect or monitor the good Senator. Why him? Why them? Why now? None of my sources know. But the questions intrigue them enough that they want to dig further for me. It will cost about seventy-five hundred for them to get to the bottom of all this. Is it worth it to you? I realize this is steep and sudden, but my guys have moles all over. They could dig up dirt on the Pope. If I were you I would consider the expense a good investment. Still no lock on any connection between the *tres banditos* with Miller and the fuzzy faces from Carter. I hope to have an answer in two days. By the way, do you ever get the feeling someone is following you? Or just watching your house? Call me with your decision."

I voicemail Mike back.

"Mike, I'll send three thousand for your associates. FedEx to your address. The balance of the requested total is payable upon receipt of real information, not just histories. The connection remains key, if any, between Miller's boys and the mugs at Carter. And, yes, I feel that I am watched. But, so does a goldfish. Stay in touch."

Out the door and head for home. No pick-up truck or small sports car. Have they given up? Are they awake at this hour? In the front door and the dogs are happy to see me. Karen is asleep. Turn on the TV for early CNN. There it is, bigger than death. The slaughter of seventeen children at a Spring Prometheus Festival sponsored by the eighth grade Classic Club. Their celebration of school completion. In the evening, by the traditional bon fires. In the soccer field of John Brown Middle School located in Ox Bow, Maryland. The killers used two Barrett Fifty Caliber 82 A-1 Rifles. These are semiautomatic sniper rifles designed to destroy armor reinforced vehicles, turn ballistic glass to sand, and abruptly ground low-lying airplanes. They are deadly accurate at more than a mile. Ammunition is available in black-tipped armor piercing and silver-tipped incendiary varieties. Killers have choices. The victims don't. These guns are easier to get than handguns. The buyers have to show proof that they are eighteen with no felony convictions. Handgun purchasers must be at least twenty-one. The children did not stand a chance. Chunks of small bodies all over the soccer field. It looked like the aftermath of an explosion in a robotic factory except for the pools of blood.

The area and school were not on our list, but the criteria matched. We were too narrow in our search. Too arrogant that we had deciphered the code. Too blinded by own importance. Pride goeth before the fall. Unfortunately this time seventeen middle-schoolers fell. I am crushed. The tears well up in my eyes. Frustration. Anger. Fear. A promise to Mary. No more. The slaughter of the innocents must stop. This is my line in the sand. Now I sob and sniffle. The dogs want to know what the hell is going on. They come into my space and give me kisses. Karen slides by my side and holds me. I am lost.

Breakfast. Karen goes back to the sites and chat rooms. She is the new Girlfromoz. Armed with knowledge and fearful respect. She reads and rereads the recent past with knowledge of the then future. Looking for signs that would have given a better indication of place and date. She is convinced that we are on the right path. Writing down everything that TruthSeeker says, as well as that which proceeds and follows the pronouncements. Where is BrokenArrow in all of this? Is anybody crowing over the events of the evening? Concentrating on the five chat rooms will consume her day. I must go to the bank for the mole money. FedEx to San Diego.

Back home, the networks are reporting on the efforts of Senator Miller and President Sessler. Each of them was stumping for success. Miller was in Duluth, Minnesota. Sixteen thousand people at the Palli Auditorium. SAFE is alive and growing in the heartland. Same faces. Same speech. It's weird. Miller's responses are not canned, but they are the same each rally. The questions are almost the same each time. At the very least, they lead him well. Are they scripted? Audience plants are called on to help the Senator get the message to the people. All the while, the people think they are getting the message to the Senator. House of mirrors like the ending in The Lady from Shanghai. Where are real bodies . . . real people? What are images? The only way to find out is to shoot all the panels. The ones that shatter were not real. The one that falls down was a person. Do the people in the audience know which speaker is an image and which one is real?

Miller's road show is working. He is getting more and more ink, as well as better and better op-ed words each week. First the small town, more conservative and traditional papers were talking about him and his crusade. Now the mid-size markets are awakening. Not all of them. And, not always positive. But, the trend is there. He's got the buzz. Soon the liberal press of the top ten markets will have to remove their blinders. Maybe they will dig up something of disrepute about the Senator. Maybe they will nominate him for sainthood.

President Sessler is in a very different position. His is a house of cards attempting to withstand a force six storm. Leslie Tremaine and Huang Tsai abruptly departed the inner circle. Miss Tremaine cited a prior movie commitment. She was replaced by Jennifer Chessman, a young actress of much lesser note, but a big favorite with the teens. How can Leslie justify her departure? No one has a prior commitment when the President asks. Master Tsai was admitted to a Dallas hospital suffering from exhaustion. He was replaced by a wannabe from the valley. The *l'fant* terrible was just fine last weekend when he was sighted surfing off Corpus Christi. The lie is too thin. Were they deposed? By whom? For what reason?

Beyond the new weaker mix of celebrities, the changing of horses in midstream does not bode well for the Commission. The A-Team is now the B+-Team. In the face of Senator Miller's onslaught, the weakening of the castle guard is dangerous. The next panel discussion is set for this Friday. It will be interesting to see how the entire mess is handled. It will be worth watching to see the emergence of the power broker or brokers. My bet is on Elizabeth Pendelton and John Wenger. They appear to be the cleanest and therefore the ones to be trusted the least. If they emerge as the king and queen of the hill, the results of this public relations spin exercise will be predictable.

Plus, there are reports that the President is lobbying Congress for a change in Constitutional Amendment Twenty-Two. It seems the good President would like to serve for at least a third term. How can he abridge this amendment or place it in abeyance for his pleasure? For what reason is a third term in the best interest of the people? He and his party are obviously afraid of Senator Miller and his believers. The tradition of running the Vice President is guaranteed to fail. Harrison Paul is a blob of tapioca. Big on brains, small on personality, and zero on experience. He has lived in the shadow of a very charismatic, often erratic world leader. Vice President Paul has lived through a six-year bull market of astonishing economic growth. And peace in the industrial world is now the norm. Both are the sole responsibility of President Sessler. Or, at least, that's what he says. The Veep just carries the bag and shows up at minor state functions. Rarely goes outside the country except for a wedding. It was his daddy's money that financed the first election. Then daddy died and Sessler took control. Now Paul is just a Vice President. Never to be President. Never to even run. In this environment and given the fact that Sessler is a megalomaniac, a change in the constitution is the logical step in Sessler's mind to retain the power. Why should little things like constitutional law and due process stand in the way of President Sessler?

Karen works in the ComRoom. She is very kind. I'm not sure she lives here although she is here every day so far. Since when? If she lives here, when did she move in? The dogs like her. And they listen to her. I do also. She is good for all three of us. I feet her presence throughout the house and it calms me. She is in the door to the den motioning me to follow her to poolside. We sit and dangle our feet.

"Gene, look what I've found. Something you and Mary, um, we missed. These are the three lines from TruthSeeker that led to the list of nine possible targets. We were on the right track. We just overlooked the input from BrokenArrow because it did not appear near the key lines. Quotes did, however, appear on all three scrolls. The first two quotes are number clues.

See, BrokenArrow tells us: 'Extensive Filly Faves' and 'In thirty-nine houses liberty has been lost.' The third quote is a date clue: 'Classic Comic Books are for the masses.' These are nonsense lines at the end of his ramblings. Clue seekers would know to look for the words, their importance relative to those of TruthSeeker, and would know how to decipher them."

"If we check the atlas, we find that Ox Bow, Maryland is roughly at longitude seventy-six and latitude thirty-nine. The Philadelphia basketball team is the Seventy Sixers. Extensive could be considered a synonym for longitude. So, we have longitude seventy-six. Following that same path, liberty is synonymous for latitude. This gives us latitude thirty-nine. And Classic is a reference to the Classics Club, which puts on the Prometheus festival. There you have it. A complete guide to what, where, and when the killings are going to occur. If all this is accurate, we must watch the chat rooms each day so we can predict the next where and when. And, make no mistake about it, there will be a next."

"Karen, this is more than I can deal with. I think we need to call in some professional help. Someone who can act with authority. The authority we don't have. We should also check the dates of the massacres. Is there any rhyme or pattern there?"

"I've done that already. Carter, Menthen, Lutztown, and Ox Bow occurred no closer than three weeks and no more than four weeks apart. This is definitely a serial killing effort. There does not appear to be shortening or lengthening of that schedule. If the timing holds, whatever will happen will do so in three weeks to four weeks. What we don't know is when the clues will be posted. But I suspect the clues will start to appear very soon. This will give the killers time to prepare. Assuming they are not part of an already armed and poised militia. We don't know if the clues will be posted by BrokenArrow and TruthSeeker. Or, which of the two will give the right clues. We don't know if the two *cluemeisters* will provide the same type of clues in the same order. We don't know a lot. So, we must be ever vigilant."

"I'll take some time from work. The three big proposals are complete and my assistant can mop up any details. I haven't had a vacation for nearly two years and I am due. My boss took his time before we began the big crunch. It'll be a sudden request, but they'll get over it. What about you?"

"I'm still on family emergency leave and can extend that for a few more days. Then I'll go on vacation. The problem is that I'll need to get to my office for communication with Mike Duncan. I told him that was our only contact point. But, I can do that at night. I'll sneak in and out under the cover of darkness."

"We can call Mister Duncan on my cell phone if you're concerned about using the house land line. We can call from the lanai or standing in the pool, as crazy as it sounds. That way we'll be safer. It's just that he can't call us here. We can even access your e-mail by using a complex trail from here to my office to your office and back again. We can read it then trash it. If someone is watching and listening, they will note our activity but not what we see."

"Will you be moving in?"

This was a big question. Suppose she had already moved in. Was I inviting her? Yes.

"Temporarily."

"That's a good thing. Your presence here on a full-time basis is desired by the three males. If we are to live in the bunker, I best go grocery shopping. And you will want to retrieve clothes and girl stuff. I'll get you a key to the front door and the back gate while I'm out. I'll be back from my chores by three. See you then. Thank you for your care."

Our kiss is brief and non-sexual. Husband-and-wife buss. Off to the grocery store, cleaners, and hardware store. Home again, naturally.

Karen arrives in about thirty minutes. She unloads her car alone. Wants no help. She moves her clothes into Mary's room, clearly establishing the social acceptability of her abiding in my house. She will sleep with me, but not sleep with me. The dogs are happy to see her. We change for a swim.

Basjar

Midnight, right after the guard change. Night absolutely clear. Black with the sparkle of stars like a disco ceiling. Sergeant Daniel Fulker was disintegrated by the explosion and its heat. Pieces of the small truck, which carried the mass of explosives, were found six blocks away. Shreds of one tire and a piston. Shards of the side mirror and a twisted ignition switch. The blast lifted the side wall of the embassy compound about six inches from the foundation, bowed it in toward the buildings, and turned the reinforced concrete into laced sand. The lattice fell into the courtyard. No one saw the three figures carrying the rocket launchers. They were kneeling in the wall's maw before the dust settled. The three blasts thrust one highly explosive, armor piercing shell and two incendiary shells into the wall of the building that housed the soldiers and a few low-level administrators. The collapsing walls and fire claimed forty-eight of America's best and brightest. Some of them wanted to be in the Middle East, in Chadar. Chadar is a strategic military point to the north of Basjar, home of the bully of the world, el Jahdiq . . . savior of the down-trodden, oil-rich masses. All of the American soldiers were proud to serve. They knew there would be some tense times and a little bit of danger. No one, top to bottom, was vaguely prescient of this event.

Precisely ninety seconds later, a small pick-up truck pulled up to the gates at the military barracks adjacent to the United States Embassy in Riatta, the seaport capital of Qratri. Riatta handles about one-fourth of the area's oil. Oil from every country. Friend and foe. One guard leaves his booth. The other stays in air conditioned comfort and calls the Officer of the Watch. Before the guard reaches the rusted bucket of smoke-blowing inefficiency, the driver is off and running. The explosion catches him about twenty-five yards from ground zero and throws him, ablaze, another thirty yards into a large lorry parked across the boulevard. The armed guard disappears in the fireball. The booth disappears in the fireball. The gate and the surrounding walls disappear in the fireball. Alarms sound and pandemonium reigns. From the back of the lorry rush five wrapped bodies wearing boots. They kneel beside the truck and fire their rocket launchers. All projectiles strike the first floor front. The wall weakened by the shock wave of the first blast, slides to the ground like mud down a hill. The entire face of the six-story building goes, revealing twisted pipes and air-conditioning tubes. Little five-sided boxes that had been six-sided rooms. The furniture, drapes and bed linens are on fire. The smoke encases the entire building. Five bodies scurry like rats back into the lorry as it pulls out and heads south. The alarms blare and orders are barked from top to bottom. Perimeter secured. Full battle alert. Just twenty seconds too late. The digging will commence shortly. Sixty-three dead.

Four hundred and eighty five miles to the east, over the fiercest mountains and most barren desert the world, is another time zone. At nearly midnight, real time, a third small pick-up truck bumps and weaves its way through the oversized walkways of Najret. Najret is a city-state that controls the oil within a two hundred-mile radius from the hub. What is pumped from Najret is shipped from Riatta. Food, clothing, medicines, and all manner of necessities for this land-locked center of wealth come through Riatta. The relationship between the two governments is one of extensive dependence yet it can be acrimonious. Their faith in Allah and hatred for the Western World seem to be their only commonalties.

The truck is stopped at the crest of a hill on the avenue that leads directly to the American Embassy and military barracks. Two men exit the track and wire the bomb in the bed of the truck. One moves to the front to activate the detonator. He leaves and the driver reenters the cab. The wheel is lashed right and left to keep the truck on target. A carefully crafted piece of metal is wedged under the old accelerator to keep the engine roaring. The onslaught begins. About one hundred yards from the gate, the pick-up's driver rolls from the cab. The truck hurtles on its appointed path. The crash and blast are simultaneous. The fireball can be seen for miles. For those in the know, it is not an oil storage tank. The blaze, smoke, and flying debris are perfect cover for the second vehicle. The old army truck grinds its way to the much enlarged gate opening and pauses. The tarpaulin on the building side of the truck is raised and six bodies become visible.

Their firepower is unleashed on the interior building. Four mortars and two rocket launchers. Three rounds each. What was a wall is now rubble. What was behind the wall is now more rubble. In less than one minute the tarp is lowered and the truck waddles off into the flame colored night. One hundred and thirty-seven lost under the aggregate of concrete, rebar, furniture, and metal doors. Never find all the bodies, just lots of components.

The scenes are replayed on the television networks. CNN, CBS, NBC, Fox, and ABC are picking up feeds from local and the international crews, allowed to cover this part of the world. The scenes play over and over. A loop in an old Moviola. The reporters are using their best English. Hand-held cams bob and weave through the soldiers, wreckage and night darkened further by the smoke and ash in the air. Small focus. High intensity bulbs of the cameras are not sufficient to light more than ten or twelve feet from the lenses. No panoramic shots of the destruction. The scenes shift one to another to another. Is one carnage worse than another? They all look alike. They were meant to. The two-star Commanders of each fortress are saying nothing. The three-star Commander for the Middle East is saying nothing. The Pentagon is saying nothing. The White House has scheduled a briefing for eight AM, Washington time. The visuals replay, the words are repeated. After an hour the shock has worn off and the pain ever so slightly diminished. How many times can I hear about and see the butchery before I just don't give a shit? The body count rises with the sun. The worker bee soldiers scamper about in the background, directing heavy equipment and lifting pieces of the structures from the bodies. Calling for the medics whose futile attempts to save lives long since lost are sad. The outcome is predetermined, but the medics must try nonetheless.

I am told this is the beginning of The Feast of Great Joy for the citizens of Basjar. For three days, there will be parades, dancing and great feasts. The natives of Basjar are controlled by a group of multinationals cobbled together by el Jahdiq and given sanctuary in his land. Hitler's iron fist of control would be more like a debutante's white gloved handshake relative to the absolute power exercised by el Jahdiq. If he smiles you may or may not smile depending on whether he meant the smile and only he knows that. Just about any day will be your last if you don't curry favor like a toady each and every moment. About every six months el Jahdiq changes his cabinet. A few retire as advisors. Most become targets for his weapons testers after being tortured for a few weeks. His marksmen are not very good and it takes several of them to kill one proven dissident. Those truly unfortunate become subjects for the chemical and biological warfare labs. This is particularly excruciating because death can take up to six weeks. Hitler was just an angry teacher next to the Beast of the East. El Jahdiq's people are poor, suffer from regular inquisitions, and have little or no western amenities. All of the basics are reserved for The Battalions of Allah. There is a never-ending supply of new recruits. Facing death on the battlefield is more desirable than starving at home. Many of the young men send all of their ration and their pay back to their families. The war machine is efficient.

El Jahdiq has been waging war with one or another of his neighbors for the past twenty years. The wars have been minor border disputes for the most part. Necessary honing steps for a much larger conflict. A struggle to lead the faithful out of the dark ages and to their rightful position as leaders of the world. He has progressed, or regressed, from soldiers, some with rifles from World War One, to an elite over-trained force that commands long-distance tanks and artillery. In the last conflict he used biological and chemical clouds to eliminate helpless, noninvolved villagers. His message was read loud and clear Don't fuck with me. Rumors are that he has nearly all the material to build nuclear warheads. Nearly. He has gotten loans from just about every nation that hates the US. Loans in the form of credits, equipment, and technology. He owes big. And, he uses big. This debt is a drug. The more he wants, the more he gets. He pays a little by taking control of another small piece of a neighbor or a mountain tribe. Then he joneses for another fix. The dealers accommodate. The only way he can pay is to expand. But the underlying question is: When does the dog become bigger and meaner than the master? When can the borrower tell the lender to eat shit?

His war machine is run and staffed by groups from all over the world, but mostly the desert region. These are troublemakers, who have been banished from their own countries. Revolutionaries. These are the men and women who have tried to depose but failed. Sometimes the US gave them aid and sometimes our global nemesis gave them weapons and training. Just enough so that they could cause trouble—not enough for an immediate and complete overthrow of power. Both superpowers used these militants to foment unrest so each could come to the aid of those who could win. Both would shore up defenses, provide basic needs, buy the country's export and build their own air bases. Now the exiled militants serve el Jahdiq and train in his country in the hope that one day very soon they will be able to go back and take back their own from the big bad international bullies. This suits el Jahdiq.

Most of the countries that ring Basjar are neutral or friendly to the US. At least, we hope so, because that's what they tell us. They receive more support each year to keep the bad guy contained. We are their dealer. We tighten the noose around el Jahdiq's neck. Restrict his trading ability by devaluing his export, oil. If we can keep the price of his oil at an artificially depressed level for another two or three years, he will self-destruct. He will have no way to kick the massive drug of debt. At least, that's what our government tells us. This is the tension that keeps the Middle East hot. El Jahdiq has no avenues of expansion. His dealers are becoming less and less likely to lend. They have their own problems and we can apply the screws to their fragile economies to heighten their woes. If they have to pay more for basics, they will have less and less to feed the junkie. If he gets less and less, he becomes more and more anxious to expand. We are working both sides of the street. But, the wall around him is resolute. We hope. Ah, the arcane joy of international politics.

The Feast of Great Joy starts with a two-hour parade and a thirty-minute diatribe from el Jahdiq. The latest tanks and artillery as well as the elite guard battalions are paraded before the people and the National Party. The people stand on the hot concrete beneath the sweltering sun while their fearless leaders sit in an air-conditioned, bulletproof viewing stand. The stand comes complete with delicacies and cold drinks. Visible on the boulevard is the best hardware the people's money and blood can secure. Tanks from Russia, mobile artillery from China, and missile launchers with appropriate warheads from Sweden. Nothing from Uncle Sam. The elite guards goose-step to a beat that is part native and part Wagnerian. The Battalions are segmented by the type of personal weapons they carry. The variety is wide—assault, field combat, sniper, and anti-tank. The banners and flags represent the various battles and wars in which the men have fought. Several of the banners are fictitious and two of the battle flags had been dropped in defeat. But, after years of rhetoric and misinformation, and thousands of deaths, including the historians, who can remember the truth? The Boulevard of the Revolution can carry sixty men across. The Arch of Allah with its golden scimitars is their goal.

"Today is truly a day of Great Joy. The dog has been taught a lesson and he flees with his tail tucked between his hind legs. For years the forces of oppression have attempted to thwart the manifest destiny of the peace-loving people of Basjar. All we have ever wished is to live in prosperity and peace with our neighbors and the world. For years we have held forth the olive branch of love and understanding. For years we have been treated as less than human by those who would take our land and our precious resources. We have been held prisoner in our own land. We have been cheated in international commerce. Our women have been raped. Our children slaughtered. Our farms and cities pillaged. Our factories sabotaged. Our borders moved at the will of those who hate."

"I say to you, my brothers and sisters, that today this evil ends. Today we stand alone against the forces of tyranny. We stand tall that others may follow. Today is the dawn of a better tomorrow. Last night, while the dog slept, the people he has enslaved rose against him and struck a blow for the freedom of us all. We have just learned that three of our brother nations have begun to throw off the shackles of slavery. These are their calls to us for help. They have begun the grand and glorious revolution and need our assistance to complete the rout of the devil. Let us dedicate this day to our fallen. Let us dedicate this day to our strong warriors. Let us dedicate this day to the death of the oppressor. Let us dedicate this day to a safe and secure tomorrow for our children and our children's children."

Well, he's done it. Sends his saboteurs into the three countries with whom he has been fighting. The guys slink around and do the dirty deeds. The countries take the heat from Uncle Sam. Why can't the allies keep their house in order? He claims his sibling nations are acting in the best interest of the region and need his help. He sends his troops in to complete the job. Takes over the country. Installs the former rebels, who have been practicing for this day in his country. They love him. He annexes the land. Basjar expands. More oil. More food. More debt repayment. More credit. We are on the horns of a dilemma. Do we fight to preserve nations about which we don't care? Do we retaliate against the accused or the real culprit? How do we save face? What do we have to do to save the world? How do we not lose? What about el Jahdiq's lender? Will he join the battle? The geography is small but very strategic.

The massacres. The phony pageantry. The twisted truth. The lies. The hatred. The set-up for revenge. Who is the biggest liar? Who is behind all the killing? Are there many forces competing in a great killing tournament? The one that gets the most deaths wins. There must be more deaths to come. Were my niece and my sister just insignificant bugs under the jackboots of the power mongers? My sister was watched. The people in the Chat rooms are watched. I am watched. Who is this woman in my house? What does she want? Is she here to help me find Mary's killers? Is she here to kill me? Will she lead me off the path of truth? Can I trust her? I can't trust the police. I can't trust anyone in government. Not Sessler or Miller. I dare not move. I cannot move.

The images and noise from the television seem to move away. The sound is so distant it is almost not there. Sort of barrel hollow, but no echo. The picture on the screen jumps as if it were skip-framed. The motions are herky-jerky. Then they are in slow motion. The timber of the voices vacillates with the changing picture. Black and white becomes color, which becomes black and white. This ebb and flow of sight, sound, and motion is soothing. Hypnotic. The pendulum swing of the gold watch. Am I trapped? Am I stuck in this chair? Why am I crying? I do not hear my sobs. Can't feel the shudder. Pants are wet. Seat is wet. Did I spill my coffee? I never got a second cup? What is the mess? Pants. Chair. Arms are locked at my side.

Who is this woman? Why is she standing before me? Is she yelling? I can barely hear her? Her hands on my shoulders. She is holding me. Rocking me. Looking into my eyes. Trying to get a response. Nothing. Her voice is far away. Telling me to move my arms. Move my legs. Just move. I cannot. I really don't want to and don't care to try. I have stopped. Is this death? The darkness surrounds us. No light from the TV. No lights in the room. Just deep dark gray. She shrinks and grows with the light. Now she is shrinking. He voice disappears. Tugs my arms. Pulls me up. I stand, but do not move. Turn around to the chair and notice big dark stain on seat. Mine? My tears? My shirt is wet. She unbuckles my belt and removes my trousers and underpants. Walks me to the bedroom and seats me on the bed. Not the right time for that now. When is the right time? Helps me on with new pants. Leads me to the door to the garage.

The light in my eye hurts. The doctor explores to be sure of something. Does anyone really know what the doctor sees? His hands are gentle and firm. His voice is soothing. I can't understand what he is saying. He is too quiet. His nurse is taking notes. That woman is not here. Did she deposit her trouble on the doorstep of another? Two pills and a small cup of tepid water. Why not a big glass of ice cold mountain spring water? The ceiling is very low. The lights are flickering to my heartbeat. It is making me nauseous. The two men help me down the chilly dank hall to my room.

Not my room where my wet pants are. My new room. Green and gray walls and ceiling. Very soft lighting. A bed and a pee pot. A window in front of me and the door behind me. Heavy metal grate on the window. Keep me in? Keep them out? The door has a small window in it. Will they watch? What will they see? Am I to stay here for a long time? Forever? Will they feed me, clothe me, and bathe me. I don't think I can do all of that. And I don't really care. I am tired. The bed linen is fresh. There is something special about freshly cleaned and lightly starched bed linen. It is comforting to the skin. Cool, but not cold. I rest. Not sleep. Not that tired. Head on pillow, I can see the window in the door. I'll watch them. Think about where I am and why.

The square root of pi is 1.7724531. Pi squared is 9.86958772. I am better with my times than my gazintas. The rule of seventy-two predicts the doubling rate of the value of money. Divide the interest or growth rate into the number seventy-two. The resultant number will approximate the time, expressed in number of years it will take the value to double. The sum of the squared values of the horizontal and vertical legs of an isosceles right triangle equals the squared value of the hypotenuse. The three-four-five rule. Why are there only three hundred sixty degrees in a complete circle? Why are there three hundred sixty five and one fourth days in a year? Who says? Time and distance are arbitrary measurements applied by mankind and womankind? Do we really age faster in space? Do Sherpas age faster than people who live below sea level? The tree falling in the forest does make a sound. We just don't hear it if we are not there. How strong is mother's love? Being rich is nice. But there is always someone who is richer. Does that mean they are nicer? The same can't be said about happiness. What constitutes a good parent? What is the proper balance between the impact of heredity and environment? When are choices programmed? 9.869587728 plus 1.7724531 equals 11.63833038. I knew that.

The light in the room comes from outside. This room is mine. Where? The doctor. The pills. They woke me up to help me sleep. How stupid can that be? Why not wait until I awaken and need the pills? Are all these pills good for me or just a way to control my mind? I need to shower and shave. Get cleaned up. I peed myself and my crotch itches. I am tired but jittery. Where are the men who brought me to my room? Where am I? Two nurses lead me to the shower. Hope it's not communal. They are toads. They take my hospital garb. The towel is so fucking small it wouldn't cover my genitalia and I'm not that big. I get a new pair of hospital pajamas, a robe, and paper slippers. Paper slippers? What's next, steel pants? They take me to the end of the hall.

Three examining rooms. I am deposited in number two and wait. And wait. And wait.

"Good morning, Mister Benton. How do you feel?"

"A little groggy from all the downers you guys dumped in me last night. What am I doing here and when can I get out? Where are my real clothes? Look, I'm over twenty-one and I can come and go as I please. And, I please to leave. So give me the forms to sign and I'll be on my way."

"Mister Benton, you were brought here to Saint Joseph's Hospital for observation. Miss Leach brought you. She was very concerned. You had become nearly catatonic. You were not responding to light, motion, or sound. She claimed to have found you in this state yesterday morning at your home. You had urinated on yourself and were sitting stock still in front of the television set. She was very worried. She could not reach you. She wanted professional advice. You have undergone the recommended twenty-four hour observation. We must now decide whether to keep you here for more tests and treatment."

"I recommend letting me go home. I may not be fine in its purest form. I'm not violent. I haven't hurt anyone, not even myself. So, I don't need or want to be here. I will endure out-patient counseling and take whatever meds you script. But, I will not stay here."

"Sir, that is not your decision to make. It is the decision of Miss Leach as the adult responsible for your care and me. She signed you in. I am your doctor. We decide."

His pronouncement rang like the gong in a Road Runner cartoon. The solid sound. The vibrations of the impact. I was stopped cold. Someone outside of my immediate and trusted family was asserting control over my life. My coming and going were controlled by a doctor I didn't know and a woman about whom I was not sure. I was the mouse in the maze. They had the corn and the keys to the doors. Better to be pliant and win than to be stubborn and stay here.

"Listen to me, doc. If I am to be held under the Baker Act, you had better get a judge's order or a signed consent form from my next of kin. Who, by the way lives one thousand miles from here. I make my own adult decisions and I decide that I like me and I want me to go home. OK? What forms must I sign? What promises must I make and keep? Tell me. I am not prone to violence or rage, but I can get very pissed if lied to or contained."

There was panic and power in my voice and he sensed it. What he didn't know was why it was critical that I get out of the rest ranch. One, I had been here before and was not crazy (oops, bad choice of word) about a repeat performance. I'm sure he was aware of my emotional coming out party of years ago. He could read the records that it was a brief run at the palace and that the shrink who saw me then gave me a clean bill of health. Two, I had some life or death information to extract from some chat rooms. This was not his concern.

"Miss Leach is here. I'd like to talk to her before I make my decision."

The pompous arrogant prick. He wants me to be sure not to miss the fact that he is holding my balls in his iron grip. He leaves the examining room. The sterile, bright, and very unpleasant examining room. Three shades of the most bilious green. Hold on there big fella. Don't get buried in all the details of everything. That's how you got here in the first place. Holding minutia under a microscope. Examining a nit on a gnat's ass. Too fucking much detail and not enough perspective. I cant tell anyone what Karen and I know. Or what we are doing. Shit, they'd lock us both in this hellhole. No one would believe the details of the conspiracy. Conspiracies are only good and fashionable among the lunatic fringe. That's us. Take the meds. See the doc. No group. Tell the doc only what he wants to hear from someone who is susceptible to episodic depression.

Just like the last time. Pressure builds until the black cloud engulfs me. Then my self-preservation system shuts off all contact with the outside. Only temporarily. Just enough time for the psyche and soul to regroup and begin working in concert. Keep still and do as I am told. Rely on Karen. She is my only true friend. I hope.

Enter the angel of mercy and the putz.

"Gene, the doctor has decided that you can come home with me. You don't need to stay here any longer. We'll stop at the drug store and get these prescriptions filled. You're going to be all right. But, you need lots of rest. You've been going too fast and too hard."

"Mister Benton, you have experienced a serious episode of depression. So serious that it took over your mind and body. I stress episode, because it is my belief that this event, just as the previous one, was triggered by something outside of you and, just as the previous event, is not a long-term, clinical situation. With rest, the proper medication, and therapy, you'll be able to get to the cause of the event. Once there, we can deal with the underlying issues. It's a process, Mister Benton. So the better we work at it the faster we can resolve the issues. Do you understand what I am saying?"

"Shit, doc, I'm not deaf or stupid. Just depressed. Yes, I know I need help. I really, really, really don't wish this event to recur. So, I'll do what is required."

"Good, you may get dressed, check out and leave with Miss Leach. We have designated her as the responsible adult. We assumed that would be suitable for both of you."

On the ride home we stopped at the drug store. I realized that my pants didn't fit. They were baggy. The waist was at least an inch too big. They hung on my hips like some latest teen fashion. I had lost weight over the past two or three weeks. How was that possible? I ate regularly. Slept well. I guess whatever I was doing was not sufficient to counterbalance the build up and impact of the episode. I had received three prescriptions: one for mood enhancement, one for energy, and one to help me sleep. These are my happy pills. A pill for every mood and a mood for every occasion. Synthetic body elements. Ain't modern technology grand.

The dogs are happy to see me. I am really happy to see healthy animals, because they love unconditionally. They don't give a damn what kind of day or night I've had, they're just happy that I'm home and with them. They will be a big part of my therapy.

The stain remains on the seat of my television chair. The local newspaper warns of war. In the President's news briefing and later in his speech to the nation, he spoke of planned, coordinated aggression, destabilization of the Middle East, our sovereign rights, slaughter of Americans, protection of the Western World, and a joint global retaliation to el Jahdiq's criminal acts. He confirmed that he had had dialogues with all the major powers, the governments of the three nations involved, and the countries of the Security Council. He could not divulge details of his conversations, but assured all Americans that the world would not stand by and permit this form of aggression. The peace-loving people of the region and the world are seeking a swift and definitive resolution to this affront on our sovereignty. He has asked the appropriate cabinet member, advisors, and military leaders of the United States to develop plans and scenarios that would be reviewed with our international allies. In the meantime, the embassies and military barracks throughout the region are being fortified and bolstered with men and materials.

The people of the United States must stand tall. We must stand together. The sooner this conflict is resolved, the better. Film at eleven.

The Navy steams into the seas and gulfs that surround the war zone. Destroyers. Aircraft carriers. Three heavy cruisers, which can lob shells from infinity. No one has called it a war. But, a state of war preparedness is what we have. So, we must be about to be at war. The Air Force speckles the sky over the three sheikdoms like starlings. F-14s, 15s. 16s. Stealths and all types of single purpose aircraft. The troop mobilization is fierce. Men, tanks and artillery are assembled, loaded onto the jumbo aircraft, and flown somewhere. Lots of pictures of wives and children kissing their heroes good by.

Most of the news editorials, electronic and printed, are calling for an international program, not one comprised solely of the US military. Then there are the usual vox populi on the left and the right. A few publications call for cooler heads, an international dialog including certain objective third parties and a withdrawal of our troops. At the other end of the spectrum, some pundits want us to take full responsibility for resolution of war. We should bomb the enemy back to dust, free el Jahdiq's people, and rid the Middle East of revolutionaries. This would be the same as ridding New York of cockroaches. Amid all this saber rattling and clamoring, normal everyday stuff like death and taxes are relegated to the sixth page of the second section or as brief filler in the soft news half-hour before the real blood and guts, doom and gloom hour.

Senator Miller and his SAFE campaign were sucking hind teat. His constituent base was in the small towns and rural areas of the country. Most of the members of the military, top to bottom, come from the small towns across the nation. Their mothers and fathers are still there. These voters, who had been expressing unrest and a lack of confidence with the federal government, were now shoulder to shoulder with the President. Yes, the safety and security of children and grandchildren are important. We will get back to that after we rain revenge on the Butcher of Basjar. A big international threat comes before the domestic slaughter of children. Are the priorities part of a grander, yet hidden, agenda? Shit, I'm doing it to myself. Diving into the turmoil, details, and hypotheses that drove me to the brink. Twenty-four hours ago the black cloud of depression had engulfed my mind and soul. I became catatonic. I peed myself. A loving stranger got me help or, at least, observation. Now I am home, safe and secure. She is here to protect me. I have drugs. I can rest. I must not think about Dorothy, Mary, the school kids, or dirty politics in any arena. Not even my job. I must concentrate on only those things that will help me return to normal. What is normal? Who are the norms? Schwarzkopf, Lincoln Rockwell, and Bates? Episodic depression can be controlled. I will do that. Why can't I get the causes from my mind? Where is Karen? Can I kiss her? Will her kiss lift this veil of confusion? I remember this from my sons: It's not over 'till I win. OK. I'm a Scot and I've just begun to play. What can I do to dig while I am recovering? How far can I push myself while I'm digging? That's what the happy pills and Karen are for. Make sure I don't fall back under the black smog.

San Diego

"Gene, I've got some interesting and disturbing information for you. Give me a call before eleven AM your time."

I got the message at eight. Mike Duncan sounded nervous.

"Mike, good morning. What have you learned?"

"Gene, thanks for the call back. I gave you another number, a safe and secure number, on your e-mail. Hang up, check your e-mail, and call me back at that number in thirty minutes. I'll tell you why then."

Karen helps me with the elaborate procedure of going from the ComRoom to her office to my office. It takes five minutes. We read and trash all the mail, the vast majority of which was business related. A message each from my boys about their aunt. Both have to beg out of my proposed trip to Grand Cayman. Children and work. The curses of the married and ambitious. I'll get back to them later today. There is a cryptic message from Mike. A second emergency telephone number and a box number at the main San Diego post office. It looks like he is going invisible. Back to the pool and the cell phone. Karen and I agree that soon the bad guys, if they are watching, will access the company cell phone records and determine who and when we called, just not what was said,

"Mike, what the hell is going on? Why this second telephone and the post office box?"

"Gene, remember when I asked you if you ever felt watched? Well, I'm sure that someone or ones are watching me. I think they even have my apartment bugged. They may even be monitoring my computer travels. Whatever you got me into is bigger and more sinister than I could have imagined. I started to dig a little deeper about the three guys in the pictures. You know—Forbes, Thompson, and Campbell. And everywhere I dug I hit a granite sarcophagus. I mean the history and even the present of these guys is buried deep and secure. My moles came up with little bits of unconnected info. I was able to piece together a tres bizarre picture. Like a jigsaw puzzle comprised of pieces from several puzzles. Nothing seemed to make sense and I was about to give up. Quit and return some of your money. However, since all the funds had been allocated to necessities for my moles and me, returning the money was out of the question. So, I, or we, had to go on. Ethics you know. Besides, I really don't like to lose any game."

"So, back to work I went. Concentrating more closely on the details. You know when you concentrate very hard on something, you can see something new out of the corner of your eye. Well I did. I noticed a sports car and a pick-up truck. And, I felt that some things were different in my apartment. Very eerie. Like I was being watched. Maybe listened to. I got the same bad feeling that Gene Hackman had at the end of the movie, *Conversation*. They are here. So, I became very angry and disoriented. So I conduct special business like ours from this phone and through a new post office box. What the fuck are we into?"

"Mike, calm down and tell me what you've learned."

"Well the Three Musketeers are definitely not good guys. It seems as if Forbes, Thompson, and Campbell are working at least two sides of the street. And, I'll bet if there were more sides than two, these guys would be working them too. All three guys work for *grande tio sucre*. All three work for the National Security Agency. Hell, they may even work for more than one government agency. Your suspicions were spot on. The three of them are visible at both Senator Miller's rallies and the Carter, Wyoming massacre. We had to do some significant computer enhancement and jiggling, but we found their faces at Carter. Hairline, profile, noses, and ear lobes are matches. So, we know that they are both places, we just don't know why. Given the interest that someone has taken in my activities, I suspect the why is deep and nefarious. Here is what I think. I think that the three guys are in both places to do more than just keep an eye on the events. I think they are in both places to facilitate the events. I think they fuel the rallies and somehow manage an event like Carter. Take that one step further. Maybe they start events like Carter. You know, like the forest rangers, who start a fire for a planned purpose. Here is the real scary scenario. Just like the rangers, My Three Sons extinguish their fires when the blazes have accomplished their objectives."

The silence was so overwhelming that we both held our breath. With no noise over the line, the pool noise in my other ear sounded like an ocean during a storm.

"What in Christ's name are you saying? Are you saying that Forbes, Thompson, and Campbell started the shooting and then killed the kids? That's impossible. The kids did the shooting and no one is sure who shot the kids."

"What I'm saying is that maybe, just maybe, the kids, the outlaw gunslingers, are given permission or encouragement to commit the atrocities by the three gentlemen in question. Then these gentlemen either snuff the poor kids or give the go ahead to snuff them."

"If they give permission to snuff them, the local and state police must be involved somehow. This could be a huge evil network."

"The locals will step aside for feds. Let the feds take the heat for anything that goes wrong. But, claim credit for a successful completion of a mission. The feds will hit and run. Disappear into the shadows or the night. They are trained to do this in their international efforts. They can then apply this training to domestic issues that need the same type of invisible death squads."

"OK. This is not yet beyond my ken. Let's take this to the extreme. We are saying that these guys are responsible for the shootings in Carter and perhaps, Menthen, Lutztown, and Ox Bow. They foment the killings and then kill the killers. Most likely to silence them. The silencing is done to keep the fomentation or permission a secret. Loose lips sink ships and all that. How about loose lips sink presidential candidates? Isn't slaughter a little extreme to set up a candidacy? Ifs hard for me to accept that Miller would commit the crime to do the time at Sixteen Hundred Pennsylvania Avenue. There has got to be something we're missing. I mean I can follow your path. But, I can't arrive at your destination."

"Gene, at this point our guesses and speculations are just that. But, if I'm being watched, it's more than for my good looks or to learn from my work habits. Someone is worried that I am on to something. And this has to be it. My moles and I have some more digging. We have to find out all the for whoms Forbes, Thompson, and Campbell work. That's the critical piece of the puzzle. It will help confirm or refute our present position. I should have that information back to you by tomorrow morning. I'll call you and then you can call me on this line at a specified time. OK? Talk to you then."

The dial tone echoes in my ear for about fifteen seconds until I disconnect. I have got to tell Karen. Can't hold any of this information inside. I think that was one of the biggest causes of my problem. Too much too fast and all held inside. This new stuff I must share. Share the paranoia. Share the burden of knowledge. Karen summarizes what I tell her as being preposterous enough to be true. Then she tells me to take my meds and the dogs for a romp. Not to think about anything but the fresh air and sunshine. I change for a swim and we three head for the backyard. I notice the pool boy left the gate ajar again. I have to talk to him. Leave a message on his voice mail after my R and R.

Hither and Yon love the game of fetch. It takes two tennis balls. The repetitive nature of the exercise reminds me of insanity, repetition of an act anticipating different results. Except they don't expect different results. I throw. They chase after the yellow orb and return it to my feet. I don't have to struggle with them for the balls. I guess they played this a lot with Mary, because every so often one of the dogs won't just drop the ball on the ground, but he will drop it in my lap. I have to think of different areas into which I can throw the balls. Just straight ahead will not do. Variety is the key. Maybe it's not the same act over and over again. Every third or fourth toss goes in the pool. They love to splash and retrieve. I notice that they will only chase their own ball. This is the territorial game to the extreme. If I throw both balls at the same time, the dogs will bring back only their own. And I know which is which by the black mark on Hither's. Trying to trick them with feints is useless. It's their game and I am just a player.

After twenty or so tosses, each dog brings a ball back to the area where I am sitting. They drop each soggy, masticated sphere and put a paw on it. Game. Set. Match. Hot and tired, they stretch out under the table. I head for the pool. Now it's my time to focus on me and not issues. Swimming, like running, allows for introspection, wool gathering, or fantasizing. Today I'll concentrate on sexual adventures. I can select anyone I please. We can do anything. As often as my mind wants. No physical limitations. My mind is clear and free from angst. The time and distance go quickly. I know it's time to quit when my muscles are warm and my mind returns to the task at hand. Time for lunch. Sandwiches, fruit, and iced tea. Karen and I on the lanai. The dogs nap. Lucky bastards. Karen leans forward and whispers.

"I think I've found the next set of clues. TruthSeeker and BrokenArrow are at it again. Copied their entire messages off the screen. Here look at these.

The bulk of TruthSeeker's message is posturing. The last sentence reads; "There is a banner on the edge of Santa's table." This sentence is repeated in one other chat room within the body of different text. BrokenArrow responds in one matching room, as well as the room in which TruthSeeker did not go: "Woolworth is open for business." I think these are the clues. Let me show you. What is a banner? A flag. What is an edge? A rim. A coast? A border. Who is Santa? Saint Nick? What is a table? A platform? A mesa? Who or what is Woolworth? A retailer? A five-and-dime store started in Lancaster, Pennsylvania? From all of this I have extrapolated. Area Code five-ten. That's in Northern California. Coastal Mesa is a town in the area. It's a small town, like all the others. There is a high school in the town named San Nichols. And, the upcoming holiday is Flag Day, June fourteenth. Four days from now. If this is accurate, we have precious little time remaining."

"But, what if it's off by only a little a bit? We guess wrong and alert the wrong place, while kids get butchered in another part of the country. Are you willing to risk that? Shouldn't we do more digging? Cross matching to be sure we have the right place and time?"

"Well, if we do nothing kids are going to die. If we are right, we save lives. The key is going to be to stop the carnage and catch Forbes, Thompson, and Campbell at the same time. We must not tip our hands or the three bad guys will cancel the event. We have to let them think the event will occur and stop it with them on the scene. We must be able to apprehend them immediately before the carnage. I know only one person who might be able to help. Someone, who is clean. My contact at the FBI, Bodrim Bogatta. He said I could contact him at any time. Day or night. I'll call and set up a meeting. Away from this house and not at his office. Some place obscure. Some place whoever is watching us can't find."

She goes about setting up the meeting. I stretch out for a nap. The happy pills facilitate napping without bad dreams. I look forward to this pleasant change. No more mountain hikes and drowning holes. The dogs and I sleep on the master bed. They know I am troubled and I need their attention. They are balms without smothering. Their eyes are not sad, but serious. They need and give contact. Touching. Leaning. Petting. Rubbing. Kisses. Basic love.

The kiss on my lips is feminine. Karen wants me to go to the meeting with her. We are to meet at seven-thirty. It's six. I shower and have a cup of Cuban coffee. Dusk is beginning by the time we leave the house.

A normal twenty-minute drive takes forty-five minutes to avoid being followed to the mall. Meet by the fountain. Running water precludes telescopic eavesdropping.

"Hello, Karen. How are you? I assume this is Mister Benton? How can I help you both?"

"Bodrim, Gene and I think we have unearthed something incredibly sinister. We think we know where and when the next school shooting will occur."

"I must tell you that I find this to be highly unlikely. But, please, go on."

Karen relays all the information about Carter through Ox Bow, Mary, Forbes, Thompson, Campbell, Senator Miller, Mike Duncan, et cetera, et cetera. Then she tells him that we want to go to Coastal Mesa with them when they create a non-event. He listens but will not agree to our travel plans. She says that we will be there whether he likes it or not. He owes us that, at the very least. He will think about it. First he must check into the evil triumvirate. Most important he needs to determine if anyone at Menthen, Lutztown, and Ox Bow remembers the three men. Do a deep check on Miller. Talk to Mike Duncan. All of this could take a week. We don't have a week. He knows this. But, allocation of such a large amount of his limited resources based on a maybe will be difficult to hide from his superiors. And, if this is to happen, he wants to keep everybody out of the loop until the last second, thereby avoiding the possibility of a leak to other branches and departments of the government. He will look into it and get back to Karen by noon tomorrow. Fair enough? Fair enough.

Head for home, the dogs, and the news. Maybe something from the Classic Movie Channel, a drink, and an early bed. Single malt Scotch Whiskey is not only the water of life, it is the water of rest. Pour two healthy, big boy-strength drinks. Karen accepts with a sneaky smile.

"We need to discuss us."

The threat in those words. The hidden meaning. The portent of conflict. When cornered, take the offense.

"Yes we do. What's on your mind? You show me yours and I'll show you mine."

"I have been avoiding you. Not because I don't care, but because I do. I was terrified by your episode. So, I shied away. Second, I have been focused on understanding this confusing mess we are in. I feel I have an obligation to Mary and to you to get to the bottom of all this. Most particularly Mary's death. So, I just want to tell you that I have missed you as much as I hope you have missed me. And I'm sorry for my reaction and diversion."

"That's enough. My episode is nothing more than just that. An episode. I had one of them before, but my divorced was the cause. And now she lives in California. I'm on happy pills. Better ones than before. I have my physical health. Two dogs that worry about me. And the love of a wonderful woman, I hope. I will get through this. I will do more than survive. I will be better than before. All I need is time and some personality adjustment. Though I was beginning to think that I had had no long-term effect on you. My virility level had sunk to a new low. I'm glad I was mistaken. Now that that is over, what's next?"

"Make room for your clothes in my new closet which is located in the master bedroom. I guess that makes me the master. Move my personal stuff into the master bath. And help me, tomorrow afternoon, retrieve more of my belongings from my house."

My heart swelled with joy.

I rearranged my clothes to accommodate the third floor of Saks. What in God's name does anyone need with twenty pairs of shoes? Four pairs of sneaks, six pairs of slip-ons, and ten pairs of business heels. Skirts, blouses, slacks, jeans, shorts, Tee shirts, eighteen dresses. I mean, this is Florida, home of casual attire. How much more awaits my trip tomorrow? I lose two-thirds of the three-panel medicine cabinet over the double sinks. I move some of my occasionally used items to the small towel closet near the shower. If she wants to take a bath, she'll have to use the other bathroom. I am so happy I am bitchy.

As we pass from one room to the next, we brush against one another. The tension created by physical contact is nearly overwhelming. We commence undressing in the bathroom. She leaves. I finish. She turns the lights out, re-enters the room, and lights a candle on the counter. The light, reflected off the corner mirrors, seems to be more six or eight. It illuminates the entire area in a sultry, flickering orange light. She slips out of her skirt, pulls her knit halter over her head, and pulls off her thong. I turn on the water. She is behind me. I turn. We embrace. Too long away. Too long lonely. Tender kisses evolve into mouths trying to engulf each other. Tongues are on archaeological digs, probing areas recently considered to be dead.

We part and slide the glass door to the shower stall. Eight feet square. We coat each other's body with lather. Rubbing deeply and slowly as the

water cascades over us. Her back is smooth and the muscles firm. Not
overly developed. Peach cheeks pliable. Thighs covered by delicate baby
hair. Calves are strong. She turns as I retrace my path up the front of
the emotional mountain. Shins. Thighs. Hips and small round tummy.
Rib cage. Breasts. Arms and shoulders. We kiss. I am aroused from the
inside out. From the depth of my soul. My heart yells for continuation
and completion. She reciprocates my lathering as the temperature in the
stall climbs. She is grabbing. Pulling me onto her. She faces the wall, leans
into it with her hips raised inviting my entry. If I wanted to I could not
resist. Loving her is easy for me. She is on fire. I match her passion. Rub
her shoulders and arms. Kiss her neck. The back of her head. Nibble her
ears. Lather her scalp and rub vigorously as we are joined. Her quivering
becomes trembling becomes shaking. I am thrusting as slowly as I can. My
mind says go slow, but my body says go, go. I can no longer be the master
of my own fate. I pulse within her. Her moan is deep and long. She turns.
Our kiss lasts forever. Soap and fluids go down the drain.

Toweling off is almost as much fun. We get to explore areas that
had been hidden by soap and water. The flame flickers with our motion.
Curves are accentuated. Skin color is a warm sensual tan. The wax flame is
extinguished. Saved for another time. Remaining nude, we slide beneath
the sheets. She settles her head on my chest. My arm under her shoulders. It
is natural. It is good. I missed this closeness: Has my heart been that hard?

The mental alarm sounds at five AM. It's coffee time. Pad to the
kitchen. The dogs eye my arrival into their night world. They have been
guarding the fort. Now it's time for them to search the grounds for any
barbarians who might have scaled the walls in the blackness. They scamper
out the sliding door. I put water and food in the four bowls for their return
from the search and destroy mission. They can rest outside this morning
until it gets too hot for man or beast. Breakfast coffee is a wonderful
experience. Truly a drug and I am needy. The first long draught calms my
spirit and lifts me. Every day the same activity. Every day the day the same
result. God, this is good.

The electronic media are frantically dissecting the President's fireside
chat of last evening. He has used phrases such as partners in peace, one
nation indivisible, cancerous growth, put aside differences, common
enemy, safe and secure, and armed right. He confirmed that the forces
were in place. The evil had been isolated from the rest of the world. El
Jahdiq's former trading partners had been briefed. The Security Council

of the United Nations was meeting. One last envoy of peace had been sent to Basjar. All the right hot buttons for both the domestic and international audiences. His smile was wide and about as deep as the Pecos River in August. His voice was mellifluous, but the words were sharply pointed. His eyes glowed with a sincerity every mother would believe. In the background, his wife and three children sat politely. The clothes of the entire group delivered the message that this family was what every American family could and should be. Light brown hair, neatly trimmed and combed. Scrubbed freckled faces. Red, white, and blue shirts and blouses. Freshly starched khaki slacks and skirts. Only the President wore a tie and blazer.

To me, the message was clear: we are God's chosen. We are the leaders of this millennium. Barring a miracle of contrition by the most evil human on the face of the earth, I have ordered a war. I mean to crush this evil for peace in the world, an increase in my international stature and reinforcement of my political party's domestic constituency.

The President was making political hay. The price would be millions of shattered lives and billions of dollars worth of buildings, roads, and infrastructure in an unstable region of the world. Our economy would benefit greatly in the rebuilding. The reopening of the region. What the fuck did he care if the process involved massive amounts of death and destruction so long as his party was able to continue in power? The question was no longer if we would go to war. The question was how soon after the envoys returned from Basjar. There was no counter point news conference by the other party. The outs just have to go along. When this blows over, in about six weeks if the knife is swift and sure, the other party will have its chance to second guess and criticize. They will urge us to get back to the most pressing business at hand, a Safe America For Everyone. It would behoove the outs to use this time wisely. Consolidate their power base. Strategize for various scenarios. Take focus on the national election next year, long after this international bump in the road.

Karen is more beautiful in dawn's light than in the candlelight of the shower. Maybe she is thus because of the shower. I pour for her. She likes the morning coffee black. Not unlike her mood, she jokes. Dressed in shorts and a New York Giants football jersey, number fifty-six, she is sexy in a teenage way. Her hair has not yet been brushed. Skin glows. Heads for the lanai. We sit at the table beneath the fan. No words. I extend my hand to hers and trace the fingers. Smiles all around. The dogs want in

125

on the attention. Hither comes to my side and plops his head on my lap. Yon does the same to Karen. God, how saccharine, it's the Nelsons with Ricky and David. The peace of the early day is broken by a ring on her cell phone. She goes back to the master bedroom and retrieves the culprit.

She moves from the lanai to the edge of the pool and commences rapt listening. We had agreed, the less spoken the better. She presses the off button and motions me to the pool.

"That was Bodrim Bogatta. He wants to help. Did some digging after he left us last night. Apparently found out more than he had anticipated. Most of which was troubling or disconcerting. Each question raised six more. Paths crisscrossed each other until he lost sight of the starting point. He promised not to go to up the chain of command until we get closer to the next event. Did you hear what I said? I said event. An objective, non-descript description of a brutal loss of life. Have I become so inured to the horror, that I describe it that way? Or, do I find the slaughter so abhorrent that I can't deal with it on its own terms? It's a planned killing!"

"Whew, that was rough. Sorry. I think I understand what you have been dealing with. Anyway Bogatta will call us again later today. We will meet either late tonight or very early tomorrow. In the meantime we are to just monitor the chat rooms like we always do. Do not post. Make no waves. Do not go under. I told him we would just hang."

The truth had sunk in. We could be in serious trouble. Like Mary. And all we can do is wait. Act normal. Act as if we don't know that they know so they won't know that we know that they know. We have become isolated. Just what the bad guys would want. This calls for my happy pills. We wait. Read. Watch the magic eye. Movies all day. Australian Football League. Old championship basketball games. Bad talk shows. The world according to schlock. The telephone rings. We both go to the pool.

"Yes. Are you sure? OK. Ready in twenty minutes. Thanks."

"Gene, we must pack and leave. Now!"

"What about the dogs?"

"We will take them with us. Pack only what you deem essential to your existence. The rest can be retrieved at a later date. Two bags. All this will be explained by Bodrim. Now, let's go."

I can pack in less time than most people, because I value little except my life, my children, and now Karen and the dogs. None of them fit into my suitcases. Two ties and a blazer are my concession to being well dressed. Slacks, sport shirts, shorts. Florida clothes plus a sweater and a windbreaker in case we are leaving the swamp. The doorbell rings. I am expecting no one. Karen is. She nods for me to answer. I move quickly and peer through the window to the right of the door.

Frank's Water Service. But not Frank. The nametag says Bodie.

"Hello Mister Benton. It's nice to see you again. I understand your water filtration system in on the blink. If you open the garage door, I'll pull my van in and check out the pump and system."

He turns and heads to the truck. I go to the door leading from the laundry room to the garage and press the garage door opener. He pulls the van inside.

Slides the side doors open and motions for me to get Karen and our bags. We are ushered into the van. No plumbing equipment or tools of any kind. A bench seat. Throw bags behind the bench. The dogs jump into the space between the bench and front seats. I slide the door closed. It's heavy and closes with a solid thud.

Bulletproof. OK, I'll do whatever they require. Bodrim is talking in a loud voice to no one. Except those who are listening. He backs the van out of the garage, presses my clicker to close it and drives off waving at the now empty house.

"Will somebody tell me what's going on?"

"Mister Benton, all I can tell you is that you are now safe. We are moving you to some place out of harm's way. You will have a guard with you at all times. Tonight I can tell you more. Just not right now. Damn it! They're trailing us. I'll just have to make a stop at the mall. Bear with me."

We head for the East Shore Mall. Bogatta calls someone on a cell phone. In a few minutes he pulls the van into the narrow loading dock. A big delivery truck slides in front of the dock for about thirty seconds. The dogs, Karen, and I hurriedly exit. The van doors are closed. Two men heft our luggage and usher us into the shipping department of a hardware outlet. The semi pulls away as we close the store door. The van stays. We wait. In about ten minutes, a Bogatta-look alike enters the van and backs out of the dock. As Frank's Water Service drives off, I note that the small pick-up truck, which had followed us, is now on a phony trail.

We are escorted to the front of the store. The dogs and luggage remain in the back. A clerk comes up and we are turned over to her. She walks us to a side entrance at the other end of the roofed retail world. Going from climate control to bright light and oppressive heat is a shock. The limo doors are opened. We enter. The doors are locked behind us. Casually the black boat glides through the parking lot and heads toward the airport. The woman in the passenger seat hands us our tickets. Destination: San Francisco. Two stops and two plane changes.

"Ladies and gentleman, before I board any plane, I want to know what the fuck is going on. I mean I am whisked out of my house in a bulletproof van by someone I don't know. The van is seemingly followed by someone I don't know. Our mode of transportation is changed because of the unknown trackers. I am now being driven to the airport and escorted by two people I don't know so that I can be shipped to a city where I know no one. What's wrong with this video?"

"Mister Benton, please relax. Everything will be explained to you in due time."

"Well, the time to do the explaining is due now. If I don't get the answers I like before we get to the airport, I won't get on the plane. I'll raise such a ruckus that the local police will have to intervene. Then you can explain the kidnapping to them. That's the deal. Talk or I walk."

"Gene, I know these people. They helped me out of my jam a few years ago. When I needed friends they were the only ones. Trust them."

"Trust them! Hell, I'm not sure I trust you! You brought them into my world. I have had to go a long way on faith. And that precious emotion is running very thin. So, somebody better tell me everything. Now!"

"OK. I'll tell you what I know. Then Jenny will tell you the rest. Bodrim determined we were in danger. The house was being monitored. We were being monitored. All because of our snooping. They were closing in on us. Maybe to do us real harm. He is convinced Mary was murdered. Bodrim learned that Mike Duncan died yesterday under strange circumstances. His car caught fire while he was pulling out of his spot in the underground parking garage. Before he could be rescued, Mike, his car and six others had become a charred mass of metal and glass. The Fire Marshall believes flame accelerant was used in the mishap. It all happened at three AM. Bodrim was convinced that we were next on the list. We were getting too close to the truth. He decided it would be best that we disappeared before we disappeared. So we're going to San Francisco. Just remember, the pretty flowers in your hair. Yes, I'm scared. But, I've had experience with Bodrim's rapid clandestine departures and I recognize a few of the other players, like Jenny here and Robert at the store. I think I've seen this driver. Jenny, it's your turn."

"Mister Bogatta is my boss. Here is my ID. Yes, we are very concerned for your lives. Our initial investigation has indicated that you may be right in many of your assumptions. There may be another school slaughter in two or three days, The three men you identified are rogues. We're not sure who is paying them. We doubt if it's Senator Miller. We are taking you to a safe house in San Francisco. Your dogs and luggage will be there when you arrive. From there, at the appropriate time, we will go to Coastal Mesa. That's all I can tell you now. Mister Bogatta will have more details when you meet him in California."

"One last item. The stops and plane changes are for security, I assume."

"We are dealing with too many unknowns and some very powerful people. Your safety is our single concern for now."

"Karen, I feel slightly better about what I am doing."

We hold hands. Fear and fondness are great motivators.

Coastal Mesa

Hither and Yon are our solace in this new place. We unpack. One bedroom. One bath. One sitting room. One kitchen. One dining area. Very singular. Spartan but practical. Our official protector is Robert. He is black. About six feet three inches tall and weighs approximately two hundred and forty pounds. Handsome. His smile is friendly but not warm. Almost sardonic. Eyes constantly darting. Searching for something, anything. Ear plug and lapel mike let him communicate with home base, wherever that is. Wears a jacket to hide the twin Glocks. Wears a Kevlar vest for protection. We wear him. We can't leave the apartment without him unlocking the door. He lets people in only after knocking. I guess he will walk the dogs. Maybe he should have one or both of them with him. They growl at him when he enters. He stares back. Does not growl back. The three protectors respect one another. I will introduce him to them the next time his watch is over. But he must go through the same ritual I did in Wyoming. How to humble the feds. The knock announces Bogatta's arrival. Now I'll get some answers.

"Mister Benton. Karen. How are you both feeling? How are the dogs?"

"Their suspicious glare is an indication of my feelings. Mister Bogatta, I need to know what the hell is going on. Why are we here? Where is here? Is there a here after here? What do you know? Tell us everything."

"Mister Benton. As you know you are in San Francisco. Actually in a suburb of no importance. We are here to stop what you have indicated and we agree will be the next school massacre. The bloodshed is planned for San Nichols High School in Coastal Mesa sometime during the Flag Day parade and picnic. It is now three-thirty in the afternoon. We have approximately thirty-six hours to set the trap for the shooters and to catch the three men identified as Forbes, Thompson, and Campbell. Now, let me tell you what we know about these men. They are rogues. Supposedly they work for the National Security Agency. Except my contact can find no record of them ever, I stress ever, having been in the employ of the NSA. They do not presently work for the CIA, although they did. They have varied and checkered pasts. Not suburb cocktail conversation, but their pasts were necessary for the safety and security of our country. They had been out of the country until they flew beneath the radar and re-entered. They dropped out of sight. Then resurfaced at Carter. Maybe before. But, Carter for sure."

"We think they were spotted at Menthen, Lutztown, and Ox Bow. We're not completely sure, but sure enough. They come into the shoot zones slightly before or just as the shooting begins. Well before the local or state authorities arrive. The three, along with a few underlings establish a command center beyond the anticipated sphere of influence of the locals. Then Forbes, Thompson, and Campbell direct the locals. When the time is propitious, our three enter the fray, most likely from behind, and execute the executioners. To do this they must have detailed knowledge about the shoot. Who. When. Where. How. And they scout the kill zone in detail so that they know the entrances and exits. The killers are recruited from the vast sea of loonies that floats beneath the surface of society. There are people ready to kill anyone and everyone. The rage is so deep, so severe that these people will explode spontaneously. All they need is the proper venue and good handling. That's what the three men in question do. They determine the desired place and time. Then they recruit from the area. They let the misguided know the details via the chat rooms. After the butchery, they eliminate the eliminators and then they leave the scene. The locals, who have taken orders from the bogey feds, are all too pleased to take credit for cleaning up the mess. Afterward, the locals know only what they have been told by these three."

"We are sure that's how all this happens. We are just not sure why. And, we are not positive about the connection between Senator Miller and the three. Our suspicion is that they are handling him as they handle the killers. If they are functioning as bodyguards and as controllers, they have a master other than Miller. The question then is who is the real master? Is Miller involved in the killings to further his campaign? Is he setting up the slaughters to prove the need for SAFE? The key will be to learn the team for whom the three rogues really work."

"You two are honored guests of the service. I am giving you the opportunity to watch the event and my promotion unfold. Yes, that's my plan. You'll be close enough to see, just not close enough to interrupt or to be hurt. You will know almost as much as I know so that you can be witness to the heroic efforts of my team. We have alerted no one. Not the locals. Not the state authorities. And certainly none of the federal agencies."

"About an hour before the planned event, I will talk to my office and let the information filter out and down. We have strategically planted personnel so that all venues are secure. We have taken over the sanitation department and will be responsible for establishing the parade route. Buildings are now being scoured. The picnic area is blanketed. We have even taken the precaution to stakeout the area around the grounds."

"We have a vague idea who and how many are the planned killers. If our suspicions are accurate, we know their weapons. Nothing long range. These guys and girls, yes girls, most likely plan to rush the revelers. The weapons of choice are Tec-Nines and Mac-Tens. But, they'll never get a chance to use any of them. Will they? You know that was the biggest question we dealt with. Do we stop them before they start? Or do we let them start, then engage in a firefight and capture the ones not killed? Or slaughter all of them just as they would have been slaughtered by the three? Do we want to be John Wayne-style heroes? Or do we want to be the heroes who prevented disaster? We opted for the latter. It gives our investigative prowess more play. I mean, we saw the train wreck coming and we diverted the runaway engine. We will be idolized. Now why don't you two rest? We will dine in the backyard at seven? Then early to bed. Tomorrow is a long day. Leave here at noon and go to Camp One. From there we will commence Operation Unsafe."

The guy is a fucking megalomaniac. Power and success on the bodies of innocents. A crisis creator and a crisis averter. What an ice cube in my shorts. Carpe deim, Bodrim Bogatta. He has the area secured. Shit, he knew the where, when and maybe the who all along. It's our beloved protector who is the instigator. Where do the bad guys fit? Between the two government forces, who is doing what to whom? If he is successful, he can leave the service and command a huge salary in the private sector of law enforcement. Maybe become a rogue like the three bad guys. Maybe just an independent contractor. I can't fault the goal of stopping the crime before it starts. And he should get credit for that. He could stop it now before anybody gets killed. He is going to use us to validate his valor. My rage is building. Whoop-dee-do.

Dinner is cordial. Not joyous. What was I expecting? This afternoon was illuminating. Unsettling. I did not introduce the dogs to anyone. In fact, I made sure they stayed very close to Karen and me. They are to be our defense against the protectors. This entire mess has become too convoluted for me. Will we die in the midst of the firefight? Oh, it was a terrible accident. That will be their story. These distant relatives from Florida just happened to be in the way. Boo-fucking-hoo. I am scared. Hither and Yon don't care for our handlers. They adore Karen. I am their pal. To them that's everything. Hither sits at my feet and Yon sits at Karen's. They are not fed from the table. They eat from bowls thoughtfully provided by our hosts. No one tries to pet them. As a stranger approaches, the dogs freeze and stare. When a dog stares, he or she is about to attack. That's why they feel threatened when a human stares at them. The men and women who surround the grill and table are kept from us by the dogs. Each of the hounds positions himself next to Karen or me and between the person with whom we are talking. They sense all is not right. Their protective instincts, honed by Mary, are sharper now. That is good. Very good. My feeling is that they would give up their lives to save us. The agents would take out the dogs without a second thought. I don't like where this is going.

Sleep is fitful. The sense of dread is now based on my understanding of facts. So much is going to happen tomorrow that the chance of something going wrong is a good bet. I didn't dream anything specific. Just the visceral, feral premonition of death. There are stories of dogs whining and moaning before a master dies. Hither and Yon knew, without knowing, that Mary had died. Maybe I should ask them what is going to happen. My eyes pop open just as I am falling asleep. It's time to rise and shine. Karen is wrapped in the arms of Morpheus. The coffee is foul. The dogs need walking. Robert has the day shift and is not yet on duty. Jenny will walk the dogs. About forty minutes. We load the van. People, dogs and hardware. The second car, agents only, is about two lengths behind us for the entire two-hour trip. We are a convoy. Camp One is a storefront with white wash on the windows. On the main drag and accessible to everywhere. The school is less than two miles away. The marshal's stand is about three hundred yards in the other direction. The picnic grounds are just beyond the school.

The place is fully operational when we arrive. Communications have been established with men in the field. Twenty-two armed and very alert agents. The shirts and coveralls of the people at Camp One have logos that match those on the vans and pick-up trucks parked in the back. Event Exposition International and Coastal Mesa Department of Sanitation. The agents will blend in, hidden in plain sight. At the rear of the space, I notice partially opened crates of guns, flack jackets, and grenades. I guess you can never have too much firepower. The pace is orderly, but driven. No anger. No loud voices. Questions. Orders. Commands. It is clear that Bogatta is in total control of this military operation. The next two in the chain of command are Jenny, our guide to the airport, and an excessively muscular Mediterranean named Joe. The others are worker bees. Completing small tasks as required by the thinkers. Each of the small tasks fits into a slightly larger combination, which, with others, forms a complex procedure or action. Coffee is gulped and sandwiches are inhaled on the fly. No time for a white tablecloth, candles, and silverware sit-down.

"Well, Mister Benton, what do you think? Have you ever been in a Command Center before? This is where we try to eliminate any possibility of mistakes. This is where we pretest our planning. This is where the adrenaline rush starts. Impressive, right?"

"Mister Bogatta, I have nothing to which I can make a comparison. My only assessment would be possible after completion of the mission. Before that time, I just sit in awe."

"Bodrim, is all this firepower necessary? I mean it looks like you are outfitting a third world country. If you have to use this, a lot of people will get hurt or made dead. How can you justify fighting fire with fire when civilians are the losers no matter what?"

Karen has taken a less-than-completely-supportive posture. Strange. She seems to be questioning God.

"Karen, these guns are not to be used unless absolutely necessary. Remember that the kids will be armed and dangerous. They will gather at this place to kill. We must prevent this action. We must show a greater amount of resolve. That resolve will be manifested in our weaponry. The strategy to achieve our primary objective is to freeze them and show them down. Bluff and bully with a show of superior fire power and tactics. Hopefully no shots will be fired. But we have to be ready. If they get ballsy, we will have to kick them real hard. The three men behind all of this pose a different problem because of their training and discipline. I believe they will offer resistance because they will think they can win a firefight. They don't know we are here or the depth of our firepower. And, they are used to winning firefights. Our superior numbers should influence them otherwise. We have to be ready to eliminate with extreme prejudice. Now, if there are no other questions, I ask you both to sit on the couch in the corner and be still for a few more hours. There is plenty to read on the table."

The afternoon throbs into the evening. Alternating between slow motion and jet speed. The sudden flurry of activity tells me something important has or is about to happen. One foot soldier brings a television set from the other room, another readies a place for the set on the long table.

"Ladies and gentlemen, the President of the United States."

"Please be seated. Today, at one-thirty Eastern Time, the combined armies of the Peace Alliance initiated a pre-emptive strike against the aggressive forces of el Jahdiq. This strike involved the armies of Egypt, Saudi Arabia, Israel, France, Great Britain, United Germany, Spain, Poland, and the United States. Combined navy and air corps struck offensive installations in Basjar with great dispatch. Missile sites, troop assemblies, and artillery emplacements suffered the concerted might of the Peace Alliance. The preemptive strike continues as we speak. Ground troops stand ready. Before I turn this briefing over to the Allied Commander, General Warren, I want to assure the people of Basjar and the world that our strike is not intended to cause the nation or its people permanent harm. Rather, we wish to rid Basjar and the region of the war mongering that began twenty years ago and has escalated recently. The attacks on our embassies and the death of hundreds of innocent civilians can not go unanswered. The peace loving people of the Middle East and of the world cannot and will not tolerate el Jahdiq's abhorrent behavior any longer. His actions have threatened to destabilize the region and drive the world into a conflagration of apocalyptic proportions. We ask that all people pray for a swift and complete resolution to this conflict. Now, General Warren."

The agents are ecstatic. High fives. Big smiles. Prancing. A lot of noise.

"People. People. People. Listen up. Calm down. I share your enthusiasm, but remember we can't let anything deter us from our appointed tasks. The children of San Nicholas High School in Coastal Mesa must be protected. The children of this country must be kept safe and secure. The perps must be apprehended. These are our jobs. Let's conduct ourselves in the most professional manner. Our mission is not yet completed. Now back to your duties. There will be time for R and R after tomorrow."

Back to work with no grumbling. These are professionals. They do their jobs so that a bigger job can be done. I take my pills. Check out the dogs. They're in the rear. Walk past the unisex restroom. Past the packing cases that carried the electronic and communications gadgets. Past a heap of scrap paper, which will be shredded and burned before lift off. Memos. Letters. Hand-written notes. Out of the corner of my right eye I notice the name, Alan Campbell. I dip and scoop up the paper on which is written the name of one of the bad guys. Stuff the paper into my pocket. Outside with Hither and Yon, I bend down to nuzzle them and fill their bowls with water. Remove the paper and smooth it so I can read whatever is on the page" . . . the subject, Alan Campbell, has been sighted at various shooting sites. He, Brent Forbes, and Roger Thompson are believed to be responsible for the incidents at Carter, Wyoming, Menthen, New Hampshire, and Lutztown, Pennsylvania . . ."

The memo, addressed to someone I assume is Bogatta's superior, is dated six weeks ago. Well before Karen and I went to Bogatta with our suspicions. What the fuck is wrong with this picture? Did they send the memo up the line? Is it bogus? If they sent it, what are we doing here? If it is bogus, is it a cover-your-ass or a post facto blame missive? Are we window dressing? Are we part of the good guy group? Part of the to-be-exterminated group? Are we here to validate? My net-net is that we will be here after all this is over. Innocent bystanders in the war on crime. Karen must know. Better hide the message. Fold the paper into a small square. Insert the square into the plastic identification box on Hither's collar. Mary used this box to carry the dog's latest vet information, her name, address and telephone number. A duplicate of the census information on the collar tag. Two dog tags just like a soldier. If the dogs strayed or were injured, a Good Samaritan would know whom to contact. Hither carries our safety deposit box of truth. Pass by paper heap and reenter Camp One.

"Hey, Agent Bogatta, would you mind if Karen and I went outside and spent some quality time with the dogs? It's getting hot and sweaty in here. And that may do a lot for Karen, but it does nothing for me. Besides, the dogs could use some TLC. They have been yanked from home, placed on an airplane, shipped to San Francisco then driven here in a van. A little schmoozing will go a long way. We want to play fetch with them."

"Mister Benton. That's fine. One of my men will accompany you and Miss Leach. I wouldn't want you to get lost in the big empty parking lot."

We exit the building. The dogs are ecstatic to see Karen. Obviously, I am not sufficient entertainment. The two tennis balls go into play. First Hither and then Yon. After a few reps of this activity, the human watchdog sits on a garbage can and lights up a smoke. He is distracted. I retrieve the memo from Hither's collar box and palm it to Karen. As she reads it her eyes grow large and her skin becomes pale. She is afraid, very afraid. Hands me back the note and I replace it two throws later. We are sitting cross-legged and side-by-side on the macadam. The sky is clear and the breeze keeps the feels-like temperature in the mid-sixties. This should be a great day. But, it's not. It may be the last day of the rest of our lives.

Karen wraps her arm around my shoulder and draws my mouth to hers. She is trembling and it's not sexual. As we break and continue the embrace, she begins to sniffle.

"What does all this mean? Who are these guys? What are they going to do? What do they want? What's to become of us?"

"I don't have any answers. Only suspicions. I think we are in deep caca. These agents are not what they purport. They may be FBI. They're probably rogues. They may be the real bad guys. If that's true, then the three men we have uncovered may be good guys or just other bad guys. There will definitely be some heavy shooting tomorrow. And I am afraid that we are to be targets to one of three or all three groups. This is not good. But, if Bogatta's Boys and Girls Club doesn't know that we know, we can prepare to avoid what they think is the inevitable."

"You're no comfort. I'm so scared I may just pee myself."

"Play with the dogs for as long as possible and let me think."

Fetch is a game that can be played while thinking about anything else. Fetch does not require concentration or mental agility. And these dogs have their own way to play the game. They have trained me well. I do as Mary had taught them the way a human should play the dogs' game. Throw the ball. The dog stays at the human's side until he is told to fetch. The dog absolutely will not move until the command is given. The dog fetches only his ball. Retrieves the ball and places it in the lap of the human. Sits by the human's side until the throw and command. This is a very regimented game. More like an aerobic workout. Between the time of throw and retrieval is blank mental space for planning. We can't stop Bogatta's operation. But, we must stop the slaughter, while we keep from becoming the slaughtered. How do we intervene and take control of a situation over which we have no control? Neat trick. If all the players know each other, we need an outsider. Someone objective, who can sort out The Good, The Bad and The Ugly, and save our asses at the same time. My only choice is the local police. I know no one. Also, Karen and I need to be armed. Handguns. Maybe the element of surprise will make the odds less formidable. Hell, they have the firepower, training, and discipline. What am I thinking? At least we can take a few of them with us. The last act of the truly desperate. Where the hell do I get these thoughts? How do I know what to do? No military training. Some gun training. No combat weapon training. I don't know what to do. But, fear is the great motivator. The father of all life saving activity. I guess if I think everything through carefully and act with authority, we might survive. I hope.

"Karen, sweetie, we need you to go to the bathroom, inside. Scout out the handguns and grenades and return. OK?"

"I have to go to the restroom. Do you mind? I'll be right back."

Our keeper's grunt is an affirmative. He is enjoying his rest. Four throws for each hound and Karen returns. She smiles at the agent and hugs me again.

"There are pistols and ammunition racked in an open box to the left of the restroom. Grenades in the open crate to the left of that box. Have no idea what kind of grenades they are. Now what? How do we get our hands on the weapons? What do we do once we have them?"

"First things first. I'll let the dogs into the building. They will no doubt continue romping and go to the front room. We will pursue in an effort to corral them. However, we must continue to stir up the dogs' activity before we actually catch them. I'll lift two guns and a few grenades during the diversion. We'll stand and they'll come to us. As we turn to head inside, we'll have to shoo them. Ready. Let's go."

The melee of two large dogs and their supposed handlers bounding around the electronic equipment in Camp One creates near panic among Bogatta and his people. The fear of destroying or disabling this lifeline with the field is strong. Finally, Karen grabs Yon and I have hold of Hither's collar. It's almost as if they came to us when we had completed our hidden agenda. Did they know their role in the roiling?

"Get those fucking dogs out of here now. They are only alive because we must control all factors. So take care of your children before we have to. Men, make sure no damage was done. Recheck all connections and reconfirm with the field."

The four of us are panting with exhilaration. It's time to re-leash the dogs, double-check their bowls, and return to the couch. One last hug.

"Gene, were you successful?"

"Yes, were you?"

"I got a bunch of ammunition clips. But, no guns. What did you get?"

"Three automatics and some clips. Everything is stuffed in my pants and under my sweater. I notice that you look a little chunky yourself. We need to plan the second step."

The couch is not for sleeping. Sitting bunches up our clothes so that our booty is not obvious. How to alert the police at the appropriate time? Bogatta will hear from his field force once they find the shooter's nest, with or without shooters. Then he will go to the spot to direct operations from nearby. A position from which he can capture both enemies. He will take us with him, hopefully. Yes, that's where all four of us are to be caught in the crossfire. We had come from Florida after discovering the evil deed and the evil doers. We were just not professional law enforcement. We got dead. The trip to the school, to the outside world, will be our only chance to contact the locals. But how? Yon. A detailed note inside his collar box. Will he be found in time? Who will find him? Will they understand? Will the police be called? God, this is like Gramps and Lassie, and Timmy in the well. We have to be very lucky and Yon has to understand. I am betting our lives on this combination long shot. What else have we? Now to write the note, surreptitiously. Paper and pen are easily found. I reread my message. It sounds utterly preposterous. Karen agrees. What civilian or cop, in his right mind, would believe the cry for help?

The foot and auto traffic outside the windows is the going home variety. The shadows of dusk are beginning to stretch across the street. The call from Camper Six is one of discovery. The vipers' nest has been found. To the north of the picnic ground is a mound of rock and earth on which is a stand of pine trees. In front of the trees is a trench, recently dug. Looks like a hunter's dig. The road behind the mound would provide easy exit, if exit were to happen. The road also provides easy access by Forbes, Thompson, and Campbell. Bogatta orders his people to sweep Camp One. Box all the communications equipment. Go mobile with the system. Shred all paper and bum it. Pour the ashes in the dumpster. Load the vans with the weapons. Make it look as if we were never there. Cleaned of debris, Camp One must not look as if it were recently swept. The entire process takes about thirty minutes. We saddle up and head for the hill. The fire keepers have to stay behind to dump the remains. They will become sanitation workers.

The trip is orderly and not in a convoy format. Do not arouse suspicion. Twenty minutes and we are all at Camp Two. The entire field force is around the site. Alert to not leave footprints or crush the grass on the mound, the troops are dispersed to a control perimeter. The van moves to the other side of the picnic area. It seems normal that the event crew would be at the festival site the night before. No one would suspect the military deployment. Bogatta advises us to get some rest.

"Wake up is at 0400. Oh, by the way, Mister Benton, sorry about your sister. She was getting to be a nuisance to our work. Nothing personal, mind you. Just business. For the greater good and my success."

I have just been kicked in the solar plexus. My sister's killer is now my keeper. It is very personal to me. I fight to not go numb. I must be sharp for Karen. She, the two dogs, and I are ushered into the school. Down the hall, beyond the gym to the teacher's lounge. The door is locked behind us. Immediately visible are the couches, the tables and chairs, and the door to the bathroom. No windows. There is one small levered widow in the bathroom. It can be opened to a horizontal plane. Too small for Karen or me. Dog size. Double check the note. Tell Yon to get the ball. Get the ball. Please get the ball. Pick him up and squeeze him out to safety. He meanders around beneath the window. Not sure what to do. What do we want? Tell him again to get the ball. The game of fetch has a much bigger meaning than ever before. He lopes into the evening. This is it. Do or die. I am not wild about our chances. We spread our weapons on the couch. Three Glocks and nine clips.

I start to show Karen how to make the handgun ready to fire. How to remove the empty clip. Reload and reactivate. Point not aim. Quarters will be too close for the time required in aiming. Remember that the discharge will pull the gun up. The noise will scare you and nearly deafen you temporarily. Hold the gun tightly. Start to shoot as the gun comes up from the side. Continue to shoot until the target drops, whether two or eight shots. Move quickly to next target. Keep moving while shooting. Hide as much as possible. This is a killing activity. Either you kill or they kill. One is good. The other is not. She hides the fact that she is insulted by my chauvinism. I am preaching to the choir. She has a previous working knowledge of handguns. Her father had many on the farm. Target practice was a regular monthly event. She was not the best shot, but her father felt comfortable she could stop a wild pig or an intruder of unknown origin at close range. Guns in the front of our belts beneath sweaters. I don't think this was an original use for the garments. But it is the primary use now.

We agree that we should disarm the guard when he comes to awaken us for the morning's activities. Can't shoot. Just disarm, tie up, and stash in the bathroom. Liberate his communication link. Then we'll have to figure out how to get out of Dodge. Has Yon been found? Was the message read by the police? What have they done? What can they do? Our only job now is to get out of here alive. Rest before we act. Who can rest? Our naptime passed in a heartbeat. The noise of footsteps is an ominous series of thuds. I go into the bathroom and turn on the water. Then return to the couch. Karen stands to the right of the door. When the agent steps through the doorway, she clobbers him with the first volume of the Encyclopedia Britannica, A-B. He staggers. She hits again. Again. Again. He drops to the floor. Blood flowing from his nose. She hits again. Again. Again. Again. Blood is splattered on her sweater, the floor and the nearby walls. He is out cold. Maybe dead. His learning curve was just shortened. Pull him to the couch.

Strip him of his clothes. A sign of our anger. Stash his clothes in the bathroom. Lash his wrists and legs. Tape his mouth and eyes. Clear packing tape in lieu of duct. So, lots of it. Two full rolls of extra wide. Hither is quiet through the entire ordeal. He knows. I peer down the hall. Empty and dark.

Down the hall as quietly as possible. The dog's nails create a rhythmic click. Outside is only slightly lighter than the hall. We sense activity and see a light emanating from the van. Must get to the road and then literally run for our lives. Wending through the picnic ground to the mound and the road is easy. We have the element of surprise. Once on the road, we lope toward safety. Suddenly we see two sets of headlights moving cautiously toward us. We become off-road travelers. Must avoid contact with anyone who is not a friendly, and everyone falls into that category. Then we hear a male voice.

"Camp Two. This is scout Baker. Do you copy?"

"Baker. This is Camp Two. We copy."

"Camp Two. Two vehicles approaching. About six clicks. Speed is slow. Unknown occupants. Advise."

"Baker. We are deploying to Perimeter Two. Hold your position. Determine occupants. Advise. Do you copy?"

"Camp Two. Baker copies. Will advise, then join you at Perimeter Two. Further information in about ten minutes."

Must give the scout and the vehicles a wide berth. Head to the hill on the left. The adrenaline is pumping. The run starts. It's difficult to run in a stooped posture. But, we must stay below the vision line or horizon. Running up hill in a stoop is something professional athletes don't attempt. We have no choice. Failure means death. And, death is not a viable option. Despite the handguns and clips, I run with authority. My years of swimming help my stamina. Karen keeps pace. She is as tough and as frightened as I am. Hither is by our side. He knows. No sound other than our legs and feet pounding on the tall grass. It's almost as if we are holding our collective breaths. Definitely no conversation. From the crest of the hill, we can see a farm, replete with two barns, a tractor shed, and three-story house. Hither bolts down the hill to our next stop.

Lancaster, California

No time for niceties. We bang on the door. Lights appear in upstairs windows. We continue to bang on the front door. Finally we hear someone and see lights on the first floor.

"What's all the ruckus about? Who are you? What do you want?"

The farmer looks to be about thirty-five. Dressed in pajamas. Right hand by his side contains a revolver. His hands are huge.

"Sir, we mean no harm. We would like to use your telephone to call the police. There is some big trouble about to happen and they need to be told so they can stop it. Can we please use your phone?"

"What kind of trouble?"

"Without meaning to be crass, one hell of a fire fight. Kids shooting picnickers. National Security Agency shooting the shooters. And FBI shooting everybody. It's too complex to explain in detail. You have to trust me. Call the police yourself. Then let me talk to them. You can be on another phone. Listen in to be sure we are telling the truth. I see you have a gun. You won't need it. We just want to use the phone. Then we'll wait until the police show up."

Then I hear a familiar whine. Yon. Hither whines back. No barking. Both dogs are outside the house. Yon is chained to a clothes line on the side. Hither rushes to him. They nuzzle. Tails wag furiously.

"Mister, what's your name?"

"Sir, I'm Gene Benton and this is Karen Leach. We're from Florida. And you have one of my dogs, Yon. He probably showed up last night. His playmate, Hither, is here with us. Did you check Yon's collar? Did you find his identification and a small box on the collar? If you opened the box, then you know about the planned slaughter. If you didn't open

143

the collar box, do it now. Read the note and warn the authorities, we have precious little time. Please?"

"The dog showed up last night, just like you said. He is real friendly. The kids love him and he is very good with them. Couldn't understand how he got here from Wyoming. You say you're from Florida. I saw his name, Yon. But, I didn't open the collar box. Stay where you are and I'll open it now."

He comes through the door with his right hand slightly raised. Walks to the clothesline. Unhooks the snap from the leash to the collar. He takes Yon's collar gently and opens the box. Hither sits by patiently. The night watchman returns to the door, passes us, and turns on a table lamp to read the note. Looks at the door with disbelief.

"I guess it's safe for you two to come in. Remember, I'm armed."

It is best not to reveal our arsenal. He heads toward the kitchen. All four of us follow.

"I don't know what is going on here. Maybe the police can sort out this mess. I'll dial and listen while you talk."

"Hey, Alex. This is Barry Welch. I got a guy and his lady friend and their two dogs here. The guy wants to talk to you. You better tape this. It's too weird for any one to just take your word for it,"

"Hello, Officer. My name is Eugene Benton . . ."

Twelve minutes and a hundred questions later, Officer Alex Blagojavitch agrees not to alert the state authorities or anyone in the federal government. He will call the Sheriff and the entire force, including the traffic squad. They can be at Barry's farm in thirty minutes. Fully operational. Ready to deal with any potential danger. Sheriff Camera will be in charge. Mister Welch offers us coffee and we try to explain to him what we know. I can see the confusion and disbelief in his expression. He has to work hard to prevent his jaw from dropping. His wife, Leia, joins us. We have to leave the kitchen so the children can be fed. No chores today, because of the picnic. We tell her nothing. The squad cars and two vans arrive. It's time.

We explain in minute detail. The Sheriff decides to set up a perimeter outside of Camp Two and slowly tighten the noose. An ever smaller circle like a wild hog hunt, until the game is surrounded. The regular police helicopter and the one borrowed from the farm bureau swoop in at the last minute and land on the grounds. Each chopper will hold five fully armed deputies in complete body armor. The head of the sanitation department, Alex's uncle, has been called. He explained the feds had warned him not to talk to anyone. The feds were on a secret mission. They took over his department and were working along side his men. Blend in so to-speak. He was aware of the event trucks, but thought nothing was unusual. Camera tells him to contact his people and tell them not to report to work today. That way the only ones on the job will be the bogeys. He will explain to the sanitation force later.

We are ready to go back over the hill. The cruisers and police vans are loaded and scattered to appropriate drop-off points. Some men are sent back to keep an eye on the parade and the sanitation department. We turn over two Glocks and a handful of clips to Camera. Just not all of our weapons. We are now officially observers. Mister and Missus Welch are asked to stay at home. Karen thanks them profusely. Fear in their eyes. The kids are inhaling cereal.

Alex, the Sheriff, Karen, the two dogs, and I head to the crest of the hill. Bogatta must now know that we are not in his fort. I'm sure the agent has been severely chastised. Will Bogatta alter his plan? I suspect he has numerous what-if scenarios in his bag. There seems to be a normal amount of non-activity at the school. Camera looks through the night scope and spots four bodies in the trench on the mound beneath the pines. They are making ready. This explains Bogatta's inactivity. The sentry had alerted the forces in time for them to go to Perimeter Two. From there, they will move back to the grounds. Not in a wave, but individually so as to avoid suspicion. The van will drive up at the proper moment.

Bogatta will take command. The shooters and their three executioners will be executed and the world will be a better place. Where are the three executioners? Where is their black van? When will that arrive? All of this has to be choreographed to the tenth of a second. And all of this planning is done by three different forces, who don't really know what is on each other's minds. On top of all that, they hate each other. Add to this unholy trinity, the local Sheriff and any thing could go wrong. The sun is painting shadows and shapes into real life.

The parade should arrive in full force in two hours. Then the games and finally the food. The kid killers most like will try to rain their destruction around mealtime when everybody is seated or at least in a concentrated area. The arrival of the NSA threesome will be an omen of the slaughter. It is at that time that Bogatta's men will move in. Upon this cue, Camera's men and choppers will become active. The plan is for it to be over before it begins. Nobody shoots and nobody dies. That's the plan. For now we just sit and wait. The Sheriff keeps everyone off the radio until the last second. All men and machines must hang tough. No small talk. Coffee and donuts, of course. Karen and I have been without sleep, but we are so jacked that pacing is relaxing. We wait. And wait. And wait.

"Well, it's a fine mess you've gotten us into now. Back there you called me sweetie. What did you mean by that? Am I your sweetheart?"

"Yes. And more, I hope. But let's save this romantic banter for Florida. We have something important to think about now. I kept one of the Glocks and three clips. I trust no one except you, me, and the two dogs until this whole thing is over. When the shooting starts, and it will, I want you to stay in the police van where it is safe."

"You chauvinist pig. I am able to take care of myself. I'm not some shrinking violet, some dainty flower who needs to be protected by the big strong man. I've been through more than you'll ever know. My ex and his playmates were pond scum. I could deal with them. I could protect myself then. Yes, I was scared. But, I never sought the safety and security of anyone other than my own wits. I will go where you go. This is as much my fight as it is yours. Mary was my friend and we know her killer. You are my lover. The dogs are my children. I put us in with the FBI. The fucks. Therefore, the damage they cause is my responsibility. Besides what do you think became of the poor guard's Colt forty-five. Remember the guard who had some sense knocked into him?"

She lifts her sweater and blouse to reveal the steel blue American-made weapon, resting sensually against her soft, tanned stomach. Her naval is stretched from round to cat's eye. The baby hairs on her belly are aroused by the motion of the fabric, the chill in the air, the metal of the gun, the excitement of the moment, or the internal engine of someone who is about to go to war. I suspect the last reason. For a brief moment she was so sexy, I started to get aroused. Not the right time or place. I'll just have to hold that thought for Florida. The sweater is pulled down over her belt. She smiles and winks. What can I say to someone who gleefully kicked the shit out of an agent, removed his pants, and stole his weapon?

"OK, then just stay beside me. I'll need protection. We better hide the dogs. Keep them back here. They wouldn't get in the way, but they could get shot. Make sure they have bowls and are properly leashed so that they don't follow us as we move into the picnic grounds."

We can hear the first part of the parade. The Drum and Bugle Corps of the local fire and police auxiliary. They are followed by members of the VFW, the American Legion, AmVets, three high school bands. Lots of patriotic theme floats, including the usual Miss Liberty, The Flag Day Queen and Her Court, Raising the Flag on Iwo Jima, The Drummer, Flag Bearer, a Space Rocket, et cetera, et cetera.

The throng, which had viewed the parade in town, was walking alongside the marchers. The parade was now a parade within a parade. The men and women who were to feed the throng had arrived ahead of the human wave.

Trucks were unloaded. Fires for the hot dogs and hamburgers were beginning to smoke. Picnic baskets. No card tables, just blankets. Lots of blankets. Picnic baskets. Long tables for the pie-eating contest. Horseshoe pegs were pounded into the ground. Sacks laid out for the three-legged race. Six long heavy ropes for the tug-of-war pulls. All of this was done with military precision. They had been doing this for years. No need to do all the work the night before. Like ants, each with his or her own chore, the tasks were completed. And they fit into the larger entity called the day. Food, non-alcoholic beverages and a ton of good, old-fashioned fun. From sun-up to sun-down. Then home to collapse. What a perfect small-town event. A picture of Americana to be destroyed by the haters. By the forces we all hope are there to protect us. But, they are the ones who want to control us. To oppress us for their own benefit. For power. National and international power. Power, the ultimate aphrodisiac. Stronger than three Viagra at one time.

Camera starts to stir. He goes live as the first of the parade unravels into the grounds. The sanitation workers are told to collect the trash. The choppers are called in. ETA five minutes. Told to stay over the Welch farm until called. The black van appears. The FBI begins to move. The noose tightens. Sheriff s men, who had infiltrated the crowd, close in on the trench on the mound beneath the pines. My heart is now pumping. The timing is everything. Camera calls Alex to apprehend Bogatta. Cut their communications, now. The commands are barked like an angry quarterback. He is directing men he can't see to people he hopes will be there. Alex answers that Bogey One is secure and the radio is dead. Local Two reports to Local Leader. The black van is in sight. What should he do? Secure the van and its contents. Cut all communication. Then we hear the first pop. Gunfire from the black van. About twelve or fifteen shots. The screaming from the crowd blankets the radio communication.

The choppers arrive. Set down in the middle of the picnic area. The dust, flying blankets, cups, and plates make the landing zone look like the path of a hurricane. The police exit with weapons at the ready. Lumbering, they fan out. The full body armor makes them look a little robotic. They search for their targets. People begin running about in a frenzy of unknowing. The crowd moves in a wave away from the van and the gunfire and away from the helicopters. The bad guys are left standing alone. Their camouflage of bodies has dissipated. Local Three and Four report that the trench is secure. The four occupants are in custody and very angry. Local Two reports that the van is secure, but two of the occupants are dead. The third is wounded. Does not appear critical. The Sheriff moves his men. Tightens the noose completely. Arrests all event staff. Leaves no one behind. Be as clean and surgical as possible. The Sheriff s van and two cruisers head to the grounds. Without much explanation, the bad guys are swept up, placed into trucks, and taken downtown. The Sheriff has already notified the State Police and the news media. No sense in missing a PR opp. The only way to get all the answers is to expose all the rats at once. We go back into the school to find our guard. Still naked, bound, and gagged, he looks like he is sleeping. Except for the large pool of blood behind his head and the quarter size hole in the middle of his forehead. The reward for failure is death. Bogatta's law. If he knew about our departure, his ego must have tricked him into thinking we were of no consequence. The reward for arrogance is failure. Benton's law.

Downtown the jail is not large enough to hold all the detainees. They'll be squeezed in until they are removed to the state facilities. A California version of the Black Hole of Calcutta. The media is swarming like flies around a broken jar of jelly in the hot sun. The press conference is set up at the parade stand. All the big guys are there: the four major networks and CNN. The Sheriff is flanked by his deputies and a State Police Colonel. The elated officials are standing on the porch reserved for the parade judges. Red, white and blue bunting festoons the superstructure. Roses and emblems of eagles are on every corner. All the trappings of a political rally.

"Today we prevented a massacre of innocent people of this community. Today we stopped the serial killings that started in Carter, Wyoming and went through Menthen, New Hampshire, Lutztown, Pennsylvania and Ox Bow, Maryland. Today we unearthed a conspiracy of killing and attempted governmental manipulation. Today your Sheriff's department single-handedly took a huge bite out of crime. We are not at liberty to give you all the details as of now. The perpetrators are being questioned. When we have all the facts, all of the who, what, when, where, and how, we will issue a report. Presently, the captured are being moved to the state correctional facility in Lancaster. Now if you'll all bear with me, I'll give you as much information as I can."

"There are three groups. First, there are three young men and a young woman who were preparing to fire into the crowd of picnickers. These four were heavily armed, but were subdued by squads led by Officers Molina and Whyte. We can't release the names of the four until we have more details as to why they were there and the reason behind their planned action. The next group we secured is comprised of three alleged members of a government agency. We have reason to believe that these three have been sighted at the previously-noted school slaughters. We are not sure who they really are or if they do, in fact, work for our government. We believe their names are Brent Forbes, Roger Thompson, and Alan Campbell. Unfortunately, Mister Forbes and Mister Thompson attempted to resist arrest and were subsequently shot and killed by our squads. Mister Campbell was wounded and is receiving medical care. He will be questioned at length as soon as the doctor says he is strong enough."

"The third group is comprised of supposed FBI agents headed by Senior Agent Bodrim Bogatta. He and his force allegedly came here to stop the shooting by the first group and the supposed subsequent shooting by the three other men. Let me clarify that. We believe that the three men we mentioned previously, Forbes, Thompson, and Campbell had foreknowledge that the four youths were going to commit the heinous butchery. How they got the knowledge, we are not sure. We further believe that the three men were going to kill the youths after the youths had killed the picnickers. This is consistent with the pattern established in the four previous shootings. We don't know why they wanted to kill the killers, but we are sure that was their plan."

"The FBI agents were here to kill the killers of the killers. How they knew the agents knew to be here is as yet to be determined. There is some very strange and evil connection among all three groups. Once we ascertain that, we will know how far up the governmental ladder this entire mess goes. For now, we are confident that the cycle of death and destruction has been broken. We have taken a giant step to make this country safe and secure. Please forgive me, but we must get about the business of getting more information."

The reporters clamor for more information. They thrust cameras and microphones into faces of the Sheriff and his deputy. Politely rebuffed, the crowd of news hounds does not dissipate. They make assumptions and final pronouncements to cameras and millions of people on the other side of the lens.

We exit stage left with dogs by our side. Head for the Sheriffs van and Motel Six where we stash the dogs and our guns. Driven to the State Prison at Lancaster for debriefing. Our day is far from over. The prison is an imposing sight. Four stories of gray ringed with razor wire and highlighted by gun turrets every one hundred feet along the outside wall. The doors swing open to permit the van and its precious cargo to enter the inner sanctum. A short drive leads to another wall and another door. This one swings open. The yard is vast now that it is empty. The recently acquired bad guys are being housed in one wing. Triple security. The former residents of this particular wing, the physically impaired, have been dispersed, for the time being, to facilities in three counties. For now Wing D is the wing of activity. All other wings are in lockdown and will stay that way until the temporary residents leave.

We are escorted to a very sterile, brightly lit, large room. This is where we will be questioned. Those in attendance include the Sheriff, someone from the State Police, and two very important people, one man and one woman from the FBI. They have the right papers and credentials. I have a low level of concern that they might be part of a cover up for Bogatta. They have assured all of us that their only objective is to get to the bottom of all this. They are more upset at the behavior of the rogue Bogatta. They have orders from the very top to rid the agency of this cancer. The questioning is excruciatingly thorough. Dates, times, activities, places, people, thoughts, suspicions. Karen and I are questioned separately. We have nothing to hide so our stories match. Even the second time with new questions. We tell them that Bogatta is responsible for Mary's death. The inquisitors are satisfied that we have given them enough to move forward with the questioning of Bogatta and his people.

The evening news carries the story with great regalia. No action shots. Only the news conference. Lots of interviews with those who were at the picnic. No one finds the Welches. Their anonymity is safe. But, overshadowing this story is the success of the Peace Alliance. Whose decision is it to put the nation's success on foreign soil in front of or above our domestic dirty laundry? Who wants this story as quiet as can be without outright censorship?

Between the carpet-bombing, the long-range missiles, and the artillery barrages, the army of el Jahdiq did not stand a chance. The rain of death endured for thirty hours straight. There is no meal break. Missile batteries disappeared into the sand. Tanks, planes, and long range artillery were in gnarled heaps. The men inside the bunkers were buried alive or burned to cinders. On the other side, the commanders of the sea and air raiders were jubilant. The smiles and the tenor of their voices a dead giveaway. The boys from the 'hood beat up the bully from across the sea.

The briefing by the Commander in Chief, General Fraser Warren, is nothing short of a party. His normal conservative countenance has given way to the heady glee of one who is in the initial stage of crushing an enemy. The high-tech warrior does not talk of quarter or peace. This will be a discussion for the diplomats. The Mastiff of the West wants to rip the throat from the Beast of the East. That is his goal. That is the reason he is in the desert.

The troops under his command have executed his plan with surgical precision. Over three hundred missiles have been fired from carriers and land-based batteries. The combined air force has flown over five hundred high and low-level bombing sorties. The armies have successfully utilized new long-range artillery technology. With this, the batteries are able to pinpoint targets over fifty miles away. Pinpoint means to hit within twenty feet of the X. The payloads of this artillery vary. Some explode upon impact. Some burrow up to two hundred feet before they explode. The army has the capability to blow away the surface protection and then deliver two of these moles. The result is a crater hundreds of feet deep and over a half-mile wide.

The enemy has lost the vast majority of its communications network. The elite fighting battalions are in flight. Tank capacity has been reduced to less than forty percent. There is little if any artillery. No enemy planes in the sky. We have avoided the large population centers, despite the fact that el Jahdiq uses his population as a shield for his military forces. Yes, some civilians have been killed. This is an unfortunate aspect of the war el Jahdiq started. The armies of the contributing countries have performed with excellence. A true international team. Coordination and cooperation are the key words. He can't reveal when the retaliation will move to the next phase, that being the intervention of ground troops. The British and Jordanian Colonels handle the film clips.

Sleep is absolutely necessary. My eyes are wide open. I can't sleep. There are too many unanswered questions. I want to be in Lancaster at the Wing D of the State Prison. I want answers. The people want answers. Karen collapsed upon entry to our room. I walked the dogs. The guard went with me. A likable young man. Wants to make a career of the service. He can't understand why Bogatta and his people would do what they have been accused of. Wants to know all about Alan Campbell. The dogs and I head for the room. They curl up on Karen's side of the bed, but not on my side. They love her. Me, they tolerate. I can't fault their attitude. She is beautiful, kind, intelligent, and trustworthy. She is a fucking Girl Scout. I suffer fits of episodic depression, am not handsome, and don't care for strangers. I'm the dirty guy the den mother warned the Girl Scouts about. Dawn arrives in about six seconds. Get coffee for the three of us. The new guard is a young woman. Not unattractive. Her body properly disguised by the government issued hardware and vest. The dogs get a walk. Karen is nuzzled awake and offered the legal drug. We shower separately. I shave for the first time in three days. Deodorant is a refreshing addition. Dressed in clean clothes, we head back to Lancaster.

The debriefing is brief. I get the distinct feeling we are told about half of what they know. Bogatta was operating outside of his jurisdiction. He had no authority to lead his people into this environment. Acting without supervision is a bad thing. Campbell was not an independent contractor. He and the other two were operatives within the National Security Agency. Why the NSA was involved in this is still unclear. Their jurisdiction is international, not domestic. The FBI agents and Campbell are being shipped to Camp Chaffee in Arkansas. Very safe and secure. They will be questioned further by other members of the agency. Everyone is satisfied they have accomplished their objectives. I am not.

"Wait a minute. These guys had planned to be killers of killers of killers of killers, ad infinitum. Surely, you can give us more information than that gibberish. Or, do you know more than you are telling us? What is the connection between the two forces? Which one is the killer of killers and which one is the killer of the killers' killers? This all sounds like an R.D. Lang poem."

"There is much we don't know yet. What I've just told you is our confirmation that we are on the right track and that we must continue to get resolution. There are too many loose ends, which need to be tied before we can go public. And you are the public. We ask that you relax and let us do our job."

"Hell, that's how Karen and I got here in the first place. We were letting Bogatta do his job. We simply didn't know what his job was or how we were not going to fit into his plans. Therefore, we more want more facts before we go home. Like who are BrokenArrow and TruthSeeker. You owe us that."

"This we can tell you. All that you saw is not what you think you saw."

"More bullshit. Who are the real guys behind the real curtains? The second these guys are stashed away at Camp Chaffee, the tighter the lid will be screwed down on the entire operation. So tell me now. Talk to me."

I have to be very careful of not completing the threat. They are not sure what I'll do. Will I go public? Will I just skulk into the shadows?

"As soon as we know more and confirm its validity, we will tell you. We hope this will be very soon. The true identities of all the people involved in this plan will be ferreted out. People, from those in the chat rooms to the agents and the killers at the schools. We know there are many connections and perhaps one main thread. But, right now we are not sure. We, your country, ask that you be patient and quiet for a little while longer. You are safe. That's all I can say. So let us take you back to the motel. Then you and the dogs can return to Florida. Thank you, Mister Benton and Miss Leach. Your service to your country will not go unnoticed or unrewarded."

With that we were dismissed. Like small children from the dinner table when adults want to have adult conversations.

As we pack at the motel. Karen holds up a mini-cassette recorder and winks.

Gulf Beach, Florida

Home again, home again, jiggity jog. The air in the house smells and feels like I imagine the air in a crypt. Stale. Damp. Dank. Even if you set your thermostat at eighty, the air would smell the same after four or five days. Fortunately, we can open the windows and doors, turn on the ceiling fans and crank up the AC. We unpack in the stale air after we make sure the dogs have bowls of food and water. Dirty clothes of our brief other life are dumped in the hamper. Toilette articles are returned to the bathroom. Candle wax is still on the counter. A fond memory rekindles. Bags are dumped in the back of the closet. The mail and newspaper accumulation has not been too severe. Into the pool with my children. We frolic, splash, and cool off. Afterward, I shop for larder replenishment. For dinner, chicken breasts in a mustard, wine, and tarragon baste, wild rice, and sliced tomatoes, and a very, very good bottle of Chardonnay. Dinner is on the lanai lit by pool lights and a few large candles. Karen's idea. Is she hinting at something? A cigar and a stiff Balvenie complete the evening.

"I am uneasy, Gene. We have to do everything we can to protect our asses. And I feel we haven't done that yet. I want to make a few copies of the two tapes I acquired in California. Then we should take a set to an attorney and make a sworn statement with other details. Charge him with holding the evidence, which would be released if anything untoward happens to us. I know a guy. Was a judge. He is so honest he is revered. And he is feisty. He'd love to get involved. I'll call him tomorrow. I promise you this time the guy can be trusted."

"What I can't get away from is what is the relationship between Campbell, et al and Bogatta? Who was the puppet and who was the puppeteer? There has to be a link. Is it at the hip? Or, above them both? The lawyer idea is good. Maybe we should go public. Should we include

Sheriff Camera in our outing? I don't know. But, I do know that I can't solve this issue tonight. I'll take care of clean up."

"I'm exhausted. I'm going to bed so you can tend to your kitchen chores without being bothered or corrected"

While I scrape, load, wash, rinse and stack, I turn on the ten o'clock news to keep me company.

"Today on Capitol Hill, the Senate initiated an investigation into the allegations concerning Senator Baldwin Miller of Pennsylvania, his SAFE campaign, and the recent school shootings. This investigation was hurriedly called based upon evidence provided by the FBI. This evidence dealt with the agency's investigation of the aborted shooting at Coastal Mesa, California. An unidentified source indicated to us that there may be evidence to prove that the Senator knew of the shootings before they occurred. There is even speculation that the shootings were choreographed to be precursors of Senator Miller's SAFE rallies. The Senator's aides deny all the allegations and innuendoes, stating that this is a smear campaign initiated and driven by President Sessler and his party. The campaign to discredit the Senator is preposterous and is the act of an obviously desperate failing politician. The battle lines have been drawn. The ad hoc committee hearing starts tomorrow. We will be live from the Senate chambers all day. This is Wendy Mynard reporting for CNN."

"On the international front, the armies of the Peace Alliance continue to hammer the beleaguered troops of el Jahdiq. At a briefing earlier today, the Allied Command issued the statement that, and we quote, 'The enemy appears to be without resolve, troops are scattering, communications are nonexistent, missile and artillery batteries are nonfunctional. Ground troops and tanks may go into Basjar only as a mop-up force after the surrender and peace terms have been reached. Obviously, the Allied Commanders are pleased with the progress of the campaign."

Due to a near blackout of news coverage, the Western world hears what the Allied Commander wants. The Eastern world sees and hears about the civilian suffering, the resolve of el Jahdiq's armed forces, and how little damage the invasion has done to the military machine. There has to be some truth in the symbiotic mixture.

Did Sessler use the war to divert attention from his domestic problems? His inability to run again? And the party's obvious lack of a viable candidate? How the hell did he get the other countries to go along with his domestic policy? If this is true, the attack on the three embassies was very convenient. Too convenient. Could these have been staged by Sessler? Does Sessler have balls big enough to sacrifice our face and the lives of hundreds of men and women in the Foreign Service for his own historical grandeur? Did Roosevelt sacrifice the troops and ships at Pearl Harbor to justify the Pacific Theater of World War Two? How many young men and women have been sacrificed by how many governments for the sake of national pride and expansion? This is too deep for tonight.

Karen is in a deep sleep when I finally pad into the master bedroom. The dogs are beside the bed next to her. All is well with my world.

Before dawn the morning fix is ingested. Dawn brings the end of tranquility. I take a cup of joe to my bedmate. The dogs are free to roam and relieve. Karen showers and breakfasts. Her preoccupation could be interpreted as aloofness. Her smile and touching of my arm rule out that possibility. We are due at the lawyer's office at eleven to make our statements. She has to dupe the tapes for the lawyer's files. I call the office. No one knows where we have been. I tell my administrative assistant that I'll be in tomorrow, rested and ready to kick ass. To coin James Brown, I feel good. I'm back at it. The morning paper repeats the news heard last night. A small item on page eight in National News. The Coastal Mesa town council has decided to cancel next year's Flag Day parade and picnic.

The trip to the lawyer was uneventful. On the return home I get the feeling we are being observed. A sedan, noticeable on the way downtown, is behind us as we turn off the interstate. Coincidence? Not likely. I tell Karen and she attempts to identify the driver and passenger via the vanity mirror on her sun visor. Nope. Who sent the eyes? Agency, service, or some other group, which has a burning interest in our activities?

We will not hunker in the bunker. We will take steps to keep everything in the open. We don't care about loose ends. We don't have to follow protocol. We must protect our own interests. And, these interests are based on living. Time to go to the chat rooms. Tell all to anyone who will listen. The risk of retaliation is real. But there is a big upside with the spread of knowledge. It's called protection by the masses. Tell them about BrokenArrow and TruthSeeker. Tell the chatters about the system of clues. Tell them about Bogatta and Campbell. About Mary. Tell them all and let the chips fall. The rush of danger brings me to life. Am I daring death? The Light Brigade dared death with an incredibly stupid move. Look what happened to them. Am I repeating the stupidity? What will happen to me? To us? I really don't want to die, but I fear inactivity. So, if I could roll over and kick once in a while, I could deal with death. I am concerned about Karen. This is a sign of caring. Love. Just your basic need-based emotion. Going public is something we must do. The best defense is a great offense.

She writes the manifesto. We review it. It is complete. She then downloads it into as many chat rooms as she can find. Even the ones for the news networks. The die is cast.

The Senate hearings hit the ground running. When they want to move with great dispatch, they can. Questions are designed to ensnare liars, not to elicit facts. It's like when your father questioned you about the dent in the car. He already knew the facts. He just wanted you to admit the truth. All else in Washington and the rest of the country seems to be on hold as if freeze-framed. Two volumes of information have been provided the Senators. The word processors and copiers throughout the Washington metro area must have been exclusively devoted to this desktop publishing. It's now time for the Committee to ask questions about the reports. The accused government agents are the first to testify. A public gallows is built in this fashion. After Sheriff Camera will be Bogatta and Campbell. The Committee promises that Senator Miller will testify tomorrow.

Sessler does not gloat publicly. Vice President Harrison issues a statement that the administration's first priority is to supervise the successful completion of the war in the Middle East and the subsequent peace agreement. His hopes are that no ground troops will be necessary. The administration will not interfere with the duly appointed Senate Committee. Harrison pledges full support of the Committee and its endeavors. He wishes swift and clean closure to this domestic blight. He must have been giggling like a fifth grader at the paddling of a classmate.

Camera confirms all the details in the report. Adds little. Keeps our names out of the events. Step-by-step the prosecutor-judge-jury Hydra nails another plank on the platform. The prima facie case is now part of the public domain. Lunch. Reconvene at two. I am now bored. What to do for two hours? Swim so that I can indulge in eating too much fat.

Karen joins me. As we exit the pool, she wraps her towel around me and we embrace. Our kisses are lingering. Stimulating. Revitalizing. A promise of the evening. Get the mail while she prepares two small steaks, green beans, and pasta. An athlete's meal. Dinner for lunch. We and the Committee reconvene in the den. Bogatta is first.

He testifies that he had been ordered to feed clues and information to dissidents via the chat rooms. He could direct them to do his bidding. He could lead the angry youth. The youth committed the heinous crimes. Since Bogatta knew where the crimes were to be committed, he could send agents to help with the mop-up. No, he and his men were not ordered to kill the killers. No, he and his men did not kill the killers. They were there to assist in the mop-up only. No, he would not divulge the name of the individual who gave the orders. Yes, he realized he would be held in contempt. Yes, he realized he would go to jail. He explained how he got his orders. Unmarked e-mail. His payment for service. Electronic deposits. How he recruited his agents. Yes, he had violated the code of the agency. He never killed anyone but criminals. He and his men were too far away to stop the events. Bogatta is taken away from the room by officers who would take him back to jail.

Jesus H. Christ, this sounds like the testimony of the Japanese and Nazi war criminals. The lack of guilt, culpability, and responsibility enjoyed by this type of mind is incomprehensible to mere humans. The thugs were just following orders. But, whose?

Campbell is helped to the witness table. He relates that he, Forbes, and Thompson were private contractors. They were employed by the federal government. He received orders from one of Sessler's supporters in the Department of Defense.

"We broke the code used by Bogatta's group before the incident at Carter. The government had been monitoring the Chat rooms for years. We followed the path each time. Our job was to observe, but not to interfere with the events or the subsequent clean up. We had hoped to learn how all this was started, who did the killing and who did the killing of the killers. We were also placed at the service of Senator Baldwin Miller. We were positioned as federal agents. We were part of the security team at his rallies. We were really there to keep an eye on him. I figured out quickly that we were working for Senator Miller and going to the shootings because somebody thought there was a connection. I assumed that the administration thought there was connection and that Miller was setting up the killings to promote SAFE. Getting elected must have been very important to him. Politics is a crappy business. Too many hidden agendas."

"We were never able to prove Senator Miller's connection. We were never able to stop the shootings. That was not our ob. We did not know what to do except what we were told. What we did know was what we saw. And we saw the bogeys, Bogatta and his men, step in before the local and state authorities could arrive and kill the shooters. They did this at every shooting except Coastal Mesa. We were there to stop them. Capture them and turn them over to the locals. But, the locals beat us to the arrest. All hell broke loose. Two very good men died. That's the risk soldiers run. Before the Coastal Mesa event, Bogatta and his men killed a freelance photographer, Mike Duncan. He was trying to dig up information of our operation. Bogatta's men were moles for Duncan. He was getting too close to us. Too close to the whole truth. He would learn that we were not dirty. He would learn that Bogatta was dirty. So Duncan had to disappear. Hell, we could have disappeared in the firefight at Coastal Mesa. Bogatta had a ton of firepower. They just got out-smarted by the locals."

The arrogance in his voice is unmistakable. The captured lion feels contempt for the lucky hunter. He is returned to a hospital jail cell. The stage is set for Senator Miller.

Vice President Harrison issues a statement that the administration has no knowledge of the illegal activities of the aforementioned member of the Department of Defense. He abhors any use of power without responsibility. That is abuse. The manipulation of the truth. It seems right for the administration to conduct a thorough investigation of the various Cabinet Departments. From top to bottom. This will require independent counsel and, to be done properly and thoroughly, will take about six months. But, for the American people and the honor of the federal government, this investigation must commence immediately. Let no stone be unturned. President Sessler has flown to the Middle East to meet with the Military Commanders and the political leaders of the Alliance. He is attempting to bring about an end to the retaliation, expedite the peace process, and initiate rebuilding of the region.

The day is over. I run to Wall-to-Wall Video and rent a chick-flick for Karen. I am a partial chauvinist. She has endured one of my nothing-but-news days. My display of male chauvinism is appreciated. I even prepare the cheese, crackers, and fruit. Uncork another bottle of wine. God, I'm good.

Ten tissues later the wife dies and the husband faces the future with two small, adorable children. Catharsis. Rewind the misery.

"This late breaking news from Washington. Senator Baldwin Miller has apparently taken his life. The facts are sketchy. We go to Wendy Mynard."

In hushed very somber tones.

"This evening at eight thirty-seven the body of Senator Baldwin Miller was found in his automobile, which was parked with motor running near the Lincoln Memorial. Apparently Senator Miller had committed suicide by firing a single large caliber bullet into his head. We have been told he placed the gun barrel in his mouth. The explosion and impact removed the back of Senator Miller's head and shattered the rear window of the sedan. As of now, there are no other details. Speculation is that Senator Miller took his own life rather than face the Senate Committee, which was investigating his involvement in the recent rash of school shootings. Police have cordoned off the area and are combing it for clues. Neither Senator Miller's family nor his office is available for comment or elaboration. We anticipate a statement from his office shortly. This is Wendy Mynard, CNN, from Washington."

My stomach churns. He just admitted his guilt and took the cowardly way out. If you can't do the time, don't do the crime. There is a sense of relief on Karen's face. Her muscles relax and tears return to her eyes. These are lachrymose relief.

"He was the culprit behind it all. He led the wolves to the sheep and then shot the wolves after they had done his bidding. He was evil. His family will suffer the stigma for about two generations. Maybe they'll change their names and move to a distant planet. Yes, I am angry that he won't stand before the people, admit his crime and take the appropriate punishment. Yes I'm relieved this is all over. I want a drink."

I pour. She takes. We toast. To bed.

Her profile is illuminated by the full moon. She is exquisite. I move to kiss her and she moves to kiss me. Tenderness gives way to passion. I kiss her neck and shoulders. She kisses my throat and rolls me over onto my back. Her legs straddle my hips. She commences a gradual grind. I am aroused. She is not yet ready. I pull her nightgown off her shoulders. Her breasts are soft and firm. She lowers her torso and drags her nipples across my lips. She likes to be nipped. I oblige. I reach behind her and remove her panties. Off the hips, down to the knees. Right leg out, then left. Synthetic fabric discarded into the corner. Passion is now rampaging. Mouth to mouth resembles resuscitation rather than kissing. She rises to insert me. The telephone rings. I am sliding in. Another ring. I withdraw. Third ring. She is upset.

"Hello."

"Is this Mister Eugene Benton?"

"Yes, it is."

"Mister Benton, this is Special Agent Weaver of the FBI. We met in Lancaster, California."

"Yes, I remember the voice. Could you give me your badge number, Sir, for purposes of verification?"

11347963-A."

I confirmed this by checking the card he gave me in California.

"Special Agent Weaver, how may I help you?"

"Mister Benton, I am sorry to bother you, but I thought you should know that Agent Bogatta escaped from his detention cell and is reported missing as of seven-thirty this evening."

"Do you think he would come to Florida?"

"Sir, we know that Agent Bogatta is desperate. We believe he knows how Senator Miller died. In fact, we have reason to believe that he shot the Senator. We feel confident he will attempt to flee the country. We have a tight surveillance on exit points. But, he just might come to Florida as a way out of the country. Therefore, we have taken the precaution to place you and Miss Leach under observation. We presently have men watching your house. We are fairly sure that he will not bother you. If I were he, I'd run to a foreign country. But, Agent Bogatta is not thinking clearly. We believe he is deranged. We just want you to know the status of the situation and that you are being protected. Sir, do you have any questions?"

"Will you call again in the morning and give me an update? Miss Leach and I may want to go to the mountains for a few days if he is not apprehended immediately."

"Yes, sir, I'll call you at seven AM. Thank you for your cooperation. Have a good night."

I tell Karen. We are both uneasy but not frightened. It must have been Agent Weaver's men who followed us.

"Now where were we?"

"You were on top. I was in the process of getting very close. I think it started this way."

I lean forward and we start the kissing again. This time my tongue follows the contour of her body from ear to rib cage. I remove her nightgown and my shorts. My kissing continues. Her breathing is more like four-four time than waltz. Her hands find my head and guide it to her zone. This joyous interaction reaches a crescendo. Release after the relief. Sleep follows rapidly thereafter.

I am awakened by incredibly primeval growls. That deep, barely audible rumble of impending disaster. Like a far distant thunderstorm. Centuries ago wolves around the camp of the hunters and gatherers growled as a warning to the intrusion of a Saber Tooth Tiger or a Mastodon. They warned man then, and Hither and Yon are instinctively doing so tonight. They can't see the danger, but they know it's there. They don't move. No reason to provide a target this soon in the conflict. The sentries are letting the pack know. I am the alpha male.

I slide from the bed and slither across the floor to the walk-in closet. Find the Glock and a clip. Insert and cock the piece. Where the hell are my shorts? Why is being clothed important now? Crawl very delicately down the short hall to the great room, den, and kitchen. During the day this distance is covered in about six seconds. Tonight, given the circumstances, my travel time is well over a minute. Each move is measured for life and death. The sliding door is open. The dogs are free to run, but they stay behind me.

Then I hear a deeper growl. The singular ominous growl that rolls from their throats is it did from time before man ruled the earth. It has reverberated from the feral Black Forest and the caves in the Balkans. The rumble has alerted the pack and warned whelps. The dogs will not move, just growl. It is like sonar. It becomes louder as the sentinels home in on the threat. They are absolutely stock-still. They will not move until they are thoroughly convinced that they can spring and kill the intruder. They are staring into the back yard. Eyes and snouts focused on the pool. I slide along the wall to the doorway.

What does this red light mean? It's on my head. Roll to the right away from the light. I never hear the report or see the flash. But, I feel the pain, heat. The impact on the left side of my chest is beyond my wildest experience. I am bounced down to the floor about six feet from the opening. Stunned and gasping for breath. I am not sure if the hit or the fall hurt more. The pain is coursing throughout my entire body. It's like a huge weight had been dumped on me and was now pressing me through the floor. The protectors respond by charging through the open door. They have committed to an offensive defense. Their growls have become barking snarls. Incredible ferocity. Ears pinned back, neck hair bristled in a natural defense, and all their teeth visible. An eight legged, lightening quick, very pissed bodyguard rushes toward the pool. The pool lights pop on. They are triggered by the ferocious mass as it exits the house.

There is a dark figure in the blue green, very bright environment. The figure appears frozen upon being discovered. Both arms are raised and joined at the gun in front of the face. The red light runs across my eyes and holds above my head as I slide to the floor. The blasts from behind me are loud and rapid. Three. Four. Five. Six. The Loch Benton monster spasms. Arms go everywhere. Body jerks back and under. The gun plops in the pool. The monster's head looks like a platter of spaghetti and meatballs. Silence.

The dogs are in the pool attacking the bobbing torso. Fulminating in basso profundo, they rip the clothing and get to the flesh. Parts of what remained after the fusillade are beginning to rise to the top of the red brown water. A human stew is roiling: bone fragments, flesh, and fabric are the ingredients. Blood and chlorinated water are the medium. A canine Waring Blender renders our intruder almost unrecognizable.

"Can you move? Are you OK? Does it hurt?"

"Yes. Yes. And what the fuck do you think. Let's go outside and see what damage the boys did."

Karen pulls me up and helps me to walk. I am dizzy to the point of collapse. But, I have to be the big brave man.

"Hither. Yon. It's OK, boys. Hither. Yon. Settle down. It's over. Hither. Yon. Come here now."

She whistles loudly. I never knew she could whistle like a New Yorker hailing a cab. I guess there's a lot I have to learn.

Karen's whistle gets their attention and her calls calm the carnivores. Women have that power over boys at play or who are fighting, regardless of age or species. As the boys rise from the pool, bits and pieces of their quarry are visible in their muzzles and mouths. They shake dry and the pieces fly away with the water. They pace between it and us.

It's our old buddy. Despite the fact that most of his face and one shoulder are missing, our intruder is none other than the recent escapee, Bodrim Bogatta. Now a just blob in the water. The main and last ingredient in the stew. Galactic justice.

"Stay right where you are. Nobody move."

"Gentlemen, we're safe. Everything is under control. Karen, catch me."

All is black before my naked body hits the ground. I feel nothing.

The light in the room is brighter than I like. The doctor is peering into my eyes. Fuzzy look to everything in the room. A warm hand takes mine.

"Mister Benton, you'll be fine. A few stitches, isolation of the arm, and bed rest. Miss Leach has decided to take you home as soon as the forms are completed and signed. We agree it would be in your best interest."

"Gene, I have Agent Weaver of the FBI on the phone."

"Mister Benton. It seems your country owes you and Miss Leach another vote of thanks. I understand Miss Leach took care of business before our men could intervene. Hope you mend quickly."

Home again, home again, jiggity-jog. The dogs are happy. They never get tired of protecting. I guess that's their expression of love. Karen has moved the TV into the bedroom so I can watch news all day, every day. The news, the History Channel, and two nature channels. Knowledge is good: it makes me feel alive.

"Your office called and wanted to know if they should reschedule the meetings. When will you be back to work? I told them in two weeks or never, whichever you decided. They understand. Call them when you get a chance."

"We interrupt our regularly scheduled programming to bring you this bulletin."

"Ladies and gentlemen, the Vice President of the United States."

"We are sad to announce that President Paul Sessler's plane, Air Force One, has crashed in the Atlantic Ocean. At this time there is no word on the cause of the accident. We do know there are no survivors. President Sessler had just completed a successful peace mission to the Middle East. We stand united in grief and extend our condolences to President Sessler's family. Personally, I have lost a good friend, the country has lost an unparalleled leader, and the world has lost a peace loving statesman. As we learn more, we will advise the nation."

How strangely serendipitous. I peer over at the pool. The gate has been left open. Damned pool boy.